MAX BARRY

MACHINE MAN

Max Barry began removing parts at an early age. In 1999, he successfully excised a steady job at tech giant HP in order to upgrade to the more compatible alternative of manufacturing fiction. While producing three novels, he developed the online nation simulation game *NationStates,* as well as contributing to various open source software projects and developing religious views on operating systems. He did not leave the house much. For *Machine Man,* Max wrote a website to deliver pages of fiction to readers via e-mail and RSS. He lives in Melbourne, Australia, with his wife and two daughters, and is thirty-eight years old. He uses vi.

www.maxbarry.com

ALSO BY MAX BARRY

Company
Jennifer Government
Syrup

Praise for Max Barry's

MACHINE MAN

"When we first encounter Dr. Charles Neumann, the hero of Max Barry's wickedly entertaining new novel, he's human in body, but sadly machinelike in spirit. Then Barry begins the long process of inverting this equation, whittling away at poor Charlie's flesh while he simultaneously prods his soul into a hesitant, wavering sort of life. It's a brilliant book: caustically funny, and—by its closing chapter—surprisingly moving."
                                    —Scott Smith, author of *The Ruins*

"Don't open this one unless you're prepared to keep reading until the last page is done. Once again, Barry delivers." —Seth Godin, author of *Linchpin*

"Fast-paced. . . . Barry is helping to reinvent publishing."

                                                    —io9.com

machine man

MAX BARRY

Vintage Contemporaries

Vintage Books

A Division of Random House, Inc. ■ New York

A VINTAGE CONTEMPORARIES ORIGINAL, AUGUST 2011

This entire work was serialized in somewhat different form from March 2009 to December 2009 on www.maxbarry.com/machineman.

Library of Congress Cataloging-in-Publication Data
Barry, Max, 1973–
    Machine man : a novel / by Max Barry.
        p. cm.
    ISBN 978-0-307-47689-0 (alk. paper)
    1. Mechanical engineers—Fiction.   2. Artificial limbs—Fiction.   I. Title.
. PS3552.A7424M33 2011
    813'.54—dc22
    2011004724

Book design by Debbie Glasserman

www.vintagebooks.com

Printed in the United States of America
10 9 8 7 6 5 4 3 2 1

FINE, IT'S FOR MINTER.

machine man

1

AS A BOY, I WANTED TO BE A TRAIN. I DIDN'T REALIZE THIS WAS unusual—that other kids played *with* trains, not as them. They liked to build tracks and have trains not fall off them. Watch them go through tunnels. I didn't understand that. What I liked was pretending my body was two hundred tons of unstoppable steel. Imagining I was pistons and valves and hydraulic compressors.

"You mean robots," said my best friend, Jeremy. "You want to play robots." I had never thought of it like that. Robots had square eyes and jerky limbs and usually wanted to destroy the Earth. Instead of doing one thing right, they did everything badly. They were general purpose. I was not a fan of robots. They were bad machines.

. . .

I WOKE AND REACHED FOR MY PHONE AND IT WAS NOT THERE. I GROPED around my bedside table, fingers sneaking between novels I didn't read anymore because once you start e-reading you can't go back. But no phone. I sat up and turned on my lamp. I crawled underneath the bed, in case my phone had somehow fallen in the night and bounced oddly. My eyes were blurry from sleep so I swept my arms across the carpet in hopeful arcs. This disturbed dust and I coughed. But I kept sweeping. I thought: *Have I been burgled?* I felt like I would have woken if someone had tried to swipe my phone. Some part of me would have realized.

I entered the kitchen. Kitchenette. It was not a big apartment. But it was clean, because I didn't cook. I would have spotted my phone. But I did not. I peered into the living room. Sometimes I sat on the sofa and watched TV while playing with my phone. Possibly the phone had slipped down between cushions. It could be there now, just out of sight. I shivered. I was naked. The living room curtains were open and the window looked onto the street. The street looked into the window. Sometimes there were dog-walkers, and school-going children. I shivered again. I should put on some clothes. My bedroom was six feet away. But my phone could be closer. It could be right there. I cupped my hands over my genitals and ran across the living room and pulled up sofa cushions. I saw black plastic and my heart leaped but it was only a remote. I got down on my hands and knees and felt around beneath the sofa. My ass tingled with the first touch of morning sun. I hoped nobody was outside that window.

The coffee table was bare on top but laden beneath with reference books I hadn't touched since Google. A phone book, for some reason. A phone book. Three million sheafs of dead tree stacked up as a monument to the inefficiency of paper as an information distribution platform. But no phone. I sat up. A dog barked. For the first time ever I wished I had a land line, so I could call my phone. I peered at the top of the TV and it was empty but maybe I had put my phone down there and it had been dislodged by minor seismic activity. As I crossed the room, my eyes met a jogger's. Her face contorted. That might have been from exertion. Behind the TV was a cord-based civilization but no phone. It wasn't on the kitchen bench. It still wasn't on my bedside table or the carpet or any of the places I had already looked. My teeth chattered. I didn't know how warm it would be today. It might rain, it might be humid, I had no idea. I had a desktop but it took forever to boot, more than a minute. I would have to choose clothes without information on the environmental conditions. It was insane.

I showered. Sometimes to solve a problem you need to stop trying solutions. You need to step back. I stood under water and mentally retreaded the previous night. I had worked late. I had arrived home around two. I don't think I ate. I went to bed and fell asleep without even using my phone at all. I realized: *It's in my car.* It made perfect sense. I turned off the water. I had not used soap or washed my hair but from water was probably 80 percent clean. That was a pass. I wrapped a towel around my waist, grabbed keys from the kitchen, and padded out of the apartment. The stairwell was ice. I almost lost my towel trying to open the door to the underground garage. My car was in the sixth bay and already I could see the empty dock. I bwip-bwipped it open anyway and crawled inside to search between seats. I could not believe I had driven all the way home without docking my phone. Or maybe I could. Sometimes I left it in my pocket and realized only when I stopped the car and reached for it. That had happened. And last night I had been tired. It wasn't inconceivable. The phone could be anywhere. It could be anywhere.

I stared out the windshield at a concrete wall and became sure my phone was at work. I had taken it out of my pocket because you couldn't take electromagnetic equipment into Lab 4. It was on my desk. Anyone could pick it up. No. There were cameras. No one would steal my phone. Especially if I arrived early. I groped for my phone, to check the time, and groaned. This was like being blind. I put the keys in the ignition and remembered I was wearing a towel. I hesitated. I took the keys out again but it felt like a tearing. I got out of the car and fixed my towel and took the steps two at a time.

DRIVING IN, I GRIPPED THE WHEEL. THE SUN BEAT THROUGH THE windshield, mocking my sweater. I had overdressed. I reached the point where I had to decide between the avenue or by the park and didn't know which had less traffic. I hadn't read a news headline for hours. War could have broken out. There could have been earthquakes. I turned on the radio for the first time in years and it jabbered about discount carpets and what an excellent medium for advertising radio was and would I like to win a thousand dollars, and I stared at it in disbelief and turned it off. I wished I had my phone. I didn't even want to do something specific. I just wanted the possibility to do things. It could do so many things.

The avenue was choked with traffic, of course. I sat there and exchanged ignorance with time. Finally I turned the car into the science district and sped past research houses and machine fabricators. At the end, on the river, was Better Future: an eight-story complex of a half-dozen connected buildings, a wide lawn out front and razor wire everywhere else. There was more underground but you wouldn't know. At the boom gate I fumbled my security pass and had to get out to pick it off the concrete. A security guard wandered out of his booth and I tried to wave him away because the last thing I needed now was conversation. But he kept coming. "Morning, sir."

"I've got it." I swiped the card. The boom rose.

"Everything all right?"

"Yes. Just dropped my card." A hot wind blew by. I tried to pull off my sweater and my security tag snagged in the sleeve and slipped from my fingers again. By the time I freed myself, the guard was offering it to me.

"Hot one today."

I looked at him. This sounded like a criticism of my information-impaired clothing choice. But I couldn't be sure. I opened my mouth to request a clarifying restatement, then realized it didn't matter and took the card. I got back in the car and drove into the bowels of Better Future.

I SWIPED FOR THE ELEVATOR AND AGAIN FOR ACCESS TO BUILDING A. We were big on swiping. You couldn't go to a bathroom in Better Future without swiping first. There was once a woman whose card stopped working and she was trapped in a corridor for three hours. It was a busy corridor but nobody was permitted to let her out. Ushering somebody through a security door on your pass was just about the worst thing you could do at Better Future. They would fire you for that. All anyone could do was bring her snacks and fluids until security finished verifying her biometrics.

I passed the atrium, which was already filling with young people in white lab coats and older managers in suits and skirts. At the central elevator bank was a young woman with dark hair. Marketing, or possibly recruitment. The call button was lit but I moved to re-press it anyway, then stopped myself because that was completely illogical, then went ahead and did it because, seriously, what was the harm. It wasn't like I was doing anything else. As I stepped back, I saw the young woman looking at me and glanced away, then realized she was starting to smile and looked back but then she was looking away and it was too late. We stood awhile. I reached into my pocket for my phone. I hissed. She said, "Take forever, don't they?"

"No, I lost my phone." She looked confused. "That's why I was . . ." I trailed off. There was silence.

"They're all on three," she said. According to the display, three cars were at Sublevel 3 and the fourth was right behind them. "All these engineers, you'd think we could figure out how to decluster the elevators." She smiled. "I'm Rebecca."

"Hmm," I said. I was familiar with the elevator algorithm. It sent cars in the same direction so long as they had a destination, then allowed them to reverse. It was supposed to be efficient. But there was an alternative that allowed people to enter their destination *before* getting in, which allowed the scheduler to make more intelligent decisions. The problem was the system could be gamed: people figured they got elevators faster by mashing buttons. I wondered if cars should move away from one another when idle. It might even be worth delaying one car to create a gap. You would slow one journey but benefit everyone who came after. I should run some numbers. I opened my mouth to say this and realized an elevator had arrived and the woman was entering it. I followed. She pulled her satchel close to her body. She seemed tense. I tried to think of something to say but all I could think was, *Takes forever, doesn't it,* which was what she had said to me. She got out at Organizational Communications without looking at me.

. . .

I AM NOT A PEOPLE PERSON. WHENEVER I'M EVALUATED, I SCORE VERY low on social metrics. My ex-boss said she had never seen anyone score a zero on Interpersonal Empathy before. And she worked with engineers. If anyone is having a party, I am not invited. In meetings, during downtime, the people I'm seated between will both talk to the person on their other side. There's something about me that is repellent. I don't mean disgusting. I mean like magnets. The closer people get, the stronger their urge to move away.

I am a smart guy. I recycle. Once I found a lost cat and took it to a shelter. Sometimes I make jokes. If there's something wrong with your car, I can tell what by listening to it. I like kids, except the ones who are rude to adults and the parents just stand there, smiling. I have a job. I own my apartment. I rarely lie. These are qualities I keep hearing people are looking for. I can only think there must be something else, something no one mentions, because I have no friends, am estranged from my family, and haven't dated in this decade. There is a guy in Lab Control who killed a woman with his car, and he gets invited to parties. I don't understand that.

I EXITED THE ELEVATOR AND SWIPED FOR ACCESS TO THE GLASS ROOM. We called it the Glass Room because it overlooked several adjoining labs, but actually the walls were green-tinged polycarbonate plastic. Apparently they were glass until an incident involving a spilled beaker, a weapons-grade pathogen, and panicked techs with office chairs. I heard two versions of this story: in one, the pathogen was harmless and served as a wake-up call to everyone concerned. In the other, two people died before the complex could be locked down, and another six afterward, when they flooded the labs with gas. It was before my time so I don't know which was true. All I know is the walls are plastic.

The moment the door opened, I could see my phone was not on my desk. I pawed through papers, just in case. I checked the drawers. I kneeled on the plastic floor. I did a circuit of the room, checking other desks, then again, slower, encompassing all horizontal surfaces. Then I reeled into my chair and closed my eyes. I had grabbed at this idea of my phone being at work without properly considering the probabilities. Would it have killed me to do one more sweep at home? My phone was probably on my bedside table, stuck between novels. I had looked there pretty thoroughly but maybe I hadn't. I opened my eyes and rotated my office chair to survey the room slice by slice. Nothing. Nothing. I had an idea and picked up my office phone to dial my cell, but froze with my finger above the buttons because I did not know the number. It was on my phone. Everything was. I sat there and did not know what to do.

MY LAB ASSISTANTS ARRIVED. I HAD THREE: JASON, ELAINE, AND Katherine. Katherine was the one who wasn't Chinese. I was supposed to be teaching them something while they worked, but I had never been sure what. I knew I was a disappointment to them. They had made it into one of the most exciting research labs in the world and their mentor turned out to be me.

They donned white coats and stood there expectantly. Elaine glanced at Katherine and Katherine rolled her eyes and Elaine jiggled her eyebrows like: *I know.* This was right in front of me. I should have come down on them but it seemed stupid to say, *Stop jiggling your eyebrows.* They probably knew this. I had no such problems with Jason, who would say what he thought, if you asked him directly.

Elaine said, "Should we get started sometime today?"

"On what?"

Another glance with Katherine. She gestured to the glass. The plastic. The lab beyond. "On durables testing, of course."

We were supposed to be bombarding a lightweight carbon polymer with radiation. The idea was to check that it wouldn't melt. On our three previous attempts, it had melted. It was interesting to watch but frustrating on a professional level. It was probably going to melt again. This was not what I wanted to be doing, with my phone missing: watching a polymer melt. But I stood and went to get my coat because, after all, it was my job.

JASON RETRIEVED THE POLYMER WHILE I SWIPED INTO LAB 4 AND powered on the Clamp. The Clamp was a pair of hydraulic-powered steel plates, good at holding things and not melting. The rest of the room housed a spectrograph, a compact accelerator, and various support equipment, all connected by dangling cables as thick as arms. As I wiggled the joystick to maneuver the Clamp into place I saw Elaine and Katherine, green-tinged and blurred, moving about in the Glass Room. I wondered if they had seen my phone. I should have asked. But I had to concentrate on what I was doing because the Clamp was approaching and that thing was so heavy it could hurt you moving at a tenth of a meter per second. Once it had left a bruise on my hip that took three weeks to heal. My own fault. The equipment had safeties but your primary piece of protective equipment was your brain. There was a presumption that anyone entering this room was intelligent enough to keep away from hot things, sharp things, and things carrying large stores of momentum. We were not factory workers.

I set the Clamp in place and pressed a rubber button to bring its plates closer together. A klaxon sounded. An orange warning light spun. That always happened. It wasn't something I noticed anymore. While I waited, I thought about that girl in the elevator. I should have told her about elevator algorithms. She might have been interested. She might have said, *I had no idea,* and when we arrived at her floor, put a hand on the door to stop it closing.

I saw my phone. I had spent so long imagining it that for a second I wasn't sure it was really there. But it was. It was on top of the spectrograph. So obvious. I had worked late and when checking my pockets for a pen had realized I still had my phone, which wasn't allowed, and none of that mattered because here it was. I went to get it. My outstretched fingers were about to close on it when my thighs brushed metal. I looked down. I had walked into the Clamp. The plates were touching me. They were actually closer than I had meant to bring them. I should have hit STOP a few seconds ago. I heard the klaxon and noticed the swirling orange light as if for the first time. I began to back out. I wasn't in real danger. The plates moved too slowly. Although that was deceptive. The gap shrank linearly but in relative terms it accelerated. My thighs jammed. I turned sideways and shuffled. My left shoe caught. I freed that but then the right did. I hadn't accounted for a self-reinforcing feedback loop: the plates increasingly obstructing movement. I had left insufficient margin for error. I lunged for freedom and fell face-first onto the floor. I pulled one leg free but my right shoe caught. I grabbed my thigh and pulled. Above the clamp, through the green glass, Elaine and Katherine gaped. Between them and me sat my phone, untouched.

I felt unbearable pressure. My intestines tried to squeeze out of my ears. I didn't hear the noise. The klaxon covered that. But I saw the spray. In the orange light, it looked black.

During Clamp operation, the lab autolocked, for safety. I

had to tear my shirt into strips to stem the bleeding. I had to flop across the floor until I could reach the controls. I'll be honest. There was a lot of screaming. I got my hands on the STOP button. The klaxon died. The orange light faded. I closed my eyes. I was going to vomit, or pass out, or one then the other. The door opened and Jason said, "Oh fuck, fuck." I felt very sad, because that seemed to confirm it.

2

A ROOM FORMED AROUND ME. IT DIDN'T HAPPEN ALL AT ONCE. IT WOVE itself out of nothing by degrees. Not really. It was just how it seemed, under medication. It was a while before I felt confident it wouldn't blow away again—the bleached sheets, the beige walls, the furniture that was all on wheels—to reveal I was still in Lab 4, bleeding to death.

A surgeon visited, a tall woman with dark frizzy hair and impatient eyes. Usually I appreciate impatience in a person. It indicates an appreciation of efficiency. But my head was full of bees and she talked too fast to follow.

"The debridement went very well. Often in the case of traumatic injury there's a great deal of bone fragment and destroyed tissue, but yours was remarkably clean. You're lucky. I had to take your femur up about six inches but that's really nothing. Very little smoothing of the bone was required. I did a closed amputation, stitching the skin closed during the operation, and that's extremely rare in a trauma case. Normally we'd have to leave the skin flaps open, to make it easier to clean any infected tissue. But as I said, it was a remarkably clean site."

"What was a site?" My voice was thick. I wasn't sure what I was asking. I just needed her to slow down.

My surgeon raised a clipboard and scanned it. Her name tag said DR. ANGELICA AUSTIN. That sounded familiar. She might have visited me earlier, when I was less conscious. Dr. Angelica Austin flipped a page. "We might look at scaling back your pain meds."

That sounded like a terrible idea. I tried to sit up. I caught sight of my leg. I had a thigh. A thigh in a stocking. Three or four tubes emerged from areas that were patched with dressing, looping to hanging plastic bags. Between these were glimpses of something pink and black and shiny that did not look like skin but was. I was short. That was the shocking part. It wasn't the stump so much. The stump was bad. But what was terrible was the air. The space. I had half a thigh. My knee was gone. My calf. I had no foot. I was missing an entire foot. I had kicked things with that foot and now I didn't have it. These were things that were wrong.

"You . . ." said Dr. Angelica Austin. "We went through the stump yesterday. I showed you."

"I don't remember."

Dr. Angelica Austin wrote something on her clipboard. She was lowering my dosage. Before I could object, she put her hand on my shoulder. It felt awkward, for both of us. "I'll come back when you're rested. This is the darkest point, Mr. Neumann. It all gets better from here."

. . .

MY ROOM HAD WINDOWS. I COULD SEE ALL THE WAY ACROSS THE GAR-
dens. At dusk, the skyscrapers flared orange. It was very
quiet, this hospital. It was like I was the only person there.

I HAD FOUR NURSES: KATIE, CHELSEA, VERONICA, AND MIKE. MIKE WAS
the one who bathed me. That struck me as unfair. All I'd
gone through and a man sponged me. It wasn't a big deal. It
was just another disappointment. Nurse Mike was friendly.
This is nothing against Nurse Mike. He taught me how to
unwind the bandages without pulling out a draining tube,
which was something I did once and never wanted to again.
He showed me how to fasten them so they wouldn't
unwind in the night. My dressings needed changing every
four hours. That's how much I was leaking, even before you
counted what came out of the tubes. It was an alarming
idea. Presumably if I disconnected the saline drip, I would
deflate to a husk. I was a junior high physics problem. *If
Charles Neumann is a human being with volume 80 liters,
oozing bodily fluid at the rate of 0.5 liters per minute, how
often must we replace his 400-milliliter saline bags?* I felt I
should have been more sophisticated than that.

The nurses were very familiar with my stump. They seized
any opportunity to whip back the sheet and probe my flesh.
"It's looking fantastic," they said. Especially Nurse Veronica.
Nurse Veronica could not love my stump more. She smiled
and opened my curtains and changed my bags and said it
wouldn't be long before I pulled on my dancing shoes. I
knew what they were doing. They were teaching me not to
be ashamed. It was a good hospital. But I was still ashamed.

THEN CAME THE PHYSICAL THERAPIST. THE SECOND HE BOUNCED IN I
realized I was back in gym class. He was fit and tan and wore

a hospital polo shirt small enough that his biceps strained the seams. Tucked beneath one was a clipboard. The only thing missing was a whistle. "Charles Neumann!" He stopped beside my bed and folded his arms. I had been watching TV, and felt guilty. "Is it Charles? Charlie? Chuck?"

"Charles."

"I'm Dave." He rolled aside a hat stand of fluid bags. "I'm here to get you out of that bed."

I looked at my bed. It had warm sheets. A few magazines near my feet. Foot. My phone nearby. I didn't see the problem with the bed.

Dave's eyes shone. He drank a lot of fruit juice, I could tell. He made me feel listless. "We're gonna work hard together, Charles. I have to warn you. Sometimes you may not like me very much."

He dragged over a chair. He stood there and grinned. I looked at the chair. I looked at him. "What?"

"Get into it."

It seemed a long way away. It was a meter lower than the bed. What if I fell? Dave waited. His grin was permanent. I placed my phone on my bedside table and folded up my magazines. I rolled back the sheet. I leaned forward to check my dressing, the tubes.

"Don't worry about all that. Just get your butt into this chair."

You just get your butt into this chair, I thought. But I edged forward. My stump scraped across the sheets. It wasn't terrible. But it wasn't good. I felt itchy. I was thirsty. I looked around for a glass of water.

"Come on, Charles."

I gripped the edge of the bed and swung my good leg over it. Then my stump. It made me want to cry, that little movement. It was so pathetic. Once entire limbs had jumped at my command. Now this.

"Almost there."

I slid off the bed and fell into the chair. The shock of impact traveled up my stump and jangled the nerves there. My surgeon, Dr. Angelica Austin, had folded them up inside my body. I had learned this from a nurse. They were places they were never meant to be, wondering what was going on. Something dripped into my eyes.

"Yes! Great! Great!" Dave dropped to his haunches and slapped my arm. "You made it!" He laughed like we were friends. But we were not. We were not.

THE NEXT DAY DAVE TURNED UP IN A STEEL WHEELCHAIR. IT WAS pretty flash. I mean for what it was. The wheels gleamed. The seat, back, and armrests were green leather. Dave parked beside my bed and climbed out. "Hi-ho, Silver!"

"What?"

"Time to mount your steed, my lord." He slapped the chair. "It'll be great."

It would not be great. We both knew that. It would be struggling and shaking and landing in the chair like a wet fish. And then what? Maybe Dave would push me around the hospital. Maybe he would make me wheel myself. Either would be difficult and humiliating. I chewed the inside of my mouth, because I am not good at getting mad with people.

"Let's do this," said Dave.

"I have to finish reading this." I showed him my phone. He plucked it from my fingers and set it on the bedside table. I didn't stop him, because I couldn't believe what he was doing. Dave didn't understand the intimacy of the phone. He couldn't have.

"Mount up."

He was trying to antagonize me so I would strive to prove him wrong. He saw I responded well to a challenge.

He would needle me mercilessly and then, on the day I was released, tell me how he'd always known I could do it.

"Let's go, big guy." He drummed his hands on the chair. "Let's tear this place up."

That was how they justified it. Gym teachers. Personal trainers. Runners. Looking down on you, despising you, it was okay, because it was for your own good.

"Don't make me come over there," said Dave. "Ha, ha."

I DREAMED I WAS BACK AT BETTER FUTURE AND COULDN'T FIND MY LEG. I hopped around the lab, searching. I spied it on top of the spectrograph. I filled with relief because now I could reattach it, then woke and realized no.

"TAKE IT IN," SAID DAVE. "RI-I-I-IGHT IN. FEEL YOUR CHEST EXPANDing. Hold it. Hold it. Now out."

I exhaled. The sun came out from behind a cloud. I squinted and shifted in my wheelchair. We were outside. I was not happy about that.

"Three more. I want you to let the relaxation in, Charles. Let it in."

"I'm hot."

"No you're not." Hospital people walked by, entered the lobby doors. Dave sucked in breath. "Three more."

"This isn't helping."

"It's not helping because you won't let it help."

"It's because I'm missing a leg. Breathing doesn't help with that. It doesn't help at all."

Dave's eyes held no pity. "Feeling sorry for yourself?"

Dave was wearing shorts. I had been trying not to let that bother me, but he was wearing shorts, with two fit, tan legs bursting out and running down to socks and sneakers, and wasn't that a little unfair to a guy in a wheelchair with a bloated, mutant, itching stump? I didn't want to be that guy. That angry cripple guy. But I was a cripple and Dave's legs were making me angry.

"Just another chapter, buddy," said Dave. "A new chapter in your life waiting to be written."

"It's not a chapter. It's a loss. It's a regression."

"All in how you see it."

"It's not. It's objectively verifiable. I'm *less*."

Dave squatted. He put a hand on my left wheel. "Let me tell you about a guy who came through here about five years ago. He'd had an industrial accident just like you. Lost both legs. Right up to the hip. Used to be a water skier. Professionally. But day one, when he came out of surgery, he decided, *That was my old life*. He said, *Now I start my new life*. I told him to write the next chapter, man, and he did. You know what he's doing now?"

I pushed Dave's hand off my wheel, got my hands on the grips, and shoved myself away. People stood aside to let me wheel by, one furious revolution at a time.

"He's winning medals!" Dave shouted. "In the Paralympics!"

I WOKE FROM AN AFTERNOON NAP TO FIND A WOMAN IN A CHAIR beside my bed. The chair hadn't been there before. She had brought it. She had a large black case, like a portfolio. She was neat and corporate. Her facial bones were prominent and symmetrical. She was blond. "Hey, you." Her lips twisted sympathetically. "How are you?"

"What?"

"I'm Cassandra Cautery. From the company." Her head tilted. "We miss you, Charlie. I hope they're taking good care of you. Are they? Your comfort is my priority."

"Um," I said.

"Good." She smiled. She was very attractive to be giving me this much eye contact. I felt strange, as if I had been mistaken for someone else. She handed me a business card. It said, *CASSANDRA CAUTERY. Crisis Manager.*

I said, "It was my fault. The accident."

"Would you mind signing a statement to that effect?" She flipped open her portfolio and handed me a paper. It was a letter, from me. "I'm sorry. This may feel abrupt. It's just . . . well, as you say, it was your fault." She popped a pen and offered it to me.

I wondered if I should get a lawyer. It felt like that kind of situation. But the letter was true. I raised the knee I still had, positioned the paper, and signed.

"Thank you." She made it disappear into her portfolio. "I appreciate that. Now let's talk about you. About what you need to get back on your feet." Her smile wavered. "I'm so sorry."

"It's okay."

"That slipped out."

"It's . . ." I shrugged.

"Ramps. Leave. We'll make it happen. We're that kind of company."

"Okay."

"Are you sure everything here is perfect? There's nothing at all?"

"No," I said. "Well. I don't like my physical therapist."

I NEVER SAW DAVE AGAIN. THAT AFTERNOON I WAS VISITED BY NURSE Veronica, who fiddled with the flowers by my bed. "Would you . . . what would you like to do this afternoon, Charlie?"

"Stay here," I said.

"In bed?"

"Yes."
"Okay," she said.

I DIDN'T GET UP FOR TWO DAYS. I'M NOT COUNTING BATHROOM VISITS. I did have to leave the bed for those. I had to shuffle into my wheelchair, steer onto the tiles, and drag myself onto the toilet. Then there was nothing to do but look at my stump. The stocking was off and the draining tubes removed. I no longer leaked. I was nothing but pink skin and black stitches. I didn't like the bathroom visits because I didn't like the stump.

But in bed, things were okay. I had my phone. I had wi-fi. I logged on to my work account and wrote notes. I streamed movies. I got addicted to a game. I won't say I was happy. Every now and again I reached to scratch my right leg and realized it wasn't there. Or I shifted my weight and found it unexpectedly easy. But I could see this might not be the end of everything.

DR. ANGELICA AUSTIN RETURNED. IT HAD BEEN A WEEK. I LAY BACK AND closed my eyes while she prodded at the disaster site.

"Very good." She flipped back the sheet. "I couldn't ask for a better result."

I said nothing. I didn't want to disrespect Dr. Angelica Austin. But I found it hard to believe she could be proud of this. Maybe I was being unfair, because she worked with living tissue and I worked with machine-fabricated metals. But if I ever produced something that ugly, I would be embarrassed.

"Have you felt sensation in the missing limb?"
"What?"
"Following an amputation, many patients report phantom sensation."

"Uh," I said. "No." I had heard of phantom pain. I just never thought I'd hear it from a doctor. I thought it belonged in the same category as ghosts and auras.

"Don't be ashamed to mention it."

"I haven't felt anything."

Dr. Angelica eyed me.

"I feel what's *there*. What's there is itchy."

"Painful?"

"Yes. It aches." I waited for Dr. Angelica to pick up the clipboard, the one for writing down pain medication doses. She didn't. "A lot."

"That's because you're not moving it. I heard you stopped physical therapy."

"Yes."

"Therapy is essential to your recovery. Why did you stop?"

"I didn't like Dave."

"You didn't have to like him. You just had to do what he said."

Dr. Angelica frowned. She wore glittery earrings. They were a little extravagance in an otherwise austere outfit. She would have to remove those for surgery. You couldn't have tiny jewels dropping into someone's chest cavity. They were counterfunctional, which implied Dr. Angelica cared more about looking good than doing her job. I was possibly being unfair again. Maybe she didn't have surgery today.

"It's time you saw the prosthetist."

For a second I thought she said *prostitute*. "Prosthetics?"

"Yes." Dr. Angelica eyeballed me, as if I should count myself lucky I was getting a prosthetist at all. I got the feeling she did not think I had really deserved her surgery. "She's very good."

"I don't need a prosthesis." I was thinking about what that would mean: more gym class. Gripping wooden rails, struggling to coordinate parts of my body. "I can use the chair. I sit down all day at work. I sit down at home. I don't play sports."

"Do you drive? Does your house have steps? Do you ever catch an escalator? How many times a day do you stand?"

I said nothing.

"You're not useless," said Dr. Angelica. "You haven't broken. You have a minor disability and you can learn to overcome it."

I WAS SICKLY AS A CHILD. I GUESS THAT COMES AS NO SURPRISE. I WAS that kid who spent a whole summer inside, curtains drawn against the hoots and laughter of kids in the street outside. Glandular fever. Then complications in the lungs. When I got back to school, in gym class I handed the teacher the note that allowed me to be excused to the library. He made me show him that note every time, even though it said *for the duration of the year.* He was waiting for me to decide I was ready for gym class, and forget what my note said. That day never came. In the library, I read about trains and DNA and how they built the Hoover Dam. Walking home, I watched a boom gate descend across a railroad crossing and knew it did so because the wheels of an approaching train had dipped the track's inductance below its preprogrammed level.

As a result, I threw like a four-year-old. I couldn't catch. When I ran, my arms and legs flailed like I was drowning. If I had to play baseball, I swung at balls with hope but no faith and was not surprised. In soccer, people wove through me like I wasn't there.

When I got older things started to change. I don't mean I improved. I mean it mattered less. By senior year, most of the kids who could run and jump and throw balls like missiles had dropped out. Being smart became valuable. No girl came up clutching textbooks to ask if I could help with her homework, but I could see it might happen. The likelihood of such an occurrence was on the rise. I attended MIT, and in mechanical engineering no one cared about sports. There was a girl in wave propagation, Jenny, and one time when I was presenting a paper on hydrodynamics she kept nodding and smiling. I spent a week thinking how to ask her out. Then I came to class and there was a guy kicking a little sack in the air, doing tricks, and Jenny was watching him in a whole other way, and I realized things were not so different after all.

THE PROSTHETIST WALKED IN WITH A BUNCH OF ARTIFICIAL LEGS under each arm, like a Hindu goddess. She dumped the legs onto my bed and ogled me through glasses. Her hair was brown and limp and dragged into a merciless ponytail. Her shirt was white and huge. "Hi! I hear you got a transfemoral." Before I could respond, she lifted up my sheet. "Oh. They weren't kidding. That is a clean stump." She rolled the sheet up to my waist and put her elbows on the bed, so she could look at it from up close. "Some kind of machine accident, yes?"

"A clamp."

"Well, you hit the jackpot. This is amazing."

I stared at her. She wasn't the first person to act like my amputation was just terrific. But she was the first I believed.

"If you're planning to do the other leg, you should definitely use the same method. I'm serious."

"What?"

"I'm joking." She sat up but one of her hands was still right next to my stump. "It's Charlie, right? I'll be honest, Charlie. I love a transfemoral. I see a lot of transtibials—that's below the knee—and, no offense to those people, but it's like fitting shoes. There's no art in it. This . . ." She patted my stump. I jumped. "This is a blank canvas. This gives us options. Want to see some legs?" She turned to rummage through her limbs. A section of hair drifted in front of her face and she jammed it behind her ear like she wanted to teach it a lesson. "Okay. Let's see what we've got here." She lifted something. A pole. The toe was rubber. Like the bottom half of a crutch. The top was a flesh-colored plastic bucket with cloth straps. "This is entry-level. I'm only showing you this so you know what's out there. Hey. Hey." My eyes jumped to her face. "I'm not putting you in this. This is horrible. This is the public option. Although, just FYI, if your employer wasn't giving you basically the best medical care in the world, this is what you'd get." She put the pole leg on the floor, where I couldn't see it. "Let's forget that. Wait. Did I introduce myself? I'm Lola Shanks."

I knew that from the ID tag dangling from her billowing shirt. She was grimacing into the camera. If my ID looked like that, I would ask them to take another picture.

"Let me show you something else." From the ankle down it resembled a real leg. A real leg that had died a few days earlier. The toes were flat and squared off. The calf was aluminum. The knee was a band of jointed metal. At the top was another bucket. "This you can put a shoe on. And I see from your face that you're not in love with it, but imagine it under long pants. The fullness here? It gives you a more natural look. Once you get practiced, nobody will know the difference. Not until you take off your pants." She grinned. She was pretty young. How much education did you need to become a prosthetist? Not much, apparently. "What do you think?"

"How does it work?"

"You're looking at the socket. Ninety percent of your satisfaction with the prosthetic will come from how well you fit the socket." I noticed her choice of words; not *how well the socket fits you*. "We wrap your limb in a stocking, pull it into the socket through this little hole at the bottom here, and tighten it with these straps. But that's not ideal. What we'll do once the swelling has subsided is take a mold of your leg and build a custom socket off that."

"How does it walk?"

"Well, you swing it. It takes some practice."

"You swing it?"

"Right. It's hinged. Your foot will fly out in front of you for a while. Steep inclines will be a challenge. Everything will be a challenge. It's going to be hard, Charlie, no matter what you wear."

I looked at the pile of legs. "What else?" I could see something black and silver poking out from behind her. That looked interesting.

She smiled. "You're spoiling it. I was trying to build up some suspense before we went to the top of the line. But before we go there, let me warn you: these don't give you a natural look. We're now trading off cosmetics for function."

"I don't care about a natural look."

Lola's breath caught. "*Really.* Well, that's good. I feel the same way. Real beauty follows function. That's why we find things attractive: because they work. Like teeth. We don't just like them straight and white for no reason. It's because they're good at biting. This leg, it's good at walking." She reached behind her. What she produced was not like a leg. It was like a machine. The foot was two arched prongs, almost skis. From a hydraulic ankle rose twin black pylons, which disappeared into an aluminum knee. Judging from the battery casing, there was a microprocessor in there. "It's an Exegesis Archion foot on a computer-controlled adaptive knee. Multiaxis rotation, polycentric swing. That heel, that's carbon polymer. The Olympics banned it because it provided an unfair advantage over regular legs. Too much energy return. The knee is programmable. We teach it your precise gait. What it does is take the thinking out of walking. You get to stop worrying about how you're going to swing your foot and just walk."

I took the leg and turned it over. It was light. Interesting design. Nothing groundbreaking. At the top was a bucket, another one of those translucent plastic sockets. I looked inside, in case there was anything innovative in there, but there wasn't.

"You don't seem very excited," said Lola.

"Is this the best?"

"It's . . . well . . . honestly, Charlie, it's pretty great."

"This is state-of-the-art?"

"Cutting-edge," said Lola, and grinned. I realized this was a joke. People in medicine have dark senses of humor. To them, no joke is complete until there's a defiled corpse or spray of blood. "No. Seriously. This is the best."

I gave her back the leg. "Okay."

"It's not a meat leg. I can't give you that. But once you get familiar with this, it'll be almost as good as the real thing."

"Okay."

She gathered up her legs. I shuffled down in the bed. It was nothing against Lola Shanks. She just didn't have anything I wanted.

THAT NIGHT I WOKE TO DISCOVER I WAS PULLING AT THE STITCHES, digging in my fingernails. I scrambled upright and flicked on the light, expecting the worst. But I seemed intact. A little clear fluid oozed out. I mopped it with a wet wipe from the drawer, switched off the light, and lay down. But it took a long time to get back to sleep, because that was really disturbing.

. . .

THERE WAS A ROOM WITH TWO WOODEN RAILS. THE RAILS WERE FOR holding on to. They were three meters long and one meter apart, waist high. Aside from a few chairs, a desk, and a potted plant, they were the only objects in the room. It was not a place for things. It was a place for movement.

Lola Shanks parked me beside a plastic chair, set down the Exegesis legs, and rolled up my pajama pants. I wasn't happy about this, about these rails.

"I notice you're not much of a talker." She clipped my pants, so they looked like shorts. I had not worn shorts for eleven years. It was another example of how I was being turned into someone I did not want to be. "That's a problem."

"Why?"

"Because you need to be social." She rolled a stocking over my stump. "Some people will be reluctant to talk to you. Afraid of saying the wrong thing. You need to break the ice." She tucked the foot under one arm and fed the end of the stocking through a hole in its socket. She pulled. I felt a terrible pressure, like my stitches were about to burst. My stump was sucked into the socket. "How's that?"

"Tight. Tight."

"Tight is good." She reached around my hips, feeding the strap. "You're not seeing the problem, are you?"

"What?"

"The social thing. You're not afraid of isolation."

"No."

She sat back on her haunches. "You can't make this an excuse to disappear. I've seen how that turns out. How you get through this depends on you, Charlie. On how you respond to the challenge."

"Okay." I didn't mean this. It wasn't that I wanted to cut myself off from the world. I just knew it would happen.

She backed away. "Stand up."

I gripped the side of the wheelchair and levered myself into the air. The leg hung from my stump. It looked even less impressive from this angle. The ski-like prongs wobbled. They seemed flimsy. They looked like they might fall off.

"Put your weight on it."

I leaned forward. The socket squeezed me in a way that felt very wrong.

"Trust the leg, Charlie."

"The stitches—"

"I haven't popped a stitch yet."

I dragged my sleeve across my forehead. I put more weight on the leg and the toe prongs bent. I knew logically they must be rated to carry a running adult male but it seemed hard to believe. I wondered how thoroughly it had been checked.

Lola Shanks held out her arms. I took a breath and let the leg absorb my weight. The pressure was bad but not unbearable. I shuffled forward and did it again. By the time I reached Lola I was losing rivers of sweat. I had traveled four paces. "Good!" She grinned, as if this was genuinely exciting for her, and I was shaky and tired but also proud and I smiled, too.

I SAT IN BED AND INSPECTED THE EXEGESIS. I REALLY NEEDED TOOLS. To take it apart. But I could figure out some things from observation. It wasn't that complicated. It was essentially a bucket on a stick. I still found it surprising that this was as good as it got. It made me suspect that there were not a lot of amputees working in mechanical engineering. They seemed to have started from the premise that you should be grateful to be walking at all.

But Lola Shanks was right: I had grown to like it. Not because it let me walk. That I could take or leave. But I did like staggering toward Lola, her eyes growing with each step, and how when I reached her she squeezed my hands.

I WAS STILL SHOCKED SOMETIMES TO SEE I WAS MISSING A LEG. I HAD moments of paralyzing fear while my mind screamed, *Where is it?* Sometimes I dreamed I was missing something but couldn't figure out what. It became annoying. I knew my brain had thirty-five years of conditioning to get over, but seriously, when was it going to realize this was real?

AT 10:45 A.M. I GREW IMPATIENT AND FIDGETY. I COULDN'T CONCEN-trate on my phone. I felt thirsty. It was because of Lola Shanks. She visited at eleven. I slid to the edge of the bed and strapped on the leg. When she arrived I was up and hobbling. She stopped in the doorway, looking outraged, in a good way. "*Charlie,*" she said. She stuck out her elbow. "Let's go for a walk."

THE HOSPITAL WAS ENCIRCLED BY A WIDE CONCRETE PATH, FROM THE emergency bay to the rear garden. There patients stood attached to IV drips, sucking cigarettes. I was getting the hang of the Exegesis. But if I walked too confidently Lola Shanks took back her arm, so the temptation was there to feign incompetence.

"Tell me about your work," said Lola. "What do you do?"

"I test things." My ski-prong toes dragged: *skrrrrch.*

"What kind of things?"

"Things. Materials."

"Is it interesting?"

I considered. It was interesting sometimes, like when you thought the copper valence was going to fall apart under particle bombardment but then it didn't. This wasn't what people meant by interesting, though. "No."

"Oh," said Lola.

"Sometimes I make things. If I have an idea, I can propose it as a project, and if they approve it I can build it."

"What do you build?"

We descended a ramp. The ski toes tried to sail away from me and I let them. Lola's arm tightened around mine. "Last year I built an oscillator. It moved a five-gram copper rod back and forth over a distance of twenty millimeters six hundred thousand times a second."

Lola was silent. "How is that useful?"

"I'm not sure. I just proposed it and they said yes. They probably used it in some other project."

"Oh."

"Six hundred thousand oscillations per second is a lot."

"It sounds like a lot."

"I had to put it in a vacuum. To stop it setting the air on fire."

"It set the air on fire?"

"Only once. In a controlled environment."

"Who do you work for again?"

"Better Future." She looked blank. "We developed depleted-uranium ordnance in the seventies. In the eighties we made amphibious tanks. They didn't really work out. I don't think we do them anymore. About ten years ago we got into medicine. We have a lot of pharmacological products. Lately we're into proprietary metals fabrication, non-lethal weaponry, and bioengineering. We also sponsor the local softball team."

An older man in a hospital gown blocked our path, gazing out over the gardens, a cigarette to his lips. He seemed irritated about something. Maybe everything. He looked like that kind of guy. "Excuse us," said Lola. His gaze dropped to the Exegesis and his lips pressed together. "Hey," said Lola. "What was that?" He pretended not to hear. "Hey. Smokey. What's your problem? You think you're a better human being because you've got two legs?" He pushed his IV hat stand back toward the building. "Yeah, congratulations on those. Good job. I'm sure you put a lot of work into them." Lola turned to me. "Can you believe that?" She shook her head. "Outrageous."

We walked.

"People with legs have no character, Charlie. Honest to God. They never once have to figure out how to get from one room to another. And if they ever realize that, they feel *clever.*" She threaded her arm through mine. "You're going to struggle. You're going to have it tough. And that will make you a better person."

We walked in silence. A breeze touched my skin. I had never, ever, been this happy.

THE NEXT DAY LOLA TOOK ME TO THE CAFETERIA. IT WAS FULL OF DOCtors and conversation and families being positive. Some patients had no hair and some were thin as wire frames and reminded me things could be worse. Lola and I took a table near the window overlooking the gardens. I had decided to ask her out. I wasn't sure what that meant. I couldn't take her anywhere. But it was what you did when you liked a girl. And if she said yes, you had a girlfriend. That was all I knew. I was very nervous because I hadn't been in a position to ask a girl out since Jenny in wave propagation.

"How many people do you think you could poison

before anyone noticed?" She was watching a woman serving coleslaw. "I think a lot."

"Can we go out?"

She bit into her burger. "Not today. I have a plan for you involving a soccer ball."

I had been unclear. I shifted my weight from one buttock to the other. My ski toes clanged against the table leg. "Bong," said Lola.

"I like your hair."

Lola's eyes widened. They lit on a few strands drifting past her face. She made a noise like *fffbrr,* grabbed them, and twisted them around her ear. "Shut up." I didn't say anything. I didn't know if I should explain that I wasn't joking or let her think I was. "When are you plucking those eyebrows?"

I took a bite of my egg sandwich. I was out of my depth. Should I pluck my eyebrows? I didn't know men did that.

Lola's hip beeped. She unclipped her pager. "Bah. That can wait."

Lola had other patients. Of course she did. Other men. She helped them walk and squeezed their hands when they took steps. I bet every one of them fell in love with her. Maybe not every one. She was kind of odd. But enough. I recalled a paper on how test subjects experiencing highly stressful events were disproportionately attracted to the first person they met afterward. The body confused arousal with attraction. I must be the latest in a long line of freshly dismembered men to fall under the spell of Lola Shanks. She was probably sick of it. If I told her I loved her she would look pained and explain that she really liked me and I was terrific but what we had was a working relationship. Then our sessions would be awkward. I should have realized this earlier.

"What?" said Lola.

I was staring. "Nothing." I picked up my sandwich.

"I can't believe you eat eggs," she said. "They're basically fetuses."

NURSE KATIE BUSTLED INTO MY ROOM. SHE SEEMED VERY HAPPY. "Good news. You're going home."

I put down my phone. "What?"

"You've been cleared for discharge."

"What?"

"Oh, you," said Katie. "Would you like me to help you dress? Or do you want to do that yourself?"

"I don't . . . why am I being discharged?"

"I guess because you're ready." Nurse Katie was happy. She had cheeks like apples.

"I don't think I am ready."

"Well," said Katie, bending to retrieve a pajama top. "That is not the medical opinion."

I didn't understand how this had happened. No one had warned me. I hadn't been consulted. It felt like an eviction.

"Your company has arranged a car. It's out front. So let's get moving! Did you want some help with your clothes?"

I looked around the room. I didn't want to leave. Here was everything I needed. "Shouldn't I talk with my doctors first?"

"Oh, I don't think you need more doctors." Nurse Katie flopped a hospital-issue bag onto the bed. "You need to get out there and start enjoying life again."

"But . . ."

"It's all taken care of," she said. "Chop-chop."

NURSE KATIE WHEELED ME OUT TO THE CURB. THIS WAS SLIGHTLY ridiculous because I was wearing the leg, but there were rules. A van was waiting, a white one, with a Better Future logo. I didn't know why they had chosen a van until Katie helped me into the passenger seat and rolled the wheelchair around to the rear. The chair was coming with me.

"Good luck!" called Katie. She waved through the window.

"Where to?" asked the driver.

Back, I thought. But that was not an option. "Home, I guess," I said.

3

I DECIDED TO JERK MYSELF OFF. I WASN'T HORNY. I HAD NOTHING ELSE
to do. I had been home a week and was sick of Netflix. I sat
at my workstation and browsed some porn. I looked at a
girl with red hair and lips and wondered what it would be
like to talk to her. I dug myself out of my pajama pants. I
was overcooked pasta. I thought: *Kind of like a stump,* and
that was a terrible idea, horrible. I began to shrink. I wondered if I should search for amputee porn, by which I
meant porn for amputees, then realized that was not what I
would find. I searched anyway. I found a beautiful woman
with one arm and another with no legs below the knee and
I thought they were pretty hot and kind of inspiring but I
did not want to masturbate to them. I remembered a study
on male chimpanzees and how those on the lowest social

rungs exhibited severely depressed sexual desire. I shut down the computer. I felt lonely.

I WOKE TO A TERRIBLE CRAMP IN MY FOOT. NOT THE FOOT I HAD. THE other one. I groped around in the dark, grimacing and clutching at empty sheets. I hauled myself upright and turned on the lamp and threw back the sheets. "See. Nothing there." I was talking to my brain. "Nothing to hurt." I leaned forward and pretended to massage the space where my toes would have been. As a scientist, I am not proud of this. But it seemed to help. I swallowed some pills and kept massaging. I was ahead of my prescriptions. But this was a temporary problem. Soon my brain would figure out it shouldn't be feeling phantom pain, because I was a pretty smart guy.

I WAS ON MY SOFA PLAYING WITH MY PHONE WHEN IT RANG. I DIDN'T know what the hell it was doing. I was scrolling through an article and suddenly the whole screen changed and it made a noise I'd never heard before. I thought: *Pop-up advertising?* I saw: BLOCKED, DECLINE, ANSWER. I moved my thumb to the ANSWER button. It felt strange, as if I were attempting to microwave something in the TV. "Hello?"

"Dr. Neumann." A woman. Not Lola. There was a lot of warmth in *Dr. Neumann,* like she enjoyed saying my name. It was a month for unfamiliar experiences. "It's Cassandra Cautery. From the company. How are you?"

"Hello," I said again. I was not good on the phone, obviously.

"I just wanted to reach out and see how things were."

There was a pause, during which I realized this was a question. "Good."

"Great!" Cassandra Cautery was quite hot, I remembered. I was talking to a hot woman right now. "I thought so. I've seen the reports from the hospital and they were glowing. I was extremely pleased. You know how much we're concerned about you."

"Okay."

"I wanted to float an idea with you. The idea of coming back to work." She paused. "This can happen completely on your timetable. We want to do it so it works for you. But—I'm not sure if you're aware—there's evidence that returning to work is extremely beneficial. For you, I mean. You get reengaged, get busy, you're not just sitting around the house. Not that you're doing that!" She laughed. My coffee table bore four half-empty boxes of cereal and half a dozen snack wrappers. On the bookshelf there was a carton of curdled milk I had been meaning to throw away for two days but always forgot about until I sat down. I had an e-mail from my internet provider telling me that although I was on a quote unlimited download plan end quote there were reasonable usage guidelines and they would appreciate it if I tried to stay within them. "I know how it is with engineers. Never happy unless you're building something. So . . . do you have any thoughts about when you'd like to come back?"

"Um," I said. "Tomorrow."

"Tomorrow? I mean . . . absolutely. Let's do tomorrow." I heard her shuffling papers. "That's terrific. I'll send a car. A van."

"A car is fine. I have a leg."

"A . . . of course you do. I'm thrilled you're being proactive about this. I really am. It's great if we can show you're able to return to full duties relatively quickly. It just reduces any potential messiness on the legal side. You know?"

"No."

She laughed. But I was not joking. "So let's get you back on your . . . on the horse. How's eight a.m. tomorrow?"

"Okay." I took the phone from my ear and tapped END CALL. The screen faded to the home page. I had an appointment. I entered it into my phone, then checked the call log. There it was. An incoming call. It had lasted three minutes, forty-two seconds. I looked at it a while, because it was kind of remarkable.

I SHOWERED, BUT NOT FOR LONG BECAUSE I DIDN'T HAVE A CHAIR LIKE in the hospital, where I could sit and feel water drain past my butt. I had to get one of those. I gripped the shower screen and hopped to my towel. I could have worn the Exegesis—it was water-resistant—but then I wouldn't have been able to wash the stump. If there was one place I needed to wash, it was the stump.

I dried myself on the toilet, pulled on the stocking, and fitted the leg. I had not been wearing it much since I got home. Lola Shanks would be disappointed. When I stood, the plastic socket squeezed me and I thought: *That's right, that's why I don't like it.* But I lumbered into the bedroom and opened the closet. When I was dressed I walked back to the bathroom and looked at myself in the mirror. I was leaning on my biological leg. I straightened. The Exegesis did not look so good poking out of the bottom of a pair of business pants. It looked like a forked tongue. Like I had stepped in something and become tangled. I felt nervous. At the hospital, lots of people had something wrong with them.

I walked into the living room and sat on the sofa. My phone rang. The driver. I sat there and did not answer. It stopped. Then it rang again. This time I tapped ANSWER. "Hello," I said. "I'm ready."

. . .

IT WAS A BLACK TOWN CAR. THE DRIVER WAS OVERWEIGHT AND HAD A cap and a little beard. He opened the rear door and told me it was a beautiful morning. Once we were on the road, he said, "That's a fancy-looking foot you have there."

I looked up from my phone. He was watching me in the mirror. "It's an Exegesis."

"Oh yeah? What does that do?"

"It converts kinetic energy into forward motion." I was describing walking.

The driver whistled. "Nice," he said. "Nice."

WE PULLED INTO THE DRIVEWAY THAT ARCED PAST THE MAIN LOBBY doors. The driver sprang out to open my door. Before I got my phone into my pants he was offering me his hand. I took it; he levered me to my feet. It was bright and I squinted. Two people came toward me: Cassandra Cautery and a tall, smiling man I didn't recognize. "There he is," said the man. "Great to have you back." His ID tag said: D. PETERS. I think he was my section head. I didn't recognize him because he was a senior manager and they didn't go into the labs. D. Peters extended a hand and I shook it. It felt strange, like I was meeting him for the first time.

"We're so pleased," added Cassandra Cautery. She was smiling, too.

"Everything's set up for you." We began to walk toward the glass doors. I was a little awkward and my ski toes dragged. "That's amazing," said D. Peters. "What is that, ah, that called?"

"It's an Exegesis Archion."

"And what's the idea there? With the design?"

"It doesn't waste so much kinetic energy."

He nodded. "Mmm. Clever."

The glass doors·parted. We entered the air-regulated coolness of Better Future. The lobby had very high ceilings, even for us, and was connected via a glass wall to the atrium. There were birds in there. They lived their whole lives inside the company. A couple of white coats crossing the floor glanced at my foot with professional interest. It was hard to walk when you were self-conscious about it.

"I'm going to let you get to work," said D. Peters. "But if there's anything I can do for you, anything at all, I'm a phone call away."

"Okay."

"Good man." For a second I thought he was going to punch my arm. But he didn't. He strode briskly away, to do whatever it was the managers did. Have meetings, I guess. Make phone calls. It was hard for us on the technical side to understand why the company required so many managers. Engineers built things. Salespeople sold things. Even Human Resources I could understand, kind of. But managers proliferated despite performing very few identifiable functions.

Cassandra Cautery swiped into Building A. I followed. "You can really move on that," she said. I nodded. We didn't talk for a while. When we reached the elevators, a few people joined us, but no one spoke. I couldn't tell if they were uncomfortable around my leg or didn't care. Cassandra Cautery inspected something on her sleeve. The elevator dinged and we stepped inside. A man tried to join us but Cassandra Cautery said, "Would you mind very much taking the next one? Thank you."

The doors closed. The car hummed. Cassandra Cautery said, "I suffer from diastema." Her face was faintly flushed. "It's a gap between the teeth." She dug a finger into her mouth and stretched back her lips. Between her canines and her molars was a space, almost a centimeter wide. She released her lips. "I saw five different specialists but they all said the same thing. It's inoperable. There's a bundle of nerves there and the way the teeth are sitting, they can't be moved without risking permanent damage. Facial paralysis." She blinked three times. "It was hard to deal with. Growing up. I dieted. I ran and swam and did Pilates. The girls in my social group in high school, well, you probably won't understand, but they were fierce. About appearance. I told my parents I wanted the operation anyway. I didn't care if I got facial paralysis. They said no. We fought for months."

The elevator doors opened. Cassandra Cautery glanced out. The corridor was empty. I shifted uncomfortably.

"But you know what? I'm glad I have this. I'm proud of it. Not proud. Grateful. For the lesson. You can't be perfect, no matter how hard you try. That's the message. You don't stop trying to improve yourself. You keep pushing yourself in the areas you can control. But when you come up against something like diastema, all you can do is accept it. You can only take a deep breath and say, 'This is who I am.'"

There was silence. "Okay," I said.

"I've never told anyone else about this. I'd appreciate it if you kept it to yourself."

"Okay."

She smiled. "I just want you to know you're not alone."

CASSANDRA CAUTERY ESCORTED ME AS FAR AS THE GLASS ROOM. Inside, my lab assistants Jason and Elaine were at their desks. Katherine I could see down in Lab 2, doing something to rats. Katherine was always messing with those rats. She'd made them little houses and ramps out of sheet fiber. One had a kind of swing. I had been meaning to take her aside and tell her she would regret this kind of thing when it came time for destructive testing.

Jason's and Elaine's eyes followed me across the floor. I landed in my office chair. Elaine said, "Welcome back, Dr. Neumann."

"Thank you."

Elaine looked at Jason. Jason said nothing. Elaine said, "We're glad you're okay."

I turned on my computer. This thing took forever to boot. I fingered my pants pocket, seeking my phone.

"We had counseling."

I looked at her. "Why?"

"To deal with it. The accident. It was pretty gruesome. Very gruesome. I have nightmares." She hesitated. Across Elaine's forehead marched a parade of acne. She had violent skin. She wore her hair in thick bangs but you could still see it. "It was good. The counseling. They encouraged us to talk. They said we should share our feelings with you, if you were comfortable with that."

I looked at Jason. He was very upright, his face stiff. His head moved left, right, left, very slightly. I felt grateful to Jason. If everybody were like him we could just move on and pretend nothing ever happened.

Elaine said, "So I don't know if . . . if you are comfortable. With talking about it. If not—"

"I don't want to talk about it."

"Oh. Okay. No problem." She turned away. Her shoulders hunched. I had consigned her to nightmares, I guess. But I wasn't responsible for her brain. I didn't control what she thought. She was a human being. She should take ownership of what occurred between her ears.

"Welcome back, Dr. Neumann," said Jason. He had visibly relaxed. He swiveled back to his desk and we got to work.

. . .

I LEFT THE GLASS ROOM FOR LUNCH. THE CORRIDORS WERE BUSY AND my ski foot attracted attention. People stared without shame. We were a company of engineers: they were interested in how things worked. I kept moving, but when I reached the Building A cafeteria there was a line. The man ahead of me turned and saw my leg. "Hey. Are you that guy?"

"Which . . ." I said. "Yes."

"You chopped off your leg?" He bent down and peered at it. "In the lab?"

"Crushed."

"Do you mind if I touch?"

"Uh . . ." Two more people in the line turned. A bearded guy got up from his table and headed toward me, trailing lab assistants. "Okay."

"Interesting shape," said a woman behind me.

"Let me just roll up the pants here." The man glanced up. "Is that okay? I can't see."

"I'll do it." I pulled up the pant leg. There was a murmur of appreciation. I flushed.

"Look at the knee," said the beard.

"It's moving with the piston here," said the man, now on his hands and knees, peering up. "That, what, makes it more comfortable to walk?"

"And his leg fits into that plastic bit."

"The socket."

"What holds that on?"

"Straps," I said. "Just cloth straps."

There was silence. The blue-shirt guy peered around for another few moments, but didn't see anything else that caught his attention. "Well, that's really amazing."

"Incredible," said the beard. "Just fantastic, what they're doing."

"Very smart," said the woman.

These people's ID tags said AERONAUTICAL DEVELOPMENT and MOLECULAR REENGINEERING and BIOMATERIALS. To the average scientist, *stupid* was failing to account for behavioral changes exhibited by magnetohydrodynamics when accelerated to supersonic speeds. It was being uncomfortable with Gödel numbering. A few months ago I had attended a presentation on living gels, and when a man in the audience said something was *smart*, he was referring to a process for tricking living cells into fusing with carbon molecules for the first time in human history. And he said it grudgingly. We did not use the word *smart* lightly. We did not use it about a hinge.

"Very nice." Someone patted me lightly on the shoulder. "Very nice." I rolled down my pants, ashamed.

I CARRIED MY LUNCH TO A BATHROOM AND LOCKED MYSELF IN A STALL. As I picked my sandwich out of the plastic wrap, I remembered what Lola Shanks had said: that things would be tough, and that would make me a better person. She said it was about *how you respond to the challenge.* I was glad she wasn't here to see this.

I RECEIVED AN E-MAIL FROM CASSANDRA CAUTERY INFORMING ME that a car would take me home whenever I wanted. I just had to call a number. I recorded this in my phone and kept working. After everybody left, I caught the elevator to the AV Center, where vending machines offered energy bars, fruit, and cola outside darkened presentation rooms. It was free, so that engineers wouldn't wander around trying to find the most efficient sources of calories per dollar. I chose some snack bars and apples and returned to the Glass

Room. I had nothing to do. Most of my work had been reassigned while I was away, the remainder had no deadline. I ate my snacks and played with some programs but was not inspired. I read a sensationalist article about the future of embedded operating systems. Around ten, I picked up my phone. The driver said he would be ten minutes. I waited five, pulled on my jacket, and left the Glass Room. When I stepped out on the ground floor, the corridor lights glowed a dim yellow and the lobby was empty. My footsteps echoed, a soft scuff from my shoe followed by a scrape of carbon polymer, like some kind of machine process.

I DISCOVERED BUILDING A HAD BUNKS. THEY WERE SMALL, FEATURE-less rooms with barely enough space for a bed, but anyone could use them. If you had two hours before the catalytic cracker finished, you could get some downtime. There were also showers and a twenty-four-hour kitchen. I half-expected to find it populated by a loud, jokey community of scientists, like island shipwreck survivors, but it was empty. I called my driver and asked if he could collect some things from my house. That night I microwaved a shrink-wrapped meal and slept in a bunk. When I woke, I showered and dressed and caught the elevator back and this entire time I didn't see a single other person. I wished I had thought of this earlier.

IT BECAME ANNOYING TO SIT. TO TRANSIT, FROM STANDING. THE EXE-gesis was good for movement but gave me nothing when I went to lower myself into a chair. It was all up to my biological leg, which was thin and weak and complained at the effort. At the hospital, when I'd been doing physical therapy, it had bulked up a little, but since then it had shrunk back to default size. So now I accelerated into chairs, making a *whoof* upon impact. It wasn't a huge problem. But it was not ideal.

When the assistants left, I removed my leg, clamped it to a workbench, and swung over some lighting. I studied the knee. Then I disassembled it. By midnight I had built a governor. It looked like a tin of peaches, affixed below the knee. When I flicked a little metal switch on the side, it limited the speed at which the knee could flex. I strapped it on and tried sitting. It worked. I could lower myself into a chair at normal speed with no effort. But I felt unsatisfied. Now that I thought about it, it was very primitive to have to flick a switch. The knee should figure out when to engage itself.

At three in the morning I gave up on the governor idea and connected the knee's microprocessor to a computer so I could unpick its code. I figured I could modify this and flash new instructions. This took eight hours. In the meantime Jason and Katherine arrived and asked through the speaker if I needed help. I had them bring me snacks. Finally I loaded new code onto the chip and powered it on. The capacitor popped and died.

I stared at it. I needed sleep. With a clear head I could figure this out. I pulled on the leg, smelling stale sweat, and hobbled out. Without a functional microprocessor, the leg swung like a garden gate. The ski foot flew out in front. I made my way to the elevators with one hand touching the wall. When I reached my bunk, I pulled off the straps and threw the whole thing on the floor.

I WANTED ELAINE TO FETCH ME A CADMIUM BATTERY BUT SHE WAS nowhere to be found. "Have you seen Elaine?" I asked Jason.

He swiveled to face me. His glasses reflected my halogen workbench light. "I thought . . ." He looked at Elaine's desk. It was very clean. "Didn't you get an e-mail?"

I rolled to my keyboard. I had lots of e-mails. I read few. I looked at the forty-character previews, and when they began, "Season's Greetings from everyone here at . . ." or, "Seminars are now open for bookings on a . . ." it was obvious they were just noise. E-mails I needed to read began, "Didn't you see this? You must . . ." or, "Your department has again failed to . . ." or something like that. I scrolled through my in-box. I had to sift through a lot of useless information about who wasn't allowed to park where and why the air conditioners would be off from four to five but then I found it. It was from Human Resources. Elaine had transferred out. The e-mail didn't say why. It just said it was *thought best.*

"Oh," I said.

THAT NIGHT THE CADMIUM BATTERY FRIED THE MICROPROCESSOR. I had known this was a possibility but still it was disappointing. I sat at my workbench and stared at the thin wisp of smoke twisting out of the plastic knee. It was fixable. I could replace the chip. But then I would be limited by the transistors. Every time I upgraded something, something new became a bottleneck.

I pushed myself away from the bench. It was late. My problem was I was tinkering around the edges. Trying to improve it beyond the capability of its fundamental design. I was thinking like everyone else: that the goal of a prosthesis was to mimic biology.

I closed my eyes. I felt warm. I opened them, found a pad and pen, and began to write. I sketched. I filled four pages and took the leg off the table and put it on the floor to make room. I had been going about this all wrong. Biology was not ideal. When you thought about it, biological legs couldn't do anything except convey a small mass from A to B, so long as A and B were not particularly far apart and you were in no hurry. That wasn't great. The only reason it was even notable was that legs did it using raw materials they grew themselves. If you were designing something within that limitation, then okay, good job. But if you weren't, it seemed to me you could build in a lot more features.

THREE WEEKS LATER I CALLED THE HOSPITAL. I WAS VERY EXCITED. I had been putting this off, waiting until I was calm, but that never happened so finally I just did it. I closed the door to my bunk room and faced the wall so nothing could distract me.

"Lola Shanks, Prosthetics."

"Hi, it's Charles Neumann, I was in there a few—"

"Charlie! Where have you been?"

I was supposed to visit the hospital for follow-up sessions. They were mandatory, but the kind with no penalties for noncompliance. "Busy. Can I see you?"

"Yes! That would be good! I hope you've been keeping up your physical therapy. You're in trouble if you haven't. When can you come in?"

"Can you come here?" I was tapping the floor with my ski toes: *tick tick tick.* I made myself stop that. "I have something to show you. I want your professional opinion."

"Um. Okay. Why not? Where are you?"

TO MEET LOLA SHANKS I HAD TO GO TO THE LOBBY. I HADN'T BEEN aboveground since I discovered the bunk rooms. But she needed to be authorized. So I rode the elevator and walked the corridors. This was harder than it sounds because I was wearing the Exegesis and had never gotten around to fixing the knee. It tended to get away from me. I stuck close to walls. But I limped past hardened engineers without a single question. This puzzled me until I realized I had become pathetic.

I reached the lobby and fell into a black sofa. I pulled out my phone and looked up every few seconds to see if she was coming through the doors. I was early. I leaned forward and peered at a scale model of a mobile weapons platform that sat in a glass case on the low coffee table. Its little plaque said, CIVIL PEACEMAKER VO.5-III. It was essentially a caravan with guns. I had been to a presentation; the idea was you towed it somewhere like a recently captured city and left it there, making peace.

"Hey!"

I jumped. Lola Shanks was coming toward me, wearing a white polo shirt, white pants, and white sneakers. Her hair was held back with a thin white headband. My first thought was she had come directly from exercising or perhaps some sort of religious event but I think it was extremely uniform fashion choices. She held out her arms. I got off the sofa, which required rocking. My unregulated ski foot flew out. Lola grabbed my hands. "Whoa! What's wrong with the leg? It shouldn't do that." Before I could explain, she rolled up my pants. "What's this?" She tapped the tin.

"I modified it."

"You what?" By now she had exposed the knee. What was left of it. It was a half-melted empty casing. "Where's the knee?"

"I broke it." I felt uncomfortable. People were watching. Lola got to her feet, her brown eyes flicking between mine. "I didn't get to say good-bye at the hospital."

"That wasn't supposed to be good-bye. You were supposed to come in for sessions."

"Oh."

"Why did you break your knee?"

"I was trying to improve it. But then I got the idea to
build a new one."

"A new knee?"

"A new leg."

"You . . . what?"

"I built a prosthesis. Well. I'm still tinkering. It can be
better."

"You built a leg?"

"I'll show you."

"Yes," she said. "Please."

LOLA WAS ESCORTED INTO AN INTERVIEW ROOM BY A GUARD AND I
returned to the sofa. While she answered questions about
everyone she had ever met, everywhere she had ever been,
and her Facebook profile, I flipped through the company
glossy, *Looking Forward*. We were immunizing children in
Nigeria, apparently. Lola took so long I went looking for
her, and was told she was in the multiscanner. This was like
a metal detector, for an advanced definition of metal. I was
surprised because that should have been the fastest part of
the process. You just had to stand there.

Finally Lola emerged, doing up her top button. "They
swabbed me," she said. "They swabbed my mouth."

The guard handed her a tag. "Please wear this at all
times. If you lose it, you can't get out."

Lola looked at me, amused, and I shook my head to tell
her no, seriously. She clipped the tag to her polo shirt.

"Was there a problem?"

"Oh. No. I just have trouble with metal detectors." She adjusted her glasses. "Forget that. Show me your leg."

"ONE OF THE PROBLEMS WITH BIOLOGICAL LEGS," I SAID IN THE ELEVA-tor, "is they can't survive on their own. They're not modular. This creates isolated points of failure and dependency issues. All of which go away if you make the leg self-sufficient."

Lola looked up from fiddling with her access badge. "Self-sufficient?"

"As in, it works by itself. It doesn't need a warm body for fuel."

"The Exegesis doesn't need fuel."

"Yes, it does. Look, I'm giving it kinetic energy right now."

"Oh. I see."

"Without me, it just *sits* there." I glanced at her. "I mean, it's better than nothing."

"That's a really good leg, Charlie."

"For what it is—"

"Go to a public hospital. See what they're making kids walk around in down there." Her eyes glistened.

"Um," I said.

"Sticks," said Lola. "Buckets on sticks."

"The Exegesis is also a bucket on a stick. That's my point. It's a terrible design. Why has nobody built a prosthesis that can walk by itself? That's what I want to know."

"A what?"

"It's obvious." I gestured with my free hand. "You put a motor in the leg."

Lola stopped walking. "*Have* you put a motor in a leg?"

"Yes. No. Not *a* motor. Several motors. You need multiple

motors to redundantly articulate the toes." I was nervous. I hadn't shown anybody the leg. Not complete. I had even hidden it from my lab assistants. "It's experimental. There's a lot I need to do. But I want your feedback. As a professional."

Lola studied me. Then she looked around. "Where is it?"

I took her to Lab 4. It was unlikely we'd bump into my assistants; Katherine spent most of her time these days with the rats, and Jason was glued to his terminal in the Glass Room. Given the opportunity, Jason would probably stay there forever. We had much in common.

"How far down are we?" She was looking at the steel buttresses lining the walls.

"About sixty feet." I swiped my ID tag on the door reader. The door clicked. "You need to swipe your thing here, too."

"Why are we down sixty feet?"

"In case something goes wrong." She followed me into Lab 4. The leg was beneath a white sheet on an insulated floor mat. It was surrounded by workbenches and lights. The sheet was because I didn't want anyone looking at it from the Glass Room and giving suggestions.

Lola looked at me. I nodded and she approached it. I looked up: no sign of Jason. Good. Lola touched the sheet. "Can I . . . ?"

I pulled off the sheet. Lola inhaled. I looked at her face to see if this was a good inhalation or a bad one. It was hard to tell. How did the leg appear to someone who hadn't seen it before? Kind of spiderlike, I guessed. The upper section was a black lattice of interlocking steel. From there two silver pistons fed into a splayed eight-toed foot. I had been very proud of this but suddenly it looked creepy.

Lola walked around it three times. She stopped near the Clamp. It was still there. You didn't decommission machin-

ery of that caliber just because some idiot managed to lose a
limb in it. "You built this?"

"Yes."

"How did you . . . how did you build this?"

"You know." I shrugged. "A little at a time."

"It looks heavy."

"It's about two hundred pounds." I pointed at dents in
the floor. "It made those."

"How do you lift it?"

"I don't. It walks by itself."

Lola looked at me.

"It's not ideal. It has to remain in contact with the
ground. But it can handle stairs. Those toes can get up to
ten inches long. And you can't see it, but underneath are two
orbital wheels on a shifting multidimensional axis. It alter-
nates between toes and wheels depending on the terrain."

She walked around the leg. "What's this?" She gestured
to a series of black aluminum cases welded up near the
socket.

"The processor housing. I'm not really happy with the
positioning."

"What's it for?"

"Systems control. Data storage, GPS, wi-fi, et cetera."

"Your leg has wi-fi?"

"It has to. Otherwise it couldn't interface with the online
path-finding API."

Lola's eyebrows rose.

"You shouldn't need to tell your leg where to step. You
should tell it where you want to go and let it figure out how
to get there. That's basic encapsulation."

Lola looked back at the leg. I don't think she really
understood encapsulation. She knelt beside the leg and ran
her fingers over the metal.

"I'll put it on." I pulled over an office chair and began

unstrapping the Exegesis. It clanked to the floor and I flicked the latch that caused the new leg to ease down into a bent position. The hydraulics hissed. I positioned my stump against the socket and slid in. That was nothing special. It was just somewhere to stick my thigh.

"There are no straps?"

I shook my head. "I basically rest in it." I steadied myself, then stood up in the leg. "Ready?" She nodded. I pressed for power. The servomagnetics started near silently. There was a line of crude buttons for simple functions and I pressed one for a short forward journey. The leg flexed in three places and glided forward. I leaned into it and performed a matching step with my biological leg. This was the clunkiest part of the whole procedure. I wasn't happy with that. The entire time Lola was silent.

I cleared my throat. "What do you think?"

"Oh, Charlie. It's beautiful. It's completely beautiful."

"Oh," I said. "Oh. Oh. Thank you."

AFTER I ESCORTED LOLA BACK ABOVEGROUND, I RETURNED TO LAB 4 and sat on the floor beside my leg. I had thought Lola might like my leg, but you never knew. Her reaction exceeded all my expectations.

Then I felt depressed. It was the opposite of a logical reaction but there it was. I always felt like this at the end of a project. I would be frantic and determined and excited then sad because it was over and there was nothing left to improve. I stared at the leg. It occurred to me that I hadn't escaped my bottlenecks. I had only pushed them back. I had made a leg that could walk by itself, which was okay, but I could see now that this was about as far as it could go. All improvement from here would be incremental, because the bottleneck was my body.

It was late. My lab assistants had left. I looked at my leg, the good one. Well. I don't mean "good." I mean the one I'd had since birth. I rolled up my pants and turned it this way and that. It was fat and weak and ordinary. The more I looked at it, the more it bugged me.

I PULLED MY PROSTHETIC LEG APART. I DIDN'T MEAN TO BUT ONCE I GOT started I kept seeing more things I could make better. When I saw it lying in pieces I panicked about what I had done, but it was okay. I could rebuild this.

I scavenged parts from adjoining labs. I sent my assistants out for hard-to-get materials. I didn't tell them what they were for. But they probably knew. You didn't become a scientist if you could resist the urge to check what was under a white sheet in a spotlit laboratory. I stopped answering e-mail and performing paid duties. I did not shave. I built the leg into a new configuration that increased its mobility by half but immediately saw a better solution and stripped it down again. Some time passed. I am not sure how much. Sometimes I fell asleep in the lab and awoke in a cold puddle of drool. When I visited the vending machine, I carted away as many snacks as my arms could bear and piled them in the corner, so I could work for longer periods. The worst thing was going to the bathroom, which was all the way at the end of the corridor, near the elevators. The best part was making it there, because then I had a six- to eight-hour uninterrupted window ahead of me, and while leaning back on the toilet with my eyes closed, I would have ideas.

Messages from Lola accumulated in my voice mail. On the nights I made it to my bunk I listened to them before falling asleep. I put her on speaker and it was like she was in the room. Her messages urged me to call her, turning increasingly anxious. It was good to feel wanted. But I did not call her back, because my legs weren't quite ready.

JASON BROUGHT ME A SET OF THIRTY-INCH COIL SPRINGS. I HAD THE leg pieces spread across my workbench. I wasn't hiding what I was doing anymore. We had passed that point.

I realized he wasn't leaving, and pushed up my goggles. "Yes?"

Jason's eyes flicked across the components. "You wanted two springs."

"Yes. Thank you."

"It looks . . . it looks like you're building *two* legs."

I looked at my pieces. It was hard to deny.

"I don't really . . ." said Jason. "I don't understand why you want two."

"Backup."

"Oh." He did not look convinced. Still he hung there. "Is there anything I can do for you, Dr. Neumann? Anything at all?"

I thought about this. "I would like some more snacks."

He brought them.

I FINISHED MY NEW LEGS. WELL. I REACHED A POINT AT WHICH I NO longer felt an urgent, clawing need to change things. I tried to stay calm but I was trembling inside. I swallowed over and over. I felt scared to look at them. It was silly. But everything about this moment seemed fragile.

I couldn't wear them, of course. They were a set; I didn't fit. But I could sit beside them and enjoy their presence. It was quiet, just me and them.

. . .

WHEN I WAS FIFTEEN, I WAS ALMOST KILLED BY A SHIRTLESS MAN IN A Dodge Viper. I was crossing a suburban street on my way home from school and he roared around the corner. I think he expected me to scurry out of the way, but I didn't, because I was fifteen and valued appearing tough to strangers over remaining alive. The shirtless man clearly shared this philosophy, because his car jagged toward me. I realized I was going to die, or at least be hurt a lot. But at the last second—too late, in a car less well engineered—the Viper slid to a smoking halt.

The driver leaned out the window and screamed abuse. This was when I saw he was shirtless. He wore mirror shades and chunky jewelry, which flew around as he gesticulated. I tensed, in case he was about to get out and beat me up, but he only stabbed fingers in my direction, punctuating insults I couldn't hear over the torrent of high-fidelity music pouring from his stereo.

Finally he put the car in gear and drove off. I watched him slingshot around the next corner, already up to forty or fifty miles per hour. I walked on. I felt vaguely outraged that such a bad person had such a good car. Because the car was the culmination of a thousand-odd years of scientific advancement. But the guy was a dick. I wondered when that had happened; that we had started making better machines than people.

MY ASSISTANTS ARRIVED IN THE GLASS ROOM HOLDING COFFEES AND talking about something they seemed to find funny. They saw me and froze.

"Dr. Neumann?" said Katherine. I inferred this from her lip movements. I was on the other side of the polymer glass and she hadn't toggled the intercom. I waited for her to realize this. "Dr. Neumann . . . what's in the syringe?"

"Morphine." This came out muffled because I was holding my shirtsleeve in my teeth. But I think she understood. I completed the injection and let my sleeve drop. "For the pain."

Katherine and Jason shared a glance. Jason leaned toward the microphone. "What pain is that, Dr. Neumann?"

I felt disappointed. These guys were supposed to be the brightest minds of their generation. Yet here I was in the Clamp with a syringe of morphine and they couldn't figure it out. "I think that will become obvious."

On one wall of the Glass Room was the Big Red Button. If you flipped up its clear plastic panel and pressed it, everything lost power. A sign said EMERGENCIES ONLY. A while ago somebody had taped beside it: DO! NOT!!! PUSH!, because lab assistants are curious. Jason's eyes flicked at the button.

"Please call Medical," I said.

To his credit, Jason made it look like he was going for the phone. He leaned in that direction and picked up the handset. Then lunged at the Big Red Button.

But my button was closer. It was in my hand. The Clamp was powered up, humming on standby. Its steel plates were positioned about—well, a foot apart. I was sitting on one edge. My left leg, the biological one, dangled.

It was just as well I took care of this in advance, because the morphine was already seeping into my neurons, fogging my synapses. If I hadn't been prepared, Jason would have reached the Big Red Button before I could activate the Clamp and crush my leg. But I was, and he didn't, and I did.

4

I WOKE BUT NOT IN THE HOSPITAL. IT TOOK ME A WHILE TO FIGURE this out because I couldn't focus my eyes and because I really, really should have been in the hospital.

". . . on its way," said someone. It sounded like that guy. My boss. D. Peters. "Two minutes, or thereabouts."

"Everyone's off this level?" This was a woman, familiar but hard to place.

"Except Medical, yes."

I felt sensations. Hands on my body: firm and professional. They did not belong to the voices. The voices were farther away. They were observing while the hands worked. The woman sighed. "This is disgusting."

"You don't have to be here."

"It's a mess. I'm a mess cleaner. I'm here."

D. Peters cleared his throat. "Not an accident this time, I'm guessing."

"No."

"Well . . . that's good. Isn't it?"

"It's great. We have a suicidal employee."

"I mean—"

"Do you know what our workplace injury rate is like *before* we add people who deliberately throw themselves into the equipment?"

"I just—"

"Maybe you should front the investigators, Dick. See how you do. Because there will be investigators."

"Cassandra, I'm not trying to—"

"When it's an accident, you show the investigators who screwed up, how they did it, and the initiatives you're putting in place to ensure it never happens again. Initiatives solve the problem. Everybody likes initiatives," said Cassandra Cautery, the crisis manager. "What's our initiative for this? Who screwed up?"

"I guess he did."

"That answer gets us a tribunal. Did we pressure him to return to work too soon? Did we provide enough counseling? What was our process for monitoring his mental state? Did he feel we provided a welcoming workplace?"

"I see."

"Honestly, it'd be easier if he bled out."

The hands hesitated. I tried to raise my head, but only managed to half open one eye. A sun hung over my face, angry and brilliant. It looked familiar. A lab light.

"He moved," said D. Peters. "Did you see that?"

Another sigh. "I hate mess. I hate it."

"But you're so good with it."

"I know," she said.

. . .

I DRIFTED IN AND OUT. I'M NOT SURE FOR HOW LONG. I FELT CONTENT. Warm. I had an urge to scratch my leg but could ignore it. At some point I opened my eyes and saw the familiar ceiling of my old hospital room and so I went back to sleep. Everything felt okay.

A NURSE CAME AND FIDDLED WITH SOMETHING BESIDE MY BED. SHE was large and beautiful. I remembered her as Katie. *Hello,* I tried to say. I was happy to see her again and wanted her to know. My hand flopped against her dress. She turned to me and folded her arms. "Yes?" Her eyes flicked over me without feeling. Finally she turned back to my bedside table and slid the drawer home with an aggressive *thunk*. I didn't know what I had done to Nurse Katie but apparently it was something pretty bad.

WHEN I WAS LESS DRUGGED, I PULLED ASIDE THE SHEET TO INSPECT the damage. I thought it wouldn't be so terrible the second time around but it was. Before, I had been able to see the space where my leg should be. I had been a man missing a leg. Now I was a creature that ended at the thighs. A different life-form. I was small. I closed my eyes and cried because it was suddenly obvious that I had been very stupid.

BUT LATER I REMEMBERED I WASN'T LEGLESS. I HAD LEGS. I JUST wasn't wearing them. They were state-of-the-art and I had built them myself. They were already more functional than my biological legs and soon they would be even better. It was easier to keep this in mind if I avoided looking at my stumps. Everything would be fine once I got my new legs, I told myself. This wasn't loss. It was transition.

NURSE KATIE CAME BACK. IT WAS DARK OUTSIDE. THE HOSPITAL WAS quiet except for the squeaky shoes of nurses. I was groggy but not so much that I didn't know my phone was missing. Last time they had brought my personal effects with me. But now nothing. I was thirsty for internet. I itched for something with a processor.

Nurse Katie inspected my drips wordlessly, even though I was lying there, looking at her. "Hi," I said.

"Hello."

"Have you seen my phone?"

Katie set her wrists on her hips. "Your phone?"

"It was in my shirt pocket. I can't see any of my clothes in here."

"You can't have your clothes."

I hesitated, because this wasn't an answer. "Do you know where they are?"

"Yes, and you can't have them."

I tried again. "I don't need my clothes. I need my phone. Can you see if my phone is in the pocket?"

"No." Katie circled the bed and lifted my sheet. I couldn't see what she was doing but she had to be checking my catheters. I had two: a urinary catheter and a bowel catheter. Nobody had explained this to me. I had figured it out myself, when the pressure to relieve myself had become too great. It was a relief in every sense. You would think a bowel catheter would be disgusting but it had major functional advantages over a bathroom visit. Everything was sealed and sanitary. When you thought about it, it was the regular system that was foul.

"Can you tell me why you can't give me my phone?"

Katie dropped my sheet. "Because you're on suicide watch."

I was too surprised to respond. She turned and squeaked away down the corridor.

SO THAT EXPLAINED WHERE MY UNDERPANTS HAD GONE. BUT IT DIDN'T tell me why everyone was angry. It wasn't just Katie. When Nurse Mike bathed me, he was subdued and noncommittal and made no jokes. Nurse Veronica let my dinner tray clatter onto my table trolley. I was too intimidated to pursue my phone. Instead I lay in bed watching TV with the sound down, so as not to annoy anybody.

MY SURGEON VISITED: DR. ANGELICA AUSTIN, WITH THE FRIZZY HAIR and impatient manner. "So you're back." She rolled aside my sheet without asking. Her fingers pressed. I couldn't feel them at all. She could have been tenderizing steaks. "Healing well." She sounded regretful.

I looked down. The difference between my stumps was kind of amazing. I hadn't thought the right was healing much but compared with the new one it was rosy with health. The other was puffy, shiny, and stuffed with tubes. It would take a lot of time before I could get that into a prosthetic without screaming. Or a lot of drugs.

"I suppose there's no need to discuss the recovery process," said Dr. Angelica Austin. "That should be fresh in your memory."

"I'm not suicidal."

Dr. Angelica Austin ignored this. "How's your pain?"

"Very bad." Not completely true. But the nurses were being lax with my medication, forcing me to compensate by demanding it earlier and in greater quantities. "I'm not suicidal."

"Discuss that with psych." She gazed at my stump. Her expression reminded me of a time in high school when out of nowhere a girl I hardly knew said, "You have beautiful eyes." The next thing she said was "What a waste." "Not my area."

"When do I get a psych consult?"

"Soon."

"How soon?" This didn't get an answer. I changed tactics. "Can I have my phone? I don't see how it's supposed to be dangerous." Dr. Angelica popped a pen and wrote on my chart. "Is Lola Shanks coming?"

"Perhaps later."

"Why is everyone mad at me?"

Dr. Angelica Austin lowered her clipboard. "No one is mad at you." She looked mad. Then she left.

That night I developed a terrible crawling sensation in both legs. I was supposed to be doped at midnight but it was 12:17 a.m. and still no drugs. I sweated and shook and eventually held down the call button for as long as it took. Nine minutes later, Nurse Veronica arrived. She glared at me like I was a stain. "Oh, I'm sorry," she said. "I was busy with the patients who want to get better."

DAYS PASSED AND NO ONE VISITED. IN THIS RESPECT IT WAS MUCH LIKE before. The difference was now I wanted them to. Well. Not *them*. Her. I wanted Lola Shanks to barge through the door, her arms full of legs.

I couldn't risk asking for her. Since the nurses had turned hostile, letting them know I wanted something was a strategic mistake. My meals were proof of that. But I couldn't wait, either. On the fifth day I formulated a plan to drag myself across the floor to the phone in the hall. Then, like a miracle, she appeared. She did not have any prosthetic limbs. It was just her, in a big hospital shirt and sweatpants. She hung in the doorway and stared at me through her glasses.

I pulled myself upright. "Hi! Hi."

She stopped short of my bed. "You crushed your other leg."

"Yeah."

"On purpose."

"Yes."

"Why?" The word slid out of her mouth like it was heavy. It dropped to the floor and lay there.

"Because . . ." I couldn't think how to explain it. It seemed obvious. She had seen my prototype.

"Do you want to die?"

"No!"

"Do you hate yourself?"

"No. Well." I considered. There were parts of which I didn't have a very high opinion. But I didn't hate them. I just thought they could be better. "No."

"Do you like pain?"

"What? Of course not."

"Then it doesn't make any sense."

"When someone gets their vision laser-corrected, nobody thinks they're trying to hurt themselves. They're just tolerating short-term pain to improve their bodies. You do physical therapy. You make people sweat and struggle and do painful exercises. You have—you have *pierced ears*. Did you puncture your earlobes because you hate yourself? Are you working your way up to suicide?" Lola sucked in a breath, but I had found a point and wanted to make it. "Pain isn't my *goal*. My pain is a side effect of the human body being so flawed that the only way to implement significant improvements is to scrap what's there and start over. I just want to upgrade. That's not weird. People go to the gym to do that. The only difference is I have access to better technology."

I realized I had gone too far. Lola began to move. "Wait," I said. "Let me rephrase that." But she was leaning closer. Before I realized what was happening, she kissed me.

ONE TIME AT AN MIT PARTY, I TALKED TO A GIRL ON A RIPPED LEATHER sofa about alternate universes. She leaned forward as if to make a point and fell onto me with her lips open. I'm not really sure how it happened. Her pupils were dilated. I guess that's how. It was shocking and I didn't know what to do. The whole time we were kissing I was terrified I would screw this up and she would stop. Her head became heavy and her kissing less urgent and then she fell asleep. I didn't realize this right away. I had to figure it out. I put my arms around her and lay there with her in my arms and it was really great.

I mention this because until Lola Shanks kissed me it was the most passionate experience of my life, and it was twelve years earlier, and that is a really long time.

"LOLA," SAID SOMEONE FROM THE DOORWAY. LOLA'S LIPS JERKED FROM mine. It was a terrible loss. I saw my surgeon, Dr. Angelica Austin, radiating fury.

"I just . . ." Lola's shoulders dropped. Dr. Angelica Austin beckoned. Lola threw me a glance full of guilt and promise. She turned away. Her hand trailed from my shoulder. Dr. Angelica stood aside and Lola slumped by. I wanted to say *Wait* or *Come back* or even *Thank you* but Dr. Angelica's eyes stopped me. *You are never to see my daughter again.* It was like that. She put a hand on the door as if to slam it then took it away, because I was on suicide watch.

LOLA DID NOT COME BACK. WHEN KATIE DELIVERED MY DINNER I ASKED if I could see Lola, and Katie said she would find out in a way that meant she already knew, and no. I couldn't call her because I had no phone. I couldn't get out of bed because I had no legs. Even if I could get my hands on a wheelchair, I was enmeshed in a web of tubes and bags. I was trapped.

IN THE MORNING I WAS VISITED BY CASSANDRA CAUTERY, THE CRISIS manager for Better Future. She wore a snug gray jacket over a pinstripe shirt with a big collar and a little skirt. It was kind of a schoolgirl–meets–Wall Street look. Her cheek-bones were full of compassion. "Oh, Charlie." She put one hand on her chest. "Oh, Charlie." She pulled a chair to the edge of my bed and looked at me with wet eyes. "I can't tell you how upset I am. With this. With myself. With this whole situation."

I recalled Cassandra Cautery and D. Peters discussing me as I lay bleeding on the floor of Lab 4. The memory was thin and I couldn't remember what they had said. But I had the feeling I should be angry about it.

"I honestly thought we were giving you the support you needed. But we weren't. Clearly, we weren't. I'm so sorry. I need to know. What more could we have done?"

"About what?"

"About . . ." She put her hand on my arm. Her fingers were surprisingly warm. For some reason I thought they would be cold. "About making you feel necessary."

This took me a moment to untangle. I am not good with indirectness. I take people literally and realize what they meant later. "Oh. I didn't try to kill myself. I've been saying this over and over. I don't want to kill myself. I just want to replace my legs."

Cassandra Cautery opened her mouth like she was about to say something, then closed it again. She tilted her head and squinted.

"Having one leg is awkward," I said. "You either use an artificial replacement that tries to mimic the real one, which is essentially impossible and limits you to the capabilities of the prosthesis. Or you build a really good prosthetic leg, but then you're stuck with a biological limb that can't keep up. It's like a car that uses the driver's leg as one wheel. At some point biology just gets ridiculous."

Cassandra Cautery said, "I'm not sure I follow."

"I can show you. My legs are at work."

"Your . . ." She touched her mouth. "Charlie, your legs are gone. They were crushed."

"Not *those* legs. My new legs. Ones I made."

She sat back.

"It's not complicated. First I built a prosthetic leg. Then I realized it would work better as a pair. So I removed my biological leg."

"To . . . so you could . . . could . . ."

"So I could wear the artificial set."

"The artificial set . . . of legs."

"Yes."

"Because . . . because . . ."

"Because the artificial ones are better."

Cassandra Cautery seemed frozen. Her hand lay on my arm like a dead thing. I shifted, uncomfortable. I didn't know how I could explain this any more clearly. Seconds passed. I coughed. Cassandra Cautery jerked out of the chair. Her face still hadn't changed. When she spoke, only her lips moved. "Well . . . you've given me . . . a lot to think about. Can I . . . I'll get back to you . . . on this." She turned and walked away like she was on strings.

"Wait," I said. "Can you send me the prosthetist? Lola Shanks?"

Cassandra Cautery turned. Moments passed. Her eyes were on me but her brain was far away. Her head spasmed a nod. But I didn't think she meant it, and from the absence of Lola Shanks that followed, she didn't.

A MAN FILLED MY DOORWAY. HIS NECK BURST OUT OF HIS COLLAR LIKE a tree. His hands were black shovels. His gray shirt pulled against muscles I didn't have. He was a security guard. "Hi." He had a book. A novel, I thought. I wondered if it was for me. Maybe Cassandra Cautery had noticed I had nothing to do. "I'm Carl. From Better Future." Seconds passed. I usually like to interact with people who don't speak until it's necessary but I was intimidated by Carl's physique. I didn't feel inferior so much as incompatible. Carl existed on a plane where success was measured by physical feats. He had a brain because his body needed it, rather than the opposite. I didn't understand such people. I didn't know what they wanted, or might do.

Carl nodded, as if we had resolved something. He left. I heard a chair scrape in the hallway. Time became punctuated by the sound of him turning pages.

WHEN A NURSE CAME INTO MY ROOM, TO GIVE ME FOOD OR MEDICATION or check I wasn't leaking, Carl followed her in. He stood with his shovel hands folded in front of him, his eyes on each of the nurse's moves. I didn't know what he was doing, but I grew to like it, because he made the nurse nervous. One time I pressed the call button, and after two minutes had passed with no response, Carl's chair scraped back. I heard his black shoes rapping down the hall. When he came back he had Nurse Mike in tow.

"I want my phone," I told Mike. "And I want to see Lola Shanks." This hadn't been why I pressed the call button. I had wanted a TV guide. But now he was here, I was testing.

Nurse Mike glanced at Carl. "I'm sorry, Dr. Neumann. I can't help you with that." Carl said nothing. Mike's shoulders eased. So it was not a victory. But still, my position had clearly improved.

CARL STOPPED TURNING PAGES. HE WAS THERE. I COULD HEAR HIS chair squeak. But he wasn't reading. I decided to talk to him. I could be social, when I'd had time to think about it beforehand. "Carl?"

His frame appeared in the doorway. "Yes, sir?"

"Why are you here?"

"Pardon me?"

"Why are you here?"

"I don't know, sir. I go where they send me."

"Are you meant to stop me escaping?"

"I don't think you're in a position to be escaping, sir. With respect."

"So why?"

He shrugged, like heaving mountains. "I guess the company wants you looked after."

I found this unsatisfying. But I couldn't think how else to probe. "Did you finish your book?"

His eyebrows raised. "Yes."

"What was it?"

"Nothing special. Just something to pass the time." I waited. He cleared his throat. "It's about a man who goes back in time. To rescue his fiancée."

"From what?"

"A fire."

"Does he do it?"

"He does. But he creates a time rift, and has to go back again and murder her."

"Oh."

"Yeah," said Carl. "It's kind of sad."

"Could I read it?"

"I don't know if you'll like it. It's not a smart book."

"I have nothing else to do."

He went out to the hall and returned with the novel. The title was *Ripples in Everwhere*. A man stood silhouetted against a burning building. Its pages were curled and yellow.

"Looks like a favorite."

"Yeah. My fiancée died."

"Oh."

"Not in a fire, though. Car crash."

"Oh." I struggled to think what to say. I hadn't planned for this. "I'm sorry."

"Thanks. It was eight years ago."

"I never had a fiancée."

"Oh," said Carl.

"I would like one."

"Yeah, I can, uh . . . recommend it." There was silence. "They understand you. You don't really get what it's like to be understood until you've had it and . . . don't."

I nodded. That was pretty much what I figured. I turned the book over in my hands.

"That cover irritates me," Carl said. "In the book, he's never standing outside a house like that. It's an apartment. And he can't get the door open. That's why his fiancée dies. She's inside and he can't bust down the door. He's not strong enough. Why would they make the cover wrong like that?"

I shook my head. I didn't know.

"It's important. It's the most important part of the book. My Lily, I couldn't pull her out of the truck. I wasn't strong enough either." He cracked his knuckles. "Back then I didn't work out. Couldn't get the truck door open."

"That's really bad."

"Yeah," he said. "It was really bad." We nodded at each other. It was a comfortable silence. Then less so. "Anyway . . ." said Carl. "I'm keeping my eyes open for any time rifts."

"Travel to the past is almost certainly prevented by the chronology projection conjecture." Carl said nothing. "I mean . . . it seems extraordinarily unlikely."

"I know."

I tried to think how to back up. But it was too late and the silence stretched.

"Hope you like the book," said Carl.

"Thanks," I said.

TWO DAYS PASSED. CARL WAS RELIEVED BY A WHITE GUY WHO TAPPED his foot and hummed themes from TV shows. He came in and asked if I had watched the Knicks game and I didn't know which sport that was so that was the end of that. I became engrossed in Carl's book. The man in it was trying to fix his life but kept being denied by the laws of physics. Or not the actual laws of physics but how they applied in this book. What I liked was how he didn't stop trying. He broke the world in several different ways but kept going back and doing it differently. I liked the doggedness. The idea that if you wanted something impossible you could get it if all you did was never give up.

I DREAMED OF TINY, SHRINKING SPACES AND WOKE WET AND GASPING for breath, my legs crawling with needles. My body was fighting back. It was telling me it did not want to lose any more pieces. I felt annoyed, because I thought I was past this. My body really needed to realize that I didn't take orders from internal organs. I was a consciousness serviced and supported by a biological host, not the other way around. These self-interested lumps of meat and synapses, they had better get with the program, because if it came down to them or me, it was going to be me.

I WOKE TO LOLA'S VOICE. IT WAS DAYTIME AND MY BRAIN WAS FOGGY. I swam toward consciousness like a drowning man. ". . . one minute?" she said.

"Sorry, ma'am." This was the new guard.

"Lola," I croaked.

"Charlie?"

"I'm sorry, ma'am. You can't go in there."

"One minute."

"No, ma'am."

"I want to see her," I called. "Let her in."

"I'm sorry, ma'am," said the guard, like I didn't exist. "I'm sorry."

ON THE FIFTH DAY THEY REMOVED MY TUBES. THIS INCLUDED MY catheters. I didn't realize what Nurse Katie was doing until it was already too late. I gazed at the plastic in dismay. "Can't you leave those?"

"No. There's a risk of infection."

Carl stood behind her like a shadow. I didn't want to discuss this in front of Carl but I really liked those catheters. "Isn't there some kind of permanent option? What do you do for people who are paralyzed?"

"You're not paralyzed." Katie dropped the tubes into a

plastic bag marked HAZARDOUS BIOLOGICAL WASTE. "You can use a bathroom like a regular person."

I said nothing. This was true. I could. But why should I? We had the technology for a superior waste-disposal system but wouldn't use it because we preferred to drop feces into an open bowl of water and rub the residue on our asses with tree pulp. But I knew it would be pointless to get into an argument about this with Katie. Before she took them away I had a good look at those catheters, so I would remember how they worked.

I BEGAN TO EXERCISE. I RAISED MY THIGHS INTO THE AIR, ONE AT A time, and rolled onto my stomach and did the same. I did three sets of ten reps. Reps were repetitions. This was terminology I had picked up. I also did push-ups. This was less impressive than it sounds because I was resting on my thighs. In high school we had called these girl push-ups. It felt good to get my body moving again, although only because my brain was releasing endorphins as encouragement. It was like being paid to wash a car. But I did it because I knew if Lola were here it's what she'd be telling me to do.

FOUR PSYCHIATRISTS VISITED, ALL TOGETHER, LIKE A CONFERENCE. Two were men and two were women and one of the men was black. They looked like an ad for property investment or a lifestyle medication targeted at the upper middle class. The black guy leaned easily against the wall. He was smooth and comfortable and he smiled at me like we knew each other.

There were introductions. They asked me how I liked the hospital. One of the women, who was blond and had sharp ears, raved about the view. You would think she had never been aboveground before. They turned the conversation toward work. This was easy for them because I wasn't saying much beyond hello and yes and no.

"I understand you're a bit of an inventor," said the white man. He lounged across his chair but was still not as smooth and comfortable as the black guy. "You build things."

"Legs," said the sharp-eared woman. She smiled, like, *Building legs, isn't that clever.*

"Yes," I said.

"I'd like to hear about those."

For the first time, no one spoke. "Well," I said. "They're legs, I don't know what to tell you." I looked at the black guy, because maybe he could jump in and make this smooth and comfortable, but he didn't. I sighed. "Look, seriously, I do not enjoy pain. I do not want to hurt myself. I'm not—"

"Oh. Yes. We get that." The man laughed. "You don't need to convince us of your mental well-being, Dr. Neumann."

I looked from one face to another. "Then what do you want to know?"

"These legs you've built," said the woman. "We understand they're superior to any other kind of prosthesis currently available."

"Yes. As far as I know."

"In fact, they're so advanced, you . . . you actually chose to crush your other leg. So you could . . . qualify for them."

"That's right."

"Are they strong?" said the black guy leaning against the wall. "They must be."

"They're okay."

"Only okay?"

"I have some work to do."

"Oh yes." He looked significantly at the others. "What kind of work?"

"He's got ideas." This was the woman with sharp ears. "Of course he does."

"I wonder if you could share some of those ideas with us," said the lounging man. "Could you do that?"

I said, "Did you say you were psychiatrists?"

"I don't think so." He looked at the others. "Did anyone say that?"

"Well, I work in Human Resources," said the sharp-eared woman. "You practically need to be a psychiatrist for that."

"What I think we said was that we wanted to talk about how you're feeling."

I checked this against my memory. It may have been true.

"These legs, you built them on company time, am I right?"

"Um . . . yes."

"Don't be alarmed," said the lounging man. "That's not a problem. That's what we thought."

"Definitely in no way a problem," said the leaning man.

"We're from Better Future, of course," said the woman who hadn't spoken until this point. She was small and brightly dressed, like a bird. "And Dr. Neumann, may I say, we are all extremely pleased and supportive and positive about the potential of your project here." She squeezed her hands together.

DR. ANGELICA AUSTIN DIDN'T WANT TO LET ME OUT OF THE HOSPITAL. It was a little funny because the nurses couldn't be rid of me fast enough. They argued across my bed, as if I were inanimate. "I don't care what his company says," said Dr.

Angelica. "I'm his doctor and I say he's not ready to be discharged."

Nurse Katie did not stop packing my bag. Behind her, Carl mutely supervised. Two more nurses hung in the doorway, spectating: Veronica and Chelsea. Katie said, "Well, the administrator says different," and Veronica said, "Mmm-hmm."

Dr. Angelica Austin flipped my chart like she was angry with it. "There's no psych consult on here." Her eyes rose to Katie. "How on earth can there be no psych consult?"

"His company said—"

"*I* ordered a psych consult," said Dr. Angelica. "I sent them to this room. Where did they go?"

Carl spoke. This gave everyone a start, including me, because we were used to him standing there like a rock. "I can't permit them in here."

"You?" Dr. Angelica drew herself to her full height. Which was not much, but still impressive. She had a bearing. Maybe they taught that in medical school. Or maybe you just picked it up from the kids around you, who owned skis and formal wear and knew their cutlery. In engineering, we slouched. "*You* can't?"

"That's right."

"And why is that?"

"Because his mind is a commercial-in-confidence intellectual asset of Better Future."

Dr. Angelica's eyebrows shifted up. Katie closed my bag zipper. It sounded authoritative. She folded her arms and settled on her heels and looked at Dr. Angelica.

"I'm going to keep him one more day."

In the doorway, Veronica and Chelsea exhaled together. Katie said, "You can't do that."

Dr. Angelica ignored her, scratching on my chart with her pen.

"He's physically fine. There's no psych hold. He wants to be discharged. His company wants him to be discharged. The administrator is telling us to discharge."

Dr. Angelica shook her head slightly, as if she spent all day being thwarted by bureaucrats and it disappointed but did not surprise her. "His doctor disagrees."

"You know what will happen," said Katie in a low voice. Dr. Angelica's pen paused. This seemed so dramatic I almost laughed, because what? Would she be fired? Would Carl snap her neck? I thought Better Future would probably just get me a different doctor. But this was enough to defeat Dr. Angelica. Her bearing sagged. She was going to go home after this and sip red wine and stare at the wall, I could tell. She would wonder why she was doing this, struggling against commercial interests at a corporate hospital when all she wanted to do was help people, and in the morning, when she walked out of her beautiful home and unlocked her convertible, she would remember.

"They're waiting," said Katie. "What do I tell them?"

Dr. Angelica tossed the clipboard onto my tray, like it was useless now. "Tell them," she said, "I strongly advise he be kept away from industrial-grade cutting and stamping equipment."

5

I COULDN'T KEEP STILL IN THE LIMOUSINE. I PATTED MY THIGHS WITH hands like skittish birds. I adjusted my seat belt and gazed out the smoked glass window and wished we could go faster. How far was it to Better Future anyway? I didn't remember all these housing developments. I leaned forward to ask the driver if he was going the right way and forced myself to sit back, because of course he was. I just wanted to see my legs.

"Not long," said Carl. I jumped. I had practically forgotten he was there, filling the opposite seat. He was big but quiet.

My hands clenched. I needed to put something in them. I thought of my phone. The bag the hospital had packed for me was on the seat beside me: I unzipped it and rummaged through my old clothes, which I had not seen in weeks. My phone was not there. I sat back and exhaled. Those assholes.

"Problem?"

"My phone."

"Missing?"

"Yes. Yes, it's missing." I didn't mean to snipe. I was misdirecting my frustration.

"Would you like to go back for it?"

I opened my mouth to say yes.

"It's no problem," said Carl.

"Could you . . . have them send it?"

"Sure."

"By courier or something."

"Yes."

"Okay," I said. "Okay, we'll do that." I looked out the window and drummed on my thighs. Buildings slid by.

THE LIMO STOPPED. CARL EXITED LIKE A CORK FROM CHAMPAGNE. I tugged my door handle but only got as far as shuffling toward the opening before he pulled the door all the way open. I squinted. Carl bent and lifted me into a waiting wheelchair. There was applause. This didn't make any sense. Then Carl moved and I saw the concrete path to the lobby lined with employees. When they saw me they cheered. I was still confused. Standing before me was Cassandra Cautery, her hands clasped, as if in prayer. She came toward me with her arms out. She bent and kissed me on the cheek. "Welcome home," she whispered. I had gone seven years without a kiss and now I'd had two in a week. It was the kind of data event that implied a serious contamination of laboratory conditions. Cassandra Cautery put one hand on my shoulder and Carl wheeled me toward the lobby. People held out hands for high-fives. I passed a woman from Vertex Processing who in meetings always chose the seat with the greatest displacement from mine, always, and she whispered, "You're an inspiration." I didn't understand what was happening.

Inside the air was cool and regulated. "I've taken the liberty of expanding your staff," said Cassandra Cautery. "What do you think of that Jason Huang? I left him, but his metrics are average."

"I like Jason."

Carl stopped pushing. Cassandra Cautery came around and looked into my eyes. She was very beautiful. She seemed constant, occupying a natural place in the world. It was difficult to imagine her any different, like upset or tired. That was a property of beauty, I guessed: permanence. "It would be no problem to get rid of him."

"Jason's fine."

"I just want you to have the best."

"Why?"

Cassandra Cautery nodded thoughtfully, like this was a weighty question and she wanted to get the answer right. "What you said in the hospital about artificial being better. Well, that sparked some interest here. Some very high-level interest. Discussions all the way up to the Manager." She searched my eyes. I didn't know who the Manager was. "What would you say to your own product line?"

"My own product line of what?"

"Of prosthetic devices." She caught herself. "Of artificial enhancements. Of quality bio-augmentations. We haven't settled on a name. But we want you to build them. We're fully funding you to explore any and all possibilities that occur to your brilliant, brilliant mind."

"You want me to build prostheses?"

"Yes."

"Why do you want me to build prostheses?"

"Don't you want to?"

"Yes. But . . . I'm not on the business side, but—"

Cassandra Cautery laughed. "Right. You're not on the business side. Leave that to us."

"But—"

"I'm a middle manager," she said. "Some people think that's a pejorative, but I don't. There are people above me who make business decisions and people below me who execute them and those people live in different realities. Very different. And my job is to bring them together. Mesh their realities. Sometimes they're not completely compatible, and sometimes I don't even completely understand how someone can live in the reality they do, but the point is I mesh them. I'm like a translator. Only more hands-on. And that's what makes the company work. Middle managers, like me, meshing. So let me take a stab at meshing your reality, Charlie. Do you know how much money there is in medical? A lot. And more every year, because you invent a better heart and it doesn't matter how much it costs, people want it. Because you're selling them life." She blinked. "You're selling them life." She patted her jacket pockets. "I need a pen. But what's the problem with medical? The market is limited to sick people. Imagine: You sink thirty million into developing the world's greatest artery valve and someone goes and cures heart disease. It would be a disaster. Not for the . . . not for the people, obviously. I mean for the company. Financially. I mean this is the kind of business risk that makes people upstairs nervous about signing off on major capital investment. But what you're talking about, what you said at the hospital . . . it's medical for healthy people. That's what excites them. They're imagining a device. Let's say a spleen. They don't know. I don't know. It's up to you. But say you come up with a spleen that works better than natural spleens. More reliable, safer, with, um, built-in monitoring of your blood pressure. I'm sure you can come up with better ideas. But that device we could sell to anybody. The market for that is every person in the world who wants their spleen to work better. And every customer is a customer for life. Literally. You mentioned upgrades at the hospital. Well, imagine you purchase a Better Spleen. And a few years later, wait a minute, here comes the Better Spleen Two. It's the same, only it can check your e-mail." She laughed. "I'm being silly. But you see the business model. There's repeat business. I sat in on this meeting, Charlie, and a man there, he said people buy a new cell phone every thirteen months. Thirteen months. They throw out their old phone, which they loved, because there's something newer. Sexier. That's the other thing. They've seen your legs. They think there's a certain . . . a certain aesthetic to them. You haven't tried to imitate real legs. That's the difference. You've made something else. Something that stands alone. Oh. I didn't mean that. I mean it's a little like art. It's a paradigm shift. Because regular prosthetics, and I hope this isn't offensive, but they look a little creepy. A little dead. So the thought is—and this is all long-term, but it's the thinking—what if Better Parts can be fashion accessories? Is that impossible? Maybe someone would buy an artificial tooth just because it looked better. Or an artificial ear. If we sponsored some athletes, some of those . . . some Paralympians, they could become objects of desire. They're fit, they're functional, they're here. They're the future. Marketing pointed out that we already pierce our bodies in the name of fashion. We physically insert metal into our earlobes, and lips, now, and chins, and who knows what else. You've seen those kids. That's the area they're looking at. Wearable accessories. Higher-functioning, supersexy cyberbodies. What you've helped the company realize, Charlie, is that there's a marketplace under our noses. Literally. Literally under and inside our noses. Inside us. And we as a company are uniquely placed to be first to market. That's why you're getting resourced. Does that help you understand?"

I thought for a while. "A little."

She smiled. "You're welcome."

CASSANDRA CAUTERY WALKED BESIDE ME AS CARL WHEELED ME TO THE labs. I thought they would take me to the Glass Room but they turned left, for Lab 4. Several young people who I gathered were my new assistants lined the corridor. As Carl pushed past them, I discovered the reason they were outside Lab 4 was that there was no room inside. It was wall-to-wall white coats. Except in the center, where my legs stood under lights. They had been polished. They were beautiful. Cassandra Cautery had been right about that. I was a little surprised anyone else saw it, because they were beautiful only in a functional sense: beautiful because they worked. Bundles of plastic-wrapped wires as thick as my wrist snaked between bare steel struts and around oiled coil pistons. Black electrical tape strapped the computer housing on to the hip. The calves bent backward, like a gazelle's. The feet were globe-encased rotary engines with one long toe pointing forward and two angled back.

People were clapping. "You're my idol," said Jason. I hadn't even noticed him.

"What?" I said. I thought I must have misheard *idol*.

"You and Isaac Newton. And Barry Marshall. And the Curies. You people who are prepared to put yourselves on the line for your science. To become your own test subjects. I salute you."

Carl wheeled me toward the legs.

"Compared to you, Kevin Warwick is a pussy!" said Jason. "He should be embarrassed with himself!"

Carl lifted me into the air as if I were a child. He carried me to the legs like he was rescuing me from a burning building. "This okay?" he said, and I said, "Yes," and he lowered me into the sockets. I grimaced as my wounded left leg scraped plastic. Then my butt touched the seat and it was okay. I didn't have to stand in these legs; I sat. I relaxed. My hands moved down to the hips. There were controls there. My thumbs found the ignition buttons and pressed. My motors were extremely quiet, for their power output. But that was not that quiet. My legs rose up on their toes, flexed, settled.

My audience cheered and whooped. Cassandra Cautery's eyes shone. I grinned. The applause went on and on. It was at once great and terrifying. I wanted them to leave so I could play with my legs in private but I also wanted them to stay forever.

I THUMBED THE LEFT LEG FORWARD. IT ROSE AND EXTENDED AND clomped down. The floor went *crack*. I hoped that was the floor. Either way could be an issue. I thumbed the right and took a matching step. The motion rocked my body back then forward and for a second I thought I was about to fall out. I took my hands off the controls and clutched at the seat. It was okay. I could adapt to it. It was like riding a horse. Or how I imagined riding a horse. I had never actually done that. I adjusted my balance and took another step. Another. *Crack. Crack.* People moved out of my way. Two held camcorders. I needed to clear this room. I couldn't work with them here. Now I thought about it, I had no idea how I was supposed to manage twenty lab assistants. I had struggled with three. Maybe I could get Cassandra

Cautery to take them away again. I looked for her in the crowd and realized she was in the Glass Room, a watery green version of herself. She was watching from a safe distance. Down here it was just me and the ocean of lab assistants. I stopped walking. Nobody spoke. Shoes shuffled. There were a lot of pairs of glasses in this room.

"Well," I said. "What do you think?"

An incredibly thin guy with nightmarish skin cleared his throat. "The interface is crude. Ideally you want to do something with nerve impulses, I think."

"Krankman's working with nerves," said a girl. "I was on his project before this. Splicing."

They drew closer. A few dropped down to inspect the legs up close. I could almost feel their fingers. "There's a lot of weight in this metal."

"You could drop that down by hollowing these columns out."

"What about titanium?"

"What about impact absorbency? I worry what happens when he steps off something."

"Hmm," the skinny boy said. And I relaxed, because this was going to work out.

OF COURSE THE CURIES DIED. THEY IDENTIFIED IONIZING RADIATION while bathing in it. There were risks involved in being your own guinea pig. But there was a long tradition of scientists doing just that: of paying for the expansion of human knowledge with their lives. I didn't deserve to be categorized with them, because honestly, I wasn't interested in the greater good. I just wanted to make myself better legs. I didn't mind other people benefiting in some longer-term indirect way but it wasn't what motivated me. I felt guilty about this for a while. Every time a lab assistant looked at me with starstruck eyes, I felt I should confess: *Look, I'm not being heroic. I'm just interested in seeing what I can do.* Then it occurred to me that maybe they all felt this way. All these great scientists who risked themselves to bring light to darkness, maybe they weren't especially altruistic either. Maybe they were like me, seeing what they could do.

I TRIED TO CALL LOLA. I DIDN'T HAVE MY PHONE, SO I WHEELED MYSELF to my desk in the Glass Room. I had to dial through reception, and it took a long time to start ringing, and that was all it did. It seemed odd that the hospital would not answer its phone so I dialed reception again and asked them to check the number. "This is the number you want," she said. So I tried again but again it rang out.

I DIVIDED MY ASSISTANTS INTO TEAMS: ALPHA, BETA, AND GAMMA. IT was the only way to keep them manageable. They worked in competition: I wheeled among them and anything I liked sparked grins and furious development. Beta came up with a whole new wheel-based leg design, almost a chariot, which I liked so much I took it over myself. Then Alpha and Gamma also got into wheels and Beta accused them of intellectual plagiarism. It was a whole thing. There were tears. I told Gamma to go build some fingers or something. They liked this. They wound up deploying four hands' worth and using them to make obscene gestures at Beta. It was like being back at college, only I was respected. Sometimes I wheeled past bodies in the corridors: assistants who had literally lain down and slept because they were too tired to make it home. Everywhere were sodas.

. . .

EVERYONE THOUGHT BETA WAS GOING TO REACH TESTING ON A NEW prototype first but the wheels were a dead end. They couldn't get good traction on uneven ground, not even in rotating sets on independent suspension with ground-sensing sticky locks. We did a lot of stairwell damage before figuring that out. We left gouges in the walls, broken steps, and a section of railing that bowed inward. But failure was just a method of learning what worked.

Then Alpha declared they had something. They were based out of Lab 2, where Katherine's rats had lived, before they'd been moved off to another lab somewhere. Katherine had followed. I imagined they'd offered her the choice to stay with me or go with the rats. I still thought I could smell them every time I came in—the rats, that is—although that couldn't be right, because when we cleaned these rooms we did it by sucking out all the air.

Alpha's legs were similar to my previous prototype, only taller, sleeker, and titanium. There was less electrical tape and more custom carbon-polymer molding. I wheeled myself around them for an inspection. I wasn't going to do anything special today, just check fit and balance. There were too many wired connections to walk. No nerve interface yet. But still, when my assistants helped me out of the chair and lowered me into the sockets, my heart thumped. I buckled in. "Okay."

Jason held the control box. He pushed for power. Nothing happened. Smoke began to pour from the legs. People shouted. Hands grabbed at me and hauled me out. They broke out the extinguishers and drenched the legs in foam. When all that was taken care of, we started over.

I DIALED RECEPTION AND ASKED FOR A THIRD-PARTY DIRECTORY ASSIStance service. "If there's a number you'd like to look up, I can do that for you," said the receptionist. I declined. When she put me through, I asked the directory robot for the hospital. It offered to connect me directly and I said yes. It rang. The hospital picked up. I opened my mouth to request Lola Shanks in Prosthetics and the line went *click*.

I lowered the phone and looked at it. Then I put it back on the cradle. Clearly it was pointless to redial reception. But at least I understood the problem now. I could apply myself to a solution.

I SPENT A LOT OF TIME BEING JABBED WITH NEEDLES. NOT SYRINGES. Tiny steel slivers with embedded electrodes. The idea was to insert these into my truncated thighs so they could read signals from my brain, and translate them into motorized movement. We created a fourth team for this, using people transferred from other projects. Initially it was called Delta but it was confusing whenever someone said *delta* meaning "change," which was often, so they renamed themselves Omega. We converted a lab into a medical room and I lay back on the table while a tall, high-cheekboned lab assistant named Mirka punctured me. This was excruciating during the first session but not so bad once we realized the equipment could read me just as well while I was hocked to the eyeballs. So I injected myself with analgesics and let my consciousness swim away while Mirka maneuvered metal slivers around, seeking the best reception for the electric language of my brain.

My legs hurt all the time. It seemed likely this was a side effect of jamming needles in there every day, but it had started before that. It was like phantom pain. I resisted this notion because it was so stupid. Physiological pain I could be on board for. Even something neurological. Neurology was the science of nerves. It was chemical reactions you could point to. Psychology, though, was the science of fairy tales. It was like explaining volcanoes with stories of angry gods and expelled half-sons and revenge and betrayal. I did not believe in psychological pain.

But I needed sleep. So one night I took a pair of legs to bed. They were early, lightweight models, really just poles, which we'd used for prototyping and since discarded. I set them beside my bunk and turned out the light. Later, when I woke with my nonexistent muscles screaming, I dragged the legs onto the bed, shoved my thighs into the sockets, grabbed the feet, and manually flexed those crude blocks of plastic up and down. I got this idea from a paper on treating phantom pain by using mirrors to form optical illusions, which convinced the patient's brain that the limb was still there. You see why I was skeptical of the whole area. As I flexed, I felt nonexistent muscles unlock and pseudo-blood begin to flow. I waggled the plastic. It was just as well no one could see this. "Ahhh," I said.

FINALLY ALPHA'S LEGS STOPPED CATCHING FIRE. I SAT IN THEM AND took a wary step. They moved smoothly, the whine of the servomagnetics almost inaudible. The floor did not break. Nothing popped or smoked. I walked to the wall. It was not a smooth ride but I was unfamiliar with the equipment. I rotated and walked back to the center. I raised a leg. I did not overbalance. I did not fall out. I flexed the foot. It was cloven. It actually looked more like a hoof. I lowered it and raised the other leg. Still upright. I looked around and saw a lot of happy faces. I smiled, too, because this was progress.

NEXT CAME THE NERVE INTERFACE. I SPENT MORE TIME ON THIS THAN anything else. When I had an idea for something mechanical, I could usually tell someone else to go make it happen. But reading nerves was personal. It was like trying to sift raindrops from a thunderstorm only I could see. I passed days in Lab 1 with thirty-eight wires dangling from my thighs, trying to read my thoughts. It was a funny way to get to know myself. For example, when I thought about wiggling my big toe, my waves spiked at 42.912 gigahertz, but so too if I imagined country music. I wouldn't have thought those were similar. But then I thought about toe-tapping and maybe they were. Either way, it was important to figure this kind of thing out before I wore the legs outside and someone put on Kenny Rogers.

Once we had a basic neurological landscape, I practiced moving in software. We loaded leg wireframes into the computer and I tried to control them with my mind. At first they wouldn't respond. Then they jerked and twitched and tried to walk in three directions at once. Mistake by mistake, I crawled toward something practical. By the end of each six-hour session, I felt dazed and unsure where I was. I wheeled along the corridor and saw the whole world as lines and vertices. I dreamed I was a wireframe, made of green light.

MY ASSISTANTS BEGAN WEARING CHUNKY GLASSES. THEY LOOKED ridiculous. The lenses were milky, like the opposite of sunglasses. By the end of the week, half of Gamma had them. I didn't pay much attention because I assumed this was some kind of young-person fashion trend, but when I arrived in Lab 1 for a date with Mirka and her needles, she pulled on a pair, and I had to ask.

"They are Z-specs," said Mirka. She seemed surprised I didn't know, although behind the glasses it was hard to tell. "You have not tried them?"

I shook my head. Mirka pulled off her set. There was a component I hadn't noticed before: two wires terminating in flat metal contacts. Mirka unpeeled these from her temples. I wasn't sure about this but I followed her directions to adhere the contacts to my own skull and fit the glasses. Everything looked flat. Then Mirka's face sprung to life. I had never known my eyes were so low-res.

"The enhancement is nice," said Mirka. "But the real benefit is the zoom. You pinch your eyebrows. Like this."

I mimicked her movement. Her face rushed toward me. I flailed my arms. Mirka laughed. "And the other way to zoom out." She helped me upright. "You see?"

I picked a corner of the lab and made it leap closer. There was a paper clip there, as big as if I were kneeling in front of it. I zoomed out and in, picking tiny objects in the room and blowing them up. I turned my head without zooming out and nausea bloomed. So that was not a good idea. Zoom out, turn, zoom in.

"They will make you a pair, of course," said Mirka. "If you ask them. Gamma."

"Gamma's making these?" I pulled off the glasses. The world went dull.

She nodded. "Gamma is doing many peripherals."

I lay back. Mirka filled the syringe with morphine. I didn't mind Gamma experimenting. That was what I had told them to do. But I wasn't sure I wanted them making glasses. I didn't know why. As Mirka filled my veins, I wondered if it was because I had not designed them. My department was not just about me, of course. It was about developing products for a general market. Cassandra Cautery had explained this to me and it had seemed okay at the time. But I wasn't sure I liked it.

. . .

I CAUGHT THE ELEVATOR TO THE FOURTH FLOOR OF BUILDING C, WHERE Cassandra Cautery worked. Cassandra Cautery had visited the labs several times but I was always drugged or busy with wireframes so we hadn't spoken. I just knew she was escorting executives around.

I wheeled myself along carpet so thick it made my arms ache. Building C was nice. The entire Better Future complex was visually attractive, but in a utilitarian, engineering kind of way, where beauty meant simplicity. We favored straight lines and parabolic curves, no bleeding of anything into anything else. Here was free-flowing color. I was not a big fan of art but I think some part of me relaxed.

I found Cassandra Cautery's office at an intersection of corridors. I had an appointment but was early. I wondered if I should do a lap. "Charlie!" Cassandra Cautery came around her desk and beckoned me inside. "Thank you so much for making time." She closed the door behind me. The office was small and filled with thick books. It had a low sofa, a painting of a circle, and a computer that looked more interested in being pretty than working fast. There were no windows. "Can I get you a drink?"

"No. Thanks."

She leaned her butt against her desk and folded her arms. Her blond hair glowed in the artificial light, picking up the UV. "I'm hearing nothing but great things about your work. Everyone is extremely, extremely excited. It's a credit to you. As a manager."

"I don't know about that."

"Don't be so modest. I know you don't consider yourself that way. But your people don't need a social boss. They need someone who inspires them on an intellectual level. Who forges within them a burning desire to invent. That's you."

I shifted in my wheelchair.

"Listen to me. Advancing within a company requires self-assessment. I should know. My first performance review, my boss said, 'Cassandra, you are diligent, intelligent, motivated, and hardworking, but you need to learn how to settle for less than perfection.' I argued at the time, but she was right. I had to train myself to accept that not everybody works as hard as me. That what I consider unacceptably sloppy is actually an okay result, and it's counterproductive to get into a whole thing where someone starts crying and threatening to quit. And you know what? Learning that not only helped me grow as a manager. It helped me grow as a person. Because back then, I was actually, well, a little obsessive." She smiled. "You haven't told anyone about my diastema, have you?"

"What?" I remembered the gap between her back teeth. "No."

"Thank you, Charlie. Because I told you that in confidence."

"Um," I said. "Anyway, I wanted to talk to you about fingers."

She nodded. "Go on."

"Gamma has been developing fingers. They got started by themselves. I only wanted them to stop fighting with Beta. But they did some interesting things and now we have a hand. It's workable. We could replace somebody's biological hand. It doesn't work as well in all respects, mainly because of the loss of sensation, but it has advantages. It's stronger. And multipurpose. You could fit a finger with a spectrograph, for example, so you could feel electromagnetic waves. That would be really useful in our line of work. And everything about it is upgradeable. So it opens up a lot of possibilities for future enhancement."

"That sounds like exactly the kind of thing we're interested in."

"That's what I thought. And it's ready. For testing."

"You want me to find someone who needs a prosthetic hand?"

I shook my head. "I can do it."

"You can . . . you mean . . ."

"I can replace my own hand."

Cassandra Cautery was silent. "That's good of you, Charlie. But I think we'll find a test subject for this one."

"I don't mind."

"Well . . . thank you. But you can't be the test case for every bionic you invent." She smiled. "Can you?"

"Well," I said.

"Charlie. You're doing an amazing job. Upstairs could not be happier with the way things are going. And neither could I. Honestly, at first, I thought this whole project had the makings of a disaster. Not a disaster. But potentially it could be very, very messy. And you've totally proved me wrong. So let's . . . let's just keep doing what we're doing. And I'll find someone who needs a hand. How about that?" I didn't say anything. "Yes," she said. "We'll do that."

WE PERFORMED A LIVE TRIAL OF THE NERVE INTERFACE. IT TURNED OUT Alpha's legs didn't bend low enough for me to attach without yanking out needles whenever I twitched, so at the last minute I switched to Beta. This triggered angst and gloating because Beta had been a long way behind since the wheel debacle. But it was all about the technology. Beta's legs were half the weight and contoured silver steel: of all the models, they most resembled real legs. Except for the feet, which were hooves. Hooves were working for us. I finished fitting the needles and two assistants slid me into the Beta legs and tilted me upright. At this point nothing was powered on. The assistants cleared the lab and began to fill the Glass Room, crowding against the green glass. I felt a twinge of nerves. It wasn't so much the fact that I was about to see what happened when you plugged your brain directly into a pair of self-powered mechanical legs but that so many people were watching. I found the power button with my thumb and put my other hand on the emergency shutdown. I looked up at the Glass Room again and saw Jason's thumbs-up. If there was a problem with both the power button and the emergency shutdown, Jason would trip a remote kill switch. None of this should be necessary because we were feeding the legs a tenth of regular power. And we had exhaustively tested in software. Everything that happened today should be unsurprising.

I pressed for power. I heard a high-pitched whine, barely detectable. I tried to ignore this. As clearly as I could, I imagined myself lifting my right leg and taking a single step.

Nothing happened. I opened my eyes, disappointed. Then I looked down and my right leg was in front of the other. I mean the Beta leg. It had done exactly as I asked, so perfectly I hadn't noticed. When I looked at the Glass Room, behind the three-inch translucent green plastic my lab assistants were jumping up and down, Z-specs bouncing, cheering in silence.

THE MORE I TINKERED WITH GAMMA'S HAND, THE MORE I LIKED IT. IT was funny how as soon as you knew there was something better, what you had seemed unbearable. Every time I had to dig around for my ID tag, I thought: *I wouldn't have to do this if it were embedded in my finger.* When I was working on a lathe or a circuit board and I reached for a tool, whenever my fingers slipped or my hands shook, I felt exasperated, like why was I still dealing with this. It was the same with the glasses: the Z-specs were heavy and hurt my nose but when I took them off I missed them. The hand was not so advanced I could honestly say it was on balance superior to its biological equivalent. But still, there was something about it I couldn't keep away from.

I INSTALLED A VOICE OVER IP CLIENT ON MY WORKSTATION AND DIALED the hospital. The packets went nowhere. I wasn't surprised: the company firewall was strict. One of the ironies of working for the world's most advanced research lab was that our internet connection was like dial-up. The filter had to sniff everything. I played with the port settings but it didn't help. I would have to jury-rig something that made audio look like Wikipedia pages. I thought about this. It seemed possible.

Another solution would have been to leave Better Future and find a pay phone, but to be honest I thought about that only later.

THE LEGS CAME ALONG IN LEAPS AND BOUNDS. NOT ACTUAL LEAPS AND bounds. The lab ceilings weren't high. We had to save that for outdoor testing. But I could tap a hoof. I could step over a knee-high obstacle without crushing it. In fact, I could step over a knee-high obstacle without noticing it, because the legs sensed terrain. I just willed them to take me somewhere and while they took care of that, I could think about other things. It felt like the way travel was supposed to work.

A twenty-four-hour period passed in which nothing went wrong. I wore the legs outside the lab, up and down the corridor. We called them Contours, on account of their sweeping lines. They were a good-looking set of legs. I wanted to show Lola. But I still hadn't been able to reach her. It had been five weeks.

One day I was fitting myself into the Contours and the legs began to retract. This was not supposed to happen. They should have been powered down. One of the assistants cried out in alarm. I looked at the pistons and the narrowing gap between them and reached out as if I could stop them.

There was a wrenching. A brilliant flash of pain. Someone screamed. Hands pulled at me. I saw Jason's face, contorted in grief. He said, "I'm sorry," over and over. I looked at my hand. It was sandwiched between the Contours' knee and the retracted socket. There was a lot of blood. I felt dizzy. "I'm so sorry," Jason said again. He was technically in charge of the Contours until I stood up. But we hadn't been strict about that for a while because everything had been going so well. "I'm so, so sorry."

"It's okay." I was about to faint but I wanted to tell him this. "It's no problem."

"CHARLIE!" SAID LOLA. SHE SOUNDED ROBOTIC, BECAUSE MY COMPUTER was untangling her audio from IP packets that to the corporate sniffer looked like a long joke e-mail. But there was unmistakable delight in her voice. I felt relief. It had been a long time and who knew what had changed. "I've been calling and calling!"

"You have?"

"Yes! They always tell me you're busy and I have to leave a message. And I got your home number, but your answering machine filled up."

"I haven't been home."

"Since when?"

I had to think about this. "March."

"Charlie." Her voice dropped. "I think you should get out of there."

"Why?" I went to scratch my cheek and missed. I looked at my hand. I wasn't wearing my index finger, that was why.

"I just think it would be a good idea."

"Okay."

"Meet me," she said. "I'm going to give you an address."
I reached for a pen, with the hand that had fingers.

A FEW YEARS BEFORE, A GUY IN GELS STABBED THREE PEOPLE WITH A broken Schlenk flask. They had to use tear gas to get him out. He kicked and screamed that no one took his lab reports seriously. One of the stabbed people died. For days afterward people congregated in corridors and asked each other, "You just can't understand it, can you?" They huddled in unusual social configurations, engineers with marketers and managers and people from accounts. Everyone wanted to make sure that everyone else agreed: you can't understand it, can you? Like they needed to hear that *no*.

At first I shook my head along with everyone else. I didn't want to seem disrespectful. But finally it got to me and I said well obviously he was frustrated. This was to Elaine, my lab assistant with the bad skin, who quit because of nightmares. Elaine looked at me like she was trying to find something. "Yes, but to get so frustrated you would do something like that . . ." I said that's what people did when they got frustrated: they displayed violent behavior. Elaine said, "But *you* would never do something like that," and I said probably not but in the same environment with the same stimulus it was fair to assume I'd have a similar response. I wasn't a different species. It's not anybody's fault for feeling violent when their brain is flooded with vaso-pressin. That's just what happens. You drop a glass, it falls toward the earth. Maybe that's not the outcome you want, but don't blame the glass. Don't pass moral judgment because cause produced effect. We're biological machines. We have chemically driven urges. You inject a nun with a particular chemical cocktail, she's going to start swinging punches. That's a fact.

This all seemed simple and self-evident to me but maybe I didn't express it well because that afternoon I got a call from Human Resources. They said counseling was available for anyone unsettled by the incident and would I like to make use of it, and I said no, and they said maybe I should anyway, and I talked to a bald man in his office for three hours. By the end he seemed to understand my point, or at least accept that I wasn't going to shoot up the office. He said part of our responsibility as civilized beings was to control our baser instincts. Which I agreed with, but it made me think what a bizarre situation that was, a world of polite, smiling men and women one serotonin dip away from savagery, pretending that they weren't. It seemed to me that situation could be improved.

I WENT TO LAB 4 AND CLIMBED INTO THE CONTOURS. A FEW GAMMAS were about, and they looked at me curiously through their Z-specs. "Are we testing?" asked one. I shook my head. I powered on and extended the Contours to walking height. I took a step and another and walked out of the lab.

By the time I exited the elevator four security guards were waiting. One of them was Carl, the human mountain. "Good afternoon, sir," he said. "Going somewhere?"

My legs were already detouring around him and it was a moment before I could persuade them to stop. They were a little feisty. I came to a juddering halt. There was no one else around, I noticed. The place had emptied. "Yes. Out."

"Where would you like to go? We'll take you."

"Just out," I said. "Part of testing."

"I'm sorry, Dr. Neumann, but external testing must be authorized."

My jaw tightened. It wasn't Carl's fault, but I was pissed about being cut off from Lola. I thought, *I should just walk out of here.* Because it wasn't like they could stop me. I didn't mean to express this as a mental instruction, of the kind the Contours could pick up. But like I said, they were feisty. And then they were moving so quickly I had to grip the sides of the bucket seat. "Whoa," I said. Carl lunged at me like a linebacker. The Contours stepped around him and thumped into the lobby. "Dr. Neumann!" Carl shouted. "Stop!" His voice bounced around the glass-ringed lobby. It sounded a little frightening and possibly in response to this the Contours broke into a run. They pistoned toward the glass lobby doors. These did not open in time, which caused the collision-detection software to stop me so suddenly that my forehead cracked against the smoked glass. That hurt. I would have to fix that. Then the gap between the doors grew wider and the Contours took off.

I WAS ATOP A JACKHAMMER. WITH EACH STRIDE, MY NECK STRETCHED and tried to detach my head. When each hoof slammed down, my chin bounced into my chest hard enough to crack teeth. Through eyes blurred with tears, I saw an approaching road and thought: *Oh please now they will stop.* But they didn't. They ran into traffic. I clawed for the emergency shutdown button and missed. That was possibly a good thing because in retrospect I didn't want to lose power in front of oncoming automobiles. A sedan whipped by so close its turbulence tore at my hair. A truck the size of a building honked. I heard a terrified shriek and realized it was me. There was a clicking deep within the Contours, something I felt rather than heard. They stopped. I was in the path of the truck. I was going to die. I was about to learn why you don't conduct a live field test of new technology while strapped to the top of it. This truck would run me down and when it stopped its driver would find a long bloody smear leading to a gleaming pair of perfect titanium legs. It would be the ultimate vindication of my work. A testament to the superiority of artificial parts and the need for comprehensive bug testing.

The legs bent and sprang. The traffic and road grew small and far away. I let go of the seat to flail my arms. I was trying to grab air, or fly. My upward velocity slowed. For the briefest moment I was moving leisurely forward sixty feet above the ground, neither rising nor falling. It was kind of beautiful. Then the world grew larger and more dangerous. My brain suggested my terminal velocity at forty miles per hour. That was how fast I would be going when I hit the sidewalk.

Below, a woman and her young son gaped up at me. They were standing at the exact point I was destined to intersect the sidewalk. It was a terrible coincidence. Then I realized it wasn't. It was calculated. These people were cushioning. Physical objects that would help absorb the shock of impact. I had programmed the legs to avoid collisions on a horizontal plane but anything lower than they were was deemed to be ground. It had seemed a reasonable assumption in the lab.

THE MOTHER YANKED HER SON'S ARM. HE WAS NO TODDLER. I HAD SEEN women wrestling with children of this age before, in supermarket aisles and parking lots, and usually the kids didn't budge. But apparently a man plummeting out of the sky triggered a major adrenaline boost, because this kid flew through the air like he was hollow. I impacted the sidewalk ten inches away. Concrete split beneath my hooves. Dust burst into the air. My spine bent in a way that felt very, very wrong. I lost my breath and sucked in a lungful of powdered concrete. I felt the Contours moving beneath me, preparing to run. I tried to tell them to wait a second, because I had to apologize to the mother, and make sure she and her son were okay, and so was I. But the legs didn't care. Their world was defined by a location, a destination, and the optimum path between the two. Nothing else was relevant. They were definitely going to kill me.

THEY RAN FOR TEN MINUTES. DURING THIS TIME I CLUNG TO THEM, begging them to stop. Apparently one of the things you couldn't simulate in the lab was that mortal terror interfered with the ability of the nerve interface to interpret mental instructions. Either that or they were willful. I tore past pedestrians. When I finally closed my eyes and gave in to them, they stopped. I looked around and saw a busy intersection. I was somewhere downtown. Seconds passed. My legs did not move. I breathed. My tie hung over my shoulder like a tongue. My shirt was soaked with sweat. My jacket was gray with concrete dust. I looked like a hobo. A mechanical hobo. And I laughed, because that was a funny thing to be, and my legs had stopped, and I was alive, and that was the most out-of-control freaking ten minutes of my life.

I CONSIDERED HEADING BACK TO BETTER FUTURE. MY CHANCES OF finding the café with Lola Shanks seemed slim. I should power down and wait for somebody to pull over and ask if

I was okay and then I could ask them to please call my company. Now I thought about it, I should have built in a cell phone. That was a major oversight. Anyway, clearly the Contours had major functional issues and could not be trusted to bear me anywhere. Then I realized I was outside a café, and inside it, sipping coffee, was Lola.

I hesitated. The café had a green awning and iron furniture and people in nice clothes eating real food. I didn't want to make a scene. But Lola was there. I thought, *Maybe* . . . and the legs took this as a green light. They strode across the road. I ducked beneath the doorway before it could hit me on the forehead. Heads turned. Pasta hung from forks. Lola's eyes found mine. Her hair was in a ponytail. She wore a long yellow dress that billowed in the chest but gripped her like death around the arms. She smiled, like nothing mattered except that I was here, and I smiled, too, because I felt the same way.

The Contours picked a path between tables. They were behaving. "Hi," I said. I couldn't stop smiling. Lola was right: I *had* been at the lab too long. I had forgotten what it felt like to interact with people for the pleasure of it.

"Hi." She looked down, then back. We were the only people talking. We looked around and eyes shifted away. People cleared their throats and forced conversation. They were being polite. I was a little insulted, because I was not disabled. "Um. Have a seat."

The Contours settled; pistons retracted. I still towered above the table, but not as much. Lola's mouth formed an O.

"These . . . look different."

"We've made a lot of progress."

"Where are the controls?"

I tapped my head. "Nerve interface."

Lola blinked. "Charlie . . . this is amazing." She stared at my hand. I had meant to keep that out of sight. It was my robot hand. At some point I intended to cover it with molded plastic but for the moment it was all metal skeleton and coiled electrical wire. I slid it under the table. "That isn't finished."

Lola looked at me through eyelashes. When she spoke, her voice was low and throaty. "Charlie . . . what have you done?"

"Well," I said. "You know."

"Show me."

I glanced around. The other patrons had returned to their business, or pretended to. I placed my hand on the table.

Lola sat rigid. She didn't seem to be breathing. "Can I touch it?"

"Yes."

Her fingers crept closer. They explored my index finger, then ran down to the back of my hand. It was the first time I had really missed sensation feedback. "Oh, Charlie." Sunlight bouncing off a building across the street played across her cheeks. A few stray hairs that had escaped her ponytail glowed orange. I felt myself lifting out of my body. That's how it felt: like I was leaving physical form behind, becoming something weightless and untouchable.

Then a hard shard of light skipped across Lola's face. I turned. I'd heard the motor. Outside the café window, a white van jumped the curb and disgorged Better Future security guards.

"Damn," I said. That was all I managed before they burst into the café and began to knock down tables. Plates hit the floor. People yelled. In the midst of this, Carl spotted me. He raised his gun and yelled, "Lie down on the floor!" He looked nervous. I didn't like Carl nervous. Not when he had a gun pointed at me. "LIE down!"

I couldn't lie down. That was physically impossible.

Didn't Carl know that? Lola grasped my biological hand. I saw fear in her eyes and felt sad, because a second ago she had been happy and Carl had ruined it.

"Lie down!"

I had been foolish to imagine Better Future wouldn't track me. I was wearing millions of dollars' worth of equipment. The guards hovered at a radius of twenty feet, bristling guns. It occurred to me that as far as they knew, my legs were armed. Conceivably, I could have built in some firepower. I wished I had.

"Charlie, don't let them take you back," Lola whispered. "They came to the hospital. They destroyed your records."

I heard a noise and turned my head. Two guards were trying to sneak up on me.

"Go, go!" said Carl. He came toward me.

"No!" Lola stepped forward and threw out her arms. It was as if she was going to fly toward Carl and wrench his gun away, or call down the wrath of the gods, or something. I don't know. All I know is Carl pivoted and shot Lola twice in the heart.

IT SOUNDED LIKE: *CLANG! CLANG!*

6

"WELL, THIS IS REALLY UNFORTUNATE," SAID CASSANDRA CAUTERY. "I feel terrible about this."

I couldn't see her. My eyes wouldn't open properly. I didn't know where I was, or had come from.

"What we need now, I think," said Cassandra Cautery, "is to take a few deep breaths."

My right eyelid peeled open. My left was still gummed up, but I could see a blob where Cassandra Cautery's face must be. A frame of watery blond hair. Beyond her was a ceiling. I recognized that ceiling. I was at work.

"Would you like some water? You must be thirsty."

I struggled to bring her into focus. I said, "Ag." I smelled something acrid and unforgiving.

Cassandra Cautery disappeared, then returned holding a small plastic cup. "Drink."

I tried to sit up. Something swam in my head, sick and heavy.

"I think there's been miscommunication on both sides," said Cassandra Cautery. "There are some real lessons to be learned."

Lola, I said.

"It's understandable you're upset. I'd be upset in your place. But please bear in mind: it was a high-pressure situation. Our people were forced into split-second decisions."

"Lola." This time it was a real word. My left eye fluttered open. In a minute, I would be able to sit up. Shortly after that I would be able to get my hand around Cassandra Cautery's tiny neck and squeeze.

"It's the unknown," she said. "It scares people. Makes everyone worry about worst-case scenarios."

I remembered Lola reaching for me. Me straining to catch her. But my legs hadn't moved. They were inert. They were anchors. I had seen slowly spreading shock on Lola's face. Her mouth opening and closing. Her fingers describing a slow arc through the air, terminating at the red flower blossoming beneath her yellow dress. The way she fell.

"That's really your fault, Charlie. I don't want to start pointing fingers. But the way you ran off . . . it made everyone wonder what you might do."

Men in uniforms had pulled me from my legs. The nerve interface tore. A syringe had pierced my shoulder.

"I'm not sure you appreciate the pressure we're under. Management. The daily stresses. The what-ifs."

I coordinated my arms and levered myself up. I was in a small windowless room. The walls were a pale, nostalgic blue. On one wall was a first aid cabinet. It was a medical room.

"She's in surgery," said Cassandra Cautery. "You can watch, if you like."

I opened my mouth. Dizziness swarmed. I wanted to say: *Surgery?* And: *Thank you* and *save her* and *or else.*

"I'd like your input on something, when you feel up to it," she said. "I'd like to know why your girlfriend has a metal heart."

SHE LEFT. IT WAS JUST ME, A BED, AND A VINYL FLOOR WITH SOME DIS-turbing stains. Compared to the rest of the company, this room was third world. I guess it said something about our priorities. We were not healers.

The door was locked. At least, I assumed so. I couldn't bring myself to drag myself off the bed and across the floor to check. I was missing my legs. I had operated without them before, but now I knew I would never leave them again. Sitting there, half a man, waiting to find out if Lola was alive or dead, I vowed I would never let anyone take pieces of me again.

EVENTUALLY THE DOOR OPENED AND THERE WAS CARL. AT FIRST NEI-ther of us spoke. The last times we had interacted, once I fled him on artificial legs and once he shot Lola in the heart. It was an unusual social situation.

"She, uh, going to be all right," said Carl. "I think." In the hallway outside, I saw a wheelchair. Carl came toward me, his arms out. I tried to push him away because I wasn't ready for him to touch me. It would be a long time before that would be okay. But he had arms like propane tanks and I was groggy and missing a hand. He lifted me off the bed. Against Carl's rock-hard pectorals, I began to blubber. It was a posttraumatic reaction. I had been through a lot.

"Everything will be all right," said Carl.

I sobbed. Carl was probably a decent man. A decent man, in a tough job.

"It was nonlethal ammunition. I wouldn't have fired otherwise."

I stopped. I was familiar enough with our company's munitions line to know our definition of *nonlethal.* When we wanted to refer to weaponry that left the target not merely alive but likely to regain full quality of life, we said *noncrippling.* I punched Carl in the shoulder. It didn't seem to affect him. I tried again and he put me in the wheelchair. "That book sucked," I said. "That stupid time travel book." Carl didn't say anything and after that neither did I.

CASSANDRA CAUTERY WAS WAITING IN A SMALL, DARK OBSERVATION room above an operating theater, a tiny, suited silhouette. As Carl wheeled me in, she glanced at me, then returned her attention to green-cloaked figures revolving around an operating table below. Carl closed the door. Before he could get his hands on my wheelchair, I found the grips and pushed myself to the glass.

Lola was on the table. I could see one of her arms poking from beneath an ocean of green cloth. It was the only piece of her on display but it was enough. A surgeon stood with his back to me, his shoulders working. It felt very wrong, Lola lying there while a man she didn't know dug into her.

"I think Miss Shanks must have got herself into a trial," said Cassandra Cautery. "The heart is a SynCardia, but very unusual."

I could see it. The top, at least. It sat in a steel bowl on a tray to a surgeon's right, a red-stained chunk of plastic and metal. It looked strange. But then, it had been deformed by two close-range impacts from Carl's not-quite-lethal ammunition.

"A great deal of steel. Please ask her about that, when she wakes up."

I wasn't talking to Cassandra Cautery. I had decided this in the wheelchair, while Carl pushed me through corridors that smelled of fresh paint. I wasn't talking to anyone until Lola was okay.

"Fortunately, we have a replacement. A little custom model of our own. And the facilities to install it." She looked at me. "This room didn't exist until two weeks ago. We just finished construction. Do you believe in luck, Charlie?"

I kept my mouth shut.

"Me neither. Someone's looking out for your girl, I think. Someone upstairs."

At first I thought she meant God. Then I realized she meant management.

"We built this place for you. For your project."

"I'm not continuing the project." It broke my vow of silence. But I couldn't let her keep talking.

Cassandra Cautery looked sympathetic. "All right, Charlie. Whatever you want." She didn't believe me.

We watched the surgery. After a while, the surgeon with his back to us moved aside. Lola's chest was a red, wet pit.

"As long as we've got her open," Cassandra Cautery said, "I wonder if we could do anything else in there." I looked at her, furious, but also embarrassed, because I had been thinking the same thing.

I WAS BY LOLA'S SIDE WHEN SHE WOKE. IT TOOK ME BY SURPRISE, even though I'd been waiting for it: her eyelids fluttered and two dozen tiny muscles contracted and suddenly her face looked different. It was a little disconcerting. I hadn't seen this before, this sudden infusion of consciousness.

"Hi," I said. Lola reached for the tubes in her nose and I guided her hand away. "You've had surgery. They had to replace your heart."

Her eyes widened. Her fingers moved down to her chest. "Bah."

"It's okay. Try to relax."

"Bah."

I leaned closer. "What?"

"Bah." Her fingers closed around my shirt. "Bah."

"Don't exert yourself. You're not supposed to raise your blood pressure."

She pulled. I went with it, because I feared that if I resisted she would pop a stitch. Her lips brushed my ear. *"Back,"* she said. *"Put . . . it . . . back."*

"WHY AREN'T YOU GETTING HER TO TALK ABOUT THE HEART?" SAID CASsandra Cautery. This was later, in the hallway. Lola had turned unresponsive. She stared at the wall and didn't answer questions. I had started thinking, *I don't really know her that well.* We had shared some intense experiences, but when I added up the time we'd spent in each other's company, it was like four hours. When a person you've just met completely changes personality, you start to wonder which one they are. Why did Lola seem to like me? I had never analyzed that. I had put it in the same category as magic.

"She won't talk about anything. She's comatose."

"You're not trying. You're just saying her name over and over."

Now I understood why one wall in Lola's recovery room was a big mirror. "You're watching?"

"Charlie," said Cassandra Cautery. "I do not want to put any pressure on you, but what we've done here, this little in-house surgery, that's not entirely legal. Do you know how that feels to a manager?" She put a hand on her chest. "It feels like I'm kicking over the baptismal font."

"What?"

"A sustainable business works within the confines of the law. This . . ." She gestured at Lola's door. "Goes against everything I stand for."

"Then why did you do it?"

Cassandra Cautery stared at me. "I thought you'd be glad we could provide such immediate, quality medical care."

"But—"

"We're cleaning up the mess. That's what I'm doing, Charlie. Cleaning up the mess. Are you on board or not?"

I didn't answer.

"Charlie," she said. "I'm trying to help you. I really am. Now get back in there and ask about the heart."

I wheeled into Lola's room. No change: she was on her side, staring out the window. Or at least that's what I thought. When I got closer I saw she was staring at the wall near the window. "Lola?" I reached out and touched her shoulder. "Lola, it's okay. Everything's okay." I stroked her hair for a while. Sometimes I repeated: "Everything's okay." I began to relax. I was soothing myself.

Lola's hand closed over mine. Our eyes met. Suddenly I didn't know why I had wondered who she was. She was Lola, of course. "I was born with a congenital heart defect," she said. Her voice was low and distant. "Hypoplastic left heart syndrome. Only one side developed properly. I had surgery three times before I turned two. It bankrupted my family. And I needed more. It was only a matter of time. I was a time bomb. We never had vacations, or a new car, or ate out. My parents never had another kid. They scraped everything together against the day I would faint and cost three hundred thousand dollars.

"So I decided to die. There was a photo album under the

coffee table I used to read, and I'd look at the pages where my parents were young and happy and went places, and I wanted them to have that again. We lived way up north, in a snow town named Chabon, and one day I walked out and took off my coat and hat and sat down next to a frozen stream. I was being romantic, I guess. But I meant it. I wanted to save my parents' lives. I sat there until I couldn't move, and then I fell asleep.

"When I woke, I was in a hospital bed and my mom was crying. My chest hurt. I had damaged my heart. It couldn't beat by itself anymore. The hospital had installed an artificial one. It was a stop-gap measure, the doctor said, because I was still growing. In a few years, it would need to be replaced.

"So there we were. Me with an expensive new heart and my parents wiped out. This time I took down my grandparents as well. I found that out later. The retirement plans that were shelved, the homes and heirlooms that were sold. All for my temporary heart. And maybe five years until I needed a new one.

"A few weeks later I was watching TV and my mom got a call. Her face went tight and she grabbed the wall. Like somebody was pushing her over. It was the auto assembly plant. Dad's work. He'd been on the factory floor and one of the robots had caught his hand. You know. The robots that make the cars. His hand was welded to a door. The foreman, when he visited, he kept saying he couldn't understand it. There were safeties. They were actually one of the things Dad was in charge of. So it was a little ironic. I mean, it seemed ironic. At the time.

"They amputated Dad's hand at the wrist. When he came home, he had a check for fifty thousand dollars. The payment schedule—there was a set amount you got for injuries on the job. Because of the union. You lose your left hand, like Dad did, and you get fifty thousand. A thumb on the dominant hand, twenty grand. Big toes, ten each. The little ones, three grand a pop. Diminished hearing is worth ten. Each foot is forty thousand dollars." Her eyes reflected the window behind me, mapping straight lines to curves. "Guess how I know that. All these amounts."

"DAD WAS HOME FOR SIX WEEKS," LOLA SAID. "I MADE HIM BREAKFASTS. He walked me to school and afterward I ran to the gate to meet him. All bundled up against the cold, you couldn't tell he was missing a hand. He didn't have a prosthesis. He didn't see the point. He liked being home. It was the first time he hadn't had to work in years. We were both so sad when it was over. I wanted him to stay. But of course we needed the money. So he went back.

"Four days later, it happened again. Another accident. The same arm. He lost it up to the elbow. We visited the hospital and Mom cried and said we were cursed. But Dad didn't look sad. He got ten weeks' recuperation. When it was over I said, 'Are you going back to work now?' and he said, 'We'll see.' It was two days. The die stamp, this time. Some toes. Mom couldn't bring herself to visit him. She was losing her mind. But I went. And I was worried, because he looked really hurt. His foot was bandaged and he was missing his arm. I climbed into bed and hugged him as hard as I could. I cried and said he was dying. He said no, I was wrong about that. He told me about the payments. He had a little booklet. He said, 'See, Lola? The sum of the parts is greater than the whole.'

"That was how it worked. The death payout was a hundred thousand dollars. But if you added up the individual body parts, they came to a lot more. Even the hand, if you lost it all at once it was fifty thousand, but each finger was between ten and fifteen, and the thumb was twenty. You could maximize the numbers.

"He said he'd been silly with the hand. Losing it all once. Now he knew what he was doing. He was getting me a new heart. He kissed me and said it would make everything okay forever.

"The company sent a man to the house. Asking questions like: Was my father depressed? Had he talked about killing himself? They couldn't see that he was happy. I lied to them. I helped Dad plan his next accident. We had a notebook. We did sums and figured out which parts to lose. When he tucked me into bed, his eyes were full of joy, and I knew I had the best Dad in the world, because nobody else's father loved them this much.

"Mom found the notebook. I woke and she was screaming. I came downstairs and she was wild, hitting him. The next day she kept me home and gave me a talk about how Dad was sick. In the head. She'd had him committed. I was so angry. She was trying to tell me he didn't really love me. That he was just crazy. We yelled. I wished her dead. We were never the same after that.

"Dad came home after a while. They tried to keep him there but he outsmarted them. And his work couldn't find a reason to fire him, so he went back. They had a guy follow him around, a tall man with a mustache. Even when Dad came to pick me up from school. Dad said they went to the bathroom together. The way he described it, it was funny. Like playing spies. We flipped through our notebook and added up the numbers and figured we were almost there. We knew how much we needed, with bank interest, for a new heart. Just a little more. Just a foot.

"It took him three weeks to find a moment when the man with the mustache wasn't there. But something happened. Mom came to school and took me to the parking lot and said Dad had died. He'd been crushed under an engine block. I didn't believe her. I ran home and dug out his notebook and it was right there. It was only supposed to be the foot.

"The company gave us a check for a hundred thousand dollars. The death payout. He would have been so annoyed. A hundred thousand for the whole, when the parts were worth so much more.

"We invested it. And it grew. When I turned eighteen there was almost six hundred thousand dollars.

"I told the doctor I wanted something to last forever. Something steel. Because it was all I had left of Dad and I wanted him to live in my heart for the rest of my life."

Her face contorted. Her fingers dug into the cotton covering her chest. "And they took it out."

ONCE LOLA HAD FALLEN ASLEEP, I WHEELED MYSELF OUT INTO THE corridor. Cassandra Cautery emerged from a door ten feet away. "Well," she said. "That was some story."

"Yeah."

"I'm always curious about what motivates people to choose their careers. It's never what you think."

I said nothing.

"She can have the heart. We haven't disposed of it. So if it has sentimental value . . . well, she can have it."

"I'll tell her."

Silence fell.

I said, "I want to continue the project."

"Yes," said Cassandra Cautery. "I thought you might."

THE NEXT DAY, CARL WHEELED ME THROUGH THE CORRIDORS OF Research to the labs. There was not much talking. While waiting for an elevator, he said, "I was very happy to hear Ms. Shanks is recovering," and I didn't say anything.

He took me to what used to be a lab in an adjoining project before we took it over. We stopped before the door. "I don't have my pass," I said. This was an accusation, because I'd had it before he shot Lola. They had taken it while I was sedated, along with my hand and legs.

Carl swiped his own ID. The lock's display blinked green. I was surprised, because as far as I knew, we did not grant lab access to security guards. Inside was a large room with many shelves. On slabs of gleaming steel lay half a dozen sets of legs in various stages of completion. The Contours were among them. On my right was a smorgasbord of fingers. Next to those, some hands. Until this moment, I had not really believed they would let me have my parts back. I had been bracing myself for Cassandra Cautery to slide into view and say there was a last-minute problem. But no.

"Should I fetch you a sweater?"

I jumped a little, because I'd forgotten Carl was here. "What?"

"You're shivering."

It was true. "Oh. No." I put my hands on the grips and pushed myself toward the Contours. Carl did not stop me; did not close his hand on my wrist and say, *Choose something else.* I ran my hands over the metal, checking connections, making sure everything was there.

"You really like those things," said Carl. "They can press, what, a ton?"

"Something like that." It was four tons. Which, frankly, was nothing compared to what they would do once I implemented some modifications I'd been thinking about. But I didn't say that, because Carl was trying to engage me, and I didn't want to be engaged.

"You can never be strong enough," Carl said. "That's for sure." He placed a card on the steel bench beside him: my ID. "I'll leave you to it." That was the last time I ever saw him. All of him, I mean.

I CHOSE A SELECTION OF METAL FINGERS AND SNAPPED THEM INTO A hand. It wasn't a full hand. It was more like a glove. In the accident I had only crushed three fingers. It seemed worse at the time. The glove allowed the artificial fingers to slot easily into position, driving the nerve interface needles between my knuckles. This hurt about as much as you'd expect, but not for long. What I had discovered was you could get used to anything. I had the feeling of being connected to something large and cold and distant and my synapses popped pleasantly. I looked at my metal fingers and they moved.

I wheeled myself back to the Contours and pressed for them to retract. Once they were a comfortable height, I lifted the nerve interface mat out of the sockets. The great thing about the hand was the fingers did not tremble. They slid the needles into my flesh as precisely as lasers.

When I had finished wiring myself, I hauled myself into the sockets. Three weeks ago I hadn't been able to do this without assistance. I had come a long way. I got comfortable and closed my eyes and the pistons hissed. The Contours' hooves *thunk-thunked* against the floor. I won't lie, it was one of the most sensual experiences of my life. As much as I had missed the legs, I had underestimated how good it would feel to have them back.

I took a step. *Thunk.* The way they'd borne me through the city, screaming out of control, I had probably imagined most of that. These legs wouldn't betray me. They were reliable. I could tell. They were practically me.

My eyes fell on the wheelchair. That thing looked like a joke. I walked to it, raised a hoof, and positioned it on the seat. I pressed down. The chair's metal struts popped and squealed and it splintered like firewood.

I WALKED TO THE ELEVATORS. WHILE I WAITED, HANDS BEHIND MY back, I hummed a little. The elevator doors opened on two assistants wearing Z-specs. "Good morning, Dr. Neumann!" They moved aside to make room.

"Hello." I couldn't remember their names.

"Are you coming back to work?"

"Yes," I said. "No." Those milky lenses were a little creepy. Of course, I was half machine. But still. "Soon."

"Good." The tall one grinned. "We have some things to show you."

The doors opened. I stepped out. I was curious about those things. But I wanted to see Lola more. It was funny, because an hour ago all I could think about was my parts. And Lola was almost certainly sleeping. There was nothing productive I could do there. Still, I made my way to her room and ducked under the doorway. Her eyelids briefly fluttered open and she smiled. It was a small smile but very beautiful, and I thought about this afterward: this perfect moment, which could not be improved.

7

I READ ONCE THAT YOU NEED TWO THINGS TO BE HAPPY: ANY TWO OF health, money, and love. You can cover the absence of one with the other two. I drew comfort from this idea while I was fully bodied, employed, and unloved. It made me feel I wasn't missing much. But now I realized this was unmitigated bullshit, because health and money did not compare with love at all. I had a girl in a hospital bed who liked me and I didn't know where that might go but I could tell it was more important than low blood pressure. It mattered more than a new car. With Lola in the same building, I walked with a spring in my step. That was true literally. But I mean I was happy, happy on an axis I had previously known about only in theory. I was glad to be alive.

· · ·

WHEN I REACHED THE GLASS ROOM I NOTICED A LOT OF Z-SPEC-
wearing lab assistants. They were grinning. At first I thought
they were pleased to see me but by the time I reached my
desk I suspected they were playing some kind of joke.
"Hello," I said to one, and she said hello and her lips
stretched wider. I settled the Contours and poked on my
computer. They hovered, eight or ten of them. When I
couldn't stand it, I said, "What?"

"Notice anything different?" I realized this was Jason. I
hadn't recognized him at first because the Z-specs occupied
half his face. I wasn't used to identifying people by their
lips. I looked from one set to another.

"No."

"Nothing at all?"

"No."

"Would you like us to take off our glasses?"

"Not really."

Someone stifled a giggle. "All right," I said. "Take them
off."

They pulled off the specs. Underneath, they had no
pupils. That's how it looked. "We can't," said Jason. There
was laughter. "We're still wearing them."

I rose in the Contours. Closer up, I could see flat silver
circles swimming in his pupils. Tiny silver floating suns.

"We miniaturized. Now they're lenses."

"Z-lenses," corrected a girl.

"Silicon and gel on flexible polycarbonate wafers," said
Jason. "You don't use your eyebrows to control the zoom.
You blink." His eyelids fluttered. His silver pupils swirled
like mist.

"I see," I said.

"No, you don't." More laughs. "Not without Z-lenses.
Not really."

I looked at their proud, smiling, pupilless faces. I was

being less enthusiastic than they wanted. But it was weird. "Okay," I said. "Good work."

I WORKED ON PARTS DURING THE DAY AND VISITED LOLA EVERY evening. Sometimes she slept. More and more she was awake. She lay with hair exploding across her pillow and put her hand on my arm as we talked. She could laugh and tell stories but she tired quickly and it was always over too soon.

"I've never liked my ears," she said. "Look. They're way too high."

"Too high for what?"

"For . . ." She smiled, let go of her hair, and slapped my arm. In the setting sun, she looked very warm. "For *looks*."

"They look great." I touched her ear. I couldn't quite believe I was allowed to do this, but I was. I was. "Your helixes follow the golden ratio."

"That's good?"

"I can prove it mathematically."

"I wish you'd gone to my high school."

"Your ears are excellent," I said. "For biology."

"Ah." She nestled a little lower in the pillow, which meant it was almost time to go. "I suppose you could do better."

"Well . . ."

"Tell me."

"I don't know. No. I couldn't."

"You could, though."

"I like your biology," I said. "You have great biology."

"But . . ."

"Well, functionally . . ."

"Yes?"

"There are areas for improvement."

"Tell me some."

"Well . . ." I glanced at the mirror. It was hard to know how private we were.

"If you had to change something."

I hesitated. I touched her shoulder. "The clavicle. I guess that's obvious. It's not very strong. That goes for bones in general, relative to modern metals. We know how to do lightweight and strong a lot better than bones."

"I don't want to break." She probed her clavicle around my fingers. In the sunlight, her hand glowed red.

"Exactly."

"I like that you see past bodies," Lola said dreamily. "To . . . something else." She closed her eyes. I stayed a while, her hand on mine, watching her breathe.

I MADE LAB 3 MY OWN SPACE, FORBIDDEN TO LAB ASSISTANTS. I couldn't concentrate with them around. They had always been loud and energetic, laughing at nothing, exclaiming over trivia like they were the first people in the world to synthesize a mated compound, but I had found this more tolerable before they had silver eyes. I began to dread walking into rooms, because of how they would look at me.

They offered to make me a pair of Z-lenses. I said I was busy. The truth was I didn't like Z-lenses. I should have. They were marvels. I might have built these. But I hadn't and that bothered me. I guess that sounds selfish. But I did not like technology I couldn't modify. I was not a user.

In Lab 3 I tinkered with the Contours, sifting through software, tightening code. For fun I drafted some arms. I was just playing around. I didn't plan on replacing my biological arms. Not right away. But the fact was I had artificial fingers and there was a limit to what you could do with those while they were attached to a biological arm. It was the bottleneck problem again. So I dabbled. It was the best way to work: with no particular goal in mind. It allowed me to explore the most intriguing ideas, not the ones most likely to meet spec.

One of those kinds of ideas came to me in the elevator after leaving Lola. I rode down to Lab 3 and locked myself inside. I took out my ideas notepad and began to doodle. It was just a thought. I didn't know much about this area. I didn't know what was possible. But still, I liked it. The idea was to make Lola a heart.

LOLA MOVED TO A LIVE-IN SUITE IN THE UPPER SECTION OF BUILDING C. It meant that to reach her I had to leave one elevator and circumnavigate the atrium, passing by the lobby. As I clomped along, Contours pistoning, hooves *clump-clumping* on the carpet, heads turned. Mouths dropped. People in suits backed out of my way and people in white coats edged closer. They wanted to ask questions and tell me about related projects and ask if I would pose with them for photos. I didn't mind the attention but I was eager to see Lola and it slowed me down. So I found a back way, avoiding the high-traffic areas. Some of it was tiled and on my first step it splintered into a web of cracks. I hesitated. Then I continued.

"You should do a presentation," said Cassandra Cautery, leaning against the wall outside Lola's suite. She had been waiting for me. "Everyone's asking about you."

"Okay."

"I'll hold you to that." She laughed a little. I felt annoyed, because I didn't want to do a presentation. "How is everything? Are you happy?"

"Yes."

"I've seen a report on these, ah, these glasses."

"Z-lenses."

"They sound wonderful." She smiled. "I've never needed

glasses myself. I've always had twenty/twenty vision. Just lucky."

"Z-lenses are better than twenty/twenty. They're about twenty/two." Cassandra Cautery looked confused. "Twenty/ twenty vision doesn't mean you have perfect eyesight. It's not twenty out of twenty. That's a misconception. It means you can see as well over twenty feet as an average human."

"I did not know that."

"If you have good eyesight, you might be twenty/eighteen. That is, you can see from twenty feet away what the average human can see from eighteen. Very good eyesight for a human is twenty/fifteen. Maybe twenty/twelve. But you'd need to be descended from a nomadic tribe." I eyed her blond hair. "I don't think you'd be twenty/twelve."

"Oh."

"Twenty/two is about the same as a hawk."

"Oh," she said. "Well."

"I'd like to see Lola," I said. "If that's okay."

Cassandra Cautery nodded. She seemed preoccupied. I left her in the corridor and went inside.

LOLA'S SUITE HAD A LITTLE TABLE. AT NIGHTS A NURSE WHEELED IN A trolley and uncovered pasta or slices of unidentifiable meat. It was not particularly good food but it was the best part of my day. I cut things with a blade installed in my machine fingers and Lola watched me do it.

One night I reached for the salt but Lola had already moved it to her side of the table. I looked at her. She was drinking from her glass of water. "Salt," I said, but she just nodded and kept drinking. She drained half the glass. When she set it down, she picked up a napkin and dabbed her lips. She tapped salt into her soup and handed it to me. I stared. "What?" she said.

"Nothing. It's just . . . nothing."

"What?"

I put down the salt. "You locked the salt while performing an unrelated task."

She blinked. "You mean drinking?"

"Yes."

"You can't wait five seconds for salt?"

"I can. But salt is a shared resource. If you're going to lock it, you should use it as quickly as possible, then release it. You can't leave it locked while accepting an interrupt."

"I got thirsty."

"Then first return the salt to general availability."

"Just in case you happen to want salt in that five seconds?"

"Yes."

She stared at me. "Really?"

"Otherwise you compromise the system."

"What system?"

"The . . ." I waved my hands. "The system."

"There isn't any system."

"Everything is a system. Look." I leaned forward. "What if I had your water and I suddenly decided I wanted the salt? And instead of giving you back the water I just sat here waiting for you to release the salt, which you didn't because you were waiting for the water? It's a deadlock, that's what. It's catastrophic system failure. And you're probably thinking, 'Well, I could just ask Charlie to give me the water in exchange for the salt.' But that requires you to understand my resource needs, and violate process encapsulation. It's a swamp. I'm not saying it's a big deal. I'm just pointing out that locking the salt like that is incredibly inefficient and systemically dangerous."

Lola snickered. "You're insane."

"I'm not insane. It's a fundamental principle. You're insane."

"Regular people don't bring fundamental principles to the dinner table."

"Well," I said.

We ate. "Explain that again," said Lola. "That stuff about locks."

LOLA BECAME WELL ENOUGH TO WALK AROUND. SHE HELD MY ARM AND shuffled along corridors in her little cotton gown. We graduated from short strolls to circuits. The floor was almost empty but for plants in large gray pots. There was an area near the elevators where one wall was all glass and we gazed out across the Better Future lawn and watched the sun set. It occurred to me that I had never seen anyone visit. I asked if there was someone I should call. She rested her head against the side of my arm and said nothing for a while and then, "No."

THE NIGHT PAINS WORSENED. I COULDN'T SHAKE THEM. I WOKE TO blinding cramps in nonexistent feet, the sensation of my legs curling back on themselves. I was still treating it by strapping on my old-model legs but it was no longer enough. I began to attach them before going to sleep. It was awkward and uncomfortable but better than fumbling with straps in the dark while my amputated muscles screamed.

I decided to leave the Contours on for a night and see what happened. It was a good idea because I didn't like taking them off anyway. It was like becoming a cripple again, every night. I wasn't sure how I could lie down but I was forgetting that compared with them, my weight was practically zero. All I needed to do was hold on while they bent in two places and rotated the bucket seat. I couldn't roll over. That was awkward. But discomfort was not pain so it

was a big improvement. Pretty soon I couldn't imagine ever
taking off my legs again.

I ARRIVED IN THE LABS ONE MORNING AND THERE WAS A GIRL IN A
white coat with eyes as blue as a Bunsen burner flame. I
didn't put it together until I passed another girl with violet
eyes and then a guy with emeralds. By the time I reached
the Glass Room I was prepared. Sure enough, Jason's eyes
glowed mahogany. "You colored the Z-lenses."

"It's only cosmetic." Jason wheeled his office chair closer.
"But people like it. What do you think?"

"Does it interfere with function?"

He shook his head. "You just set the chip to filter a particular frequency."

"That sounds like extra complexity. Another potential
point of failure."

"It's working pretty well."

"Never sacrifice function for appearance," I said. "It's
poor engineering." But they did look nice.

I SET ALPHA TO WORK ON HORMONE REGULATION. BETA ON SENSORY
enhancement. Gamma on a bunch of things around arms.
My ulterior motive was to deprive them of free time, to
slow the progress of Z-lenses. It seemed to work. Then I got
interested in them myself and realized I could make them
shift into the nonvisible spectrum, so I could see infrared or
ultraviolet. I didn't know how exactly this would be useful
but I could see it could be done. I spent a few days hacking
out a prototype, in glasses rather than lenses because the
technology was the same but without the delays of minia-
turization, and put them on. In infrared, the world flared
red and purple and people looked like glowing brains and

hearts. My Contours had three hot spots around the battery and hooves, but were otherwise frozen black. In ultraviolet not much was different except lab coats and some lights and surfaces, which shone. That was a little disappointing. But I felt better about Z-lenses, and stopped trying to delay them.

I CAME OUT OF LAB 3 AND THEY WERE WAITING FOR ME. MIRKA, WHO used to infiltrate me with needles, stood awkwardly at the front. She looked different. I mean, besides the fluorescent green eyes. Jason nudged her, but she didn't speak. "We did it," he said.

"Did what?"

"Found a way to regulate the spleen." He reached for Mirka, then hesitated. "Show him."

Mirka lifted her shirt. She had a very toned stomach. I noticed this first. Then the metal patch.

"Basic electrical stimulation," said Jason. "The tricky part is hitting the right nerves. But of course we could leverage a lot of our earlier leg work."

"Leg work," sniggered somebody.

"Notice Mirka's skin. We're flooding her with estrogen and thylacine. Can you see the difference?"

I looked her over. She didn't smile. But she looked good. The difference I had noticed was *health*. She was a more attractive version of herself.

"Her hair is thickening, too."

"You went to human testing without asking me?"

"Um," said Jason. "Yes. Sorry. We were going to ask. But you said not to disturb you."

"You could have waited."

"We could have. Yeah. Sorry."

I stared at Mirka.

"Did we do wrong? Because we just wanted to be like you. Be our own guinea pigs."

Mirka said, "I am happy to do it." Against her flawless skin, her eyes shone like a cat's.

"It's just a harmless way to test our organ-management techs," said Jason. "Just proof of concept. That's okay, isn't it?"

I couldn't think of a way to say no. "Yes."

Jason looked relieved. There was some laughter. "I thought it would be." Somebody elbowed him. "We're so excited about where this is going." I nodded, still distracted by Mirka. "It's all happening," said Jason.

SO OF COURSE BY THE END OF THE WEEK HALF MY LAB ASSISTANTS HAD beautiful skin and glowing hair. I kind of saw this coming but still it was a surprise. In the sciences, looking good was usually a negative. It implied you wasted time on outdoor activities instead of building something useful. Even using hair product or makeup suggested misguided priorities. Like you thought how things looked mattered, instead of how they worked. We liked to look at attractive people. We expected it of our movie stars and TV characters. But we did not respect it. We knew physical attractiveness was inversely correlated with intelligence, because look at us.

I was used to gazing around a lab and seeing acne and dark-ringed eyes and skin the color of a corpse dragged from a lake. Hair all over the place, or strangled in ponytails. These were signs of a good lab. Now it was like a laboratory in a TV commercial for skin-care products. Not quite. They were still awkward and poorly dressed and overweight or deathly thin. But still. It didn't look right.

. . .

CASSANDRA CAUTERY LEFT A MESSAGE. WHEN I DIDN'T RESPOND SHE left three more and eventually a young guy in a neat suit with thin glasses came into the Glass Room and knocked. Everyone looked at him because nobody knocked in the Glass Room. You came in, did what you had to, and left. He looked from one assistant to the next and finally his eyes landed on me. "Dr. Neumann?" I stared at him, because come on, I had titanium legs. The suits were like that, at pains to not notice me below the waist. It made me yearn for engineers, who stared and pointed and stopped me for questions. Although then that made me miss the suits. "Cassandra Cautery is wondering if you have a moment." I looked through the green glass at my assistants running through remote-control tests on a pair of robot arms. The second I left, they would start dueling with them, I knew. "If not, I'm happy to wait." He looked around for a chair.

When we reached Cassandra Cautery's office, he knocked, smiled once, and walked away. "Enter," said Cassandra Cautery. I opened the door and *thunk-thunked* inside. Her desk was piled high with sky-blue folders. "Charlie." She came around her desk and peered into my eyes. "Are you good?"

"Yes."

She closed the door. When I turned around, she was staring at my hooves. I had torn up some carpet.

"Sorry."

"You're just walking around in those now?"

"Yes."

"We should discuss that. I'm not sure it's a good idea to take them outside the labs. From a product-testing point of view."

"I need to spend time in them to refine the nerve interface." This was kind of true.

She waved this away. "That's not why I brought you

here." I waited for her to say why she had brought me here. She walked to her desk, shuffled some papers, turned back, rested her butt against the desk, and folded her arms. It was a very comfortable pose. Like from a catalog. "There's a lot of excitement about the products coming out of your area."

"Okay."

"In particular, the Better Eyes and Better Skin."

"You mean the, uh, Z-lenses and the hormone-regulating—"

"I'm using their marketing names. It's what . . ." She fluttered her hands. "This is all coming down from on high."

"Okay."

"I didn't actually expect you to go cosmetic, Charlie. I thought this was going to be more, you know, hard-core medical." The skin between her eyes sharpened. "Are you wearing Better Eyes?"

"No."

"I haven't tried them." She shrugged lightly. Her eyes were a light blue. Attractive. But not neon. "A few of the senior managers have. They were a big hit. These are the colored ones I'm talking about. No one was really in love with them before that. We thought they were a strictly scientific product. Because, obviously, you wouldn't want to walk around with white eyes. Now they're functional *and* cosmetic. It's . . . well, it's a dream." Silence. "I went down to your lab yesterday. You were locked away. But I saw your assistants. Using the, uh, the Eyes and the Skin. It's . . . well, it's amazing. They look great. I couldn't believe it. I literally could not believe they were the same people. Because I've been down many times, Charlie, and it used to be, no offense, but they were not an attractive bunch. Which is fine. That's how we expect our scientific people to be. I don't mean *expect*. I mean that's how it usually is. The people with technical smarts go into the labs and those of us with, you know, social skills, if you like, we go into management. I'm not saying we're better looking. I'm just saying, there's usually that division. If all of a sudden someone like me suddenly, I don't know, put a metal patch on my head that made me supergood with computers, you lab people would freak right out. Wouldn't you? You'd think, 'Wait, who's this chick with the cheekbones taking over?' You'd think, 'Hold on, I spent my whole life figuring out how to be good with computers. I work out every day on computers. Now somebody can have that from a patch? That's not fair.'" She nodded. "It's like worlds colliding. It's a little like that. And I'm not saying stop. Absolutely not. This is what they hoped you'd do, times a thousand. It's a success, but so much of a success it almost becomes something else entirely. Do you see what I mean?" She tucked a lock of hair behind her ear. As her hand came down, it stroked her jawline. "Do you know how often I go to the gym, Charlie? Every single day." She laughed. "I don't know why I told you that. That has nothing to do with anything. So where do you think you'll go next?" She placed her palms on the edge of the desk. "Tell me."

"Um . . . well . . . arms."

Her eyes flicked to my metal fingers. "I'm up to speed on the arms. They like where you're going there. How about teeth?"

"Teeth?"

"I'm just throwing ideas out there. Spitballing. Are you thinking of doing anything with teeth?"

"No."

She stared at me.

"If you're talking about . . . some kind of solution to your . . ." I gestured toward my jaw.

"No. Of course not."

"Because if a dentist said your teeth were too close to nerves to move, that's probably right."

"I don't care about the diastema, Charlie. Okay? Let's be clear. This is not about me. This is about you wanting to chop off your goddamn arms." I blinked. "And let me tell you right now we are going to have a serious conversation about that, because I'm still pissed about the fingers. You didn't go through proper channels. You took it upon yourself to crush your hand and I didn't know until afterward. I took care of it. I did what had to be done. But I did not appreciate being cut out of the loop. You want to do destructive testing, you come to me first. Is that clear? I can be reasonable." She spread her arms. "I'm here to help. But keep me in the loop, Charlie. Keep me in the loop."

I coughed. "Okay."

"Here's the thing. Imagine we're building a body." I opened my mouth to say I *was* building a body, but she held up a finger. "And it's a wonderful body, one everyone is very interested in getting right. The ideas for how to build this body, they mostly come from one particular brain. That brain is important, wouldn't you say? Crucial. While we're building this body, the one thing we must do, the absolute top priority, is to keep the brain safe. Well, to me, Charlie, the body isn't those Better Legs you're wearing. It's not the parts. The prostheses. It's the capacity to produce them. The body I'm supposed to be building, Charlie, is a department with the ability to create bio-enhancement products. Do you see?" She nodded. "I think you do. And you're the brain. You're the one part I must keep safe." Her brow furrowed. "What are you doing?"

I looked down. I was rubbing the heel of one hand against my titanium thigh. I guess I had been trying to knead it, to restore blood flow to a part that ached. "Nothing."

"Don't say 'nothing.'"

"It's phantom pain. Nothing serious."

"Phantom . . . ?"

"It's common. It's nothing. A glitch. A technical hiccup."

Her jaw set. "This is precisely what I'm talking about. When I hear things like this, do you know how I feel? These . . ." She gestured at my legs. "These technical phantoms? They make me feel like plucking the brain right out of the body and putting it in a jar. That's what I want to do. Put the brain somewhere safe, so no matter what happens to the body, what mistakes may be made, it will be okay. Do you understand? The need to separate the brain from the body?"

"But I'm the body. I'm the brain and the body. They can't be separated."

"Imagine they could," she said.

Silence. "I'm interested in making parts for me," I said. "Not just other people."

She stared. Then she smiled. "Well, I think we understand each other. Tell you what. You keep doing what you're doing, I'll see what I can do from this end. To mesh your reality with that of the company's."

"Okay."

"What about a tooth with a phone in it?" she said. "I think I saw that on TV one time."

"Um."

"That would be functional. That would be very functional. Not that you should cancel the cosmetic stuff. Everyone loves the cosmetics. But if you felt the urge to, I don't know, put phones in teeth, I think that would be your call. Because you're the scientist. You're the ideas man. You know?" She laughed.

"Yes," I said, although I didn't think I did.

"I'm glad we had this chat. I really am. Thanks for making time, Charlie."

"Okay," I said.

"And keep me in the loop."

"Okay." When I reached the door, I looked back. Her cheek was bulging, her tongue in there, exploring.

LOLA'S SUITE HAD A BALCONY. THE SEASON WAS TURNING BUT IF SHE wrapped up in a blanket we could still sit and watch the flitting of car headlights and streetlamps. She leaned over the railing and shivered. "If you close one eye, the cars look like toys," she said. "Like you could flick them with your finger."

I put my arm around her waist. Or where her waist must be. It was a thick blanket. She looked up. Her lips parted. Then we both turned to look inside, at the nurse moving around Lola's bed, collecting crumpled tissues from Lola's bedside table and dropping them into the trash. "She always turns up right before you," said Lola.

"Really?"

"When you're not here, I hardly ever see her."

The nurse caught my eye and smiled through the glass.

"I would like to leave." Lola put her arms around me and squeezed. "I would like to go somewhere nobody is watching."

It was a good idea. I hesitated.

"When you've finished your work, I mean."

"Yes."

"I don't mean you should stop your work."

"There could be a recuperative stage coming," I said. "To do with the arms."

"Really," Lola said. She touched my sleeve. Every one of

my hairs stood up. There was nothing like biology for sensory feedback. I hadn't been able to get close to it. "I like your arms." Her hand kept moving. It reached my metal fingers. "But I like these, too." She rested her head against me. "The ones you made yourself."

HEADING BACK TO MY BUNK, I DECIDED TO SWIPE A POTTED PLANT. Lola's floor had dozens, and those cheerful splashes of green really made a difference. I wished I could put some in the labs, but couldn't, because of contamination. I could brighten up my room, though. I carried the plant and set it in the corner.

The next day I got serious about feedback. The surprising thing was how little research there was. Papers were speculative, describing experiments that might be useful if other people filled in other great gaping voids. They opened with statements like: *To date there has been little interest in the problem of replacing sensory function lost in amputation.*

It irritated me. You could walk into an electronics store and for three hundred dollars take home a game console with a gyroscope-equipped dual-feedback resistance controller that shook and pushed to emulate in eighteen different ways the sensation of driving a tank across a battlefield. But restoring touch to someone who'd lost an arm, that wasn't of interest. Those people got a claw from the 1970s. That was problem solved. We had the technology but in the wrong places. It wasn't the morality that bothered me so much as the inefficiency. It was a misallocation of resources. And I knew that logically companies should spend a hundred million dollars on a game controller rather than a prosthesis that let a man feel again. But every time I read that, *lack of interest,* I wanted to kick someone.

I pulled the entire team onto it. Alpha, Beta, Gamma,

and Omega: about a hundred people. By the end of the day they had self-organized into hierarchical structures for task delegation and reporting. I didn't care about this. I just told them what I wanted done and let them figure it out. In this sense they were like a subroutine. Like the path-finding tech in my legs. I could see the sense of Cassandra Cautery's body analogy. On the third day, Omega hooked a girl into a nerve grid and made her taste colors. Alpha built a skin-like alloy that seemed promising until it put three thousand volts through one of them and they had to deal with Human Resources. But despite setbacks, we made progress. By the end of the week the nerve interface was two-way, capable of transmitting gross sensation. It was indistinct, every touch wrapped in cotton wool, but I could close my eyes and know when an assistant poked a mesh array. Everyone was very proud. But this wasn't because of our brilliance. It was because nobody else had tried.

I went back to the arms. They were titanium and servo-magnetic and could rotate 360 degrees on three independent axes. One night I sat there staring at them and realized there was nothing else to do. They were the smartest things I had ever built. And, not wanting to boast, I had built some smart things. Once I created a microbe that ate garbage. You could open your trash can, throw in your scraps, and an hour later they would be gone. The microbe ate them. It didn't get through QA because if the microbe got out, it would eat everything. There were concerns about a trashcan-eats-man scenario. Which was not the fault of the microbe, in my opinion. My feeling was that someone should come up with a safe receptacle. But anyway. There were no such problems with the arms, because the only person whose opinion mattered was me.

I retired to my bunk and retracted the Contours. The plant I'd stolen the week before was slumped over, brown and shriveled. I hadn't watered it. The lack of natural light may have been a problem, too. I felt annoyed. There was something pathetic about an organism that couldn't even live if you left it alone. This was maybe a little hard on the plant, which had been removed to a hostile environment, but still, it reminded me why I was doing this.

8

I WROTE AN E-MAIL TO CASSANDRA CAUTERY. BY THE THIRD DRAFT IT
said:

> You said you wanted to be kept in the loop re: destructive
> testing, well we are at that stage so just letting you know. CN.

I put it all on one line so she might miss it. I clicked
SEND and waited. Ten seconds later the e-mail notification
window slid up and my heart sank because the subject was
STOP DO NOT PROCEED WRT DESTRUCT TEST-
ING. I clicked it open. All it said was: *call me pls.* My desk
phone rang. I looked at it for a while. But there was no
escape. "Hello?"

"Where are you? What's happening?"

"Nothing. I'm in the Glass Room."

"Stay there. Okay? Don't do anything. I'm coming down. I have to make a call first. But I'll be there. Don't move."

"I wasn't saying *today*. I'm just keeping you informed."

"Great. Yes. Thank you. But I do not want you hurting yourself. Is that clear?"

"I thought you were helping me. You said you would help." My hand holding the phone, the metal one, tightened. I did not usually get angry at people. I was not a confrontational guy. But I was annoyed to discover Cassandra Cautery's true allegiance, because it should have been obvious. "I'm making these parts for *me*."

"That's not practical, Charlie."

"It is practical. Don't tell me what's practical. My job is all about practical. I know more about what's practical than you ever will."

"Calm down. We don't need to argue."

"They're *my arms*."

"I'm sending security."

Assistants had gathered in the Glass Room. They watched with huge, neon eyes. I turned my back on them. "We've been working toward this for weeks and suddenly we can't proceed with testing? You can't bring in someone else. You can't just go find some random amputee. This is a secure lab. It will take weeks to clear someone."

"I have that covered. I don't need . . . just stay calm. Sit there and don't do anything, okay?"

"What do you mean, you have that covered?"

"That's not important. Just . . ." I heard clicking fingers. She was signaling to someone. "Sit tight."

"How do you have that covered?"

"*Go,*" Cassandra Cautery hissed, but not to me. I put down the phone. When I turned I was confronted with a dozen sets of cats' eyes. Jason cleared his throat. "Is everything all right?"

I didn't say anything. I was thinking. Security was on its way. I wasn't sure what they would do when they got here. Maybe nothing. But maybe I had a limited window in which to act unfettered. "Go back to work," I told the cats. I *thunk-thunked* out of the Glass Room and down to Lab 5. This was where the arms were housed, the most recent incarnation of the servomagnetic sensory-feedback technology. They hung on plastic thread supports, spotlit. Of course they did. I didn't know why I'd felt the urge to check them. I headed to Lab 1. We had started calling this the Repository because it was where we stored the parts that never worked right, never got finished, or were exciting until we invented something better. Some were entire fingers and spleens and stomachs. I touched my metal ring finger to the security panel. It glowed red. I stared. This lock had never shown red to me, ever. There was no reason for it to do so. It was my room. It was where I kept my parts.

A groan slipped out of my mouth. I tried the finger again. Red. I thought: *Maybe there's something wrong with the finger.* But there wasn't. It was the lock. Cassandra Cautery had disabled my access. No door in Better Future would open for me now. I felt dizzy. I grabbed at the wall for balance, which was stupid, because I was in the Contours, which would keep me upright whether I was conscious or not, not like treacherous meat legs, and then I did start to faint, and my skull hit the wall. "Ow," I said. The Contours took a stuttering step. I did not ask them to do that. I was freaking out. I was brainstorming the nerve interface. That was bad. That might have unintended consequences. And the bottom line was I needed to get into the Repository and see if my parts were okay.

I kicked the door. It burst inward and ricocheted off steel shelves on the far wall. I flinched at my own violence. The lab lights fuzzed on. I walked inside. We tried to keep it tidy but it looked like an army of robots had exploded in here. I scanned gleaming shelves, running inventory. I couldn't remember everything we had but it seemed full. I felt myself calming. I had been silly. I had gotten carried away. Of course my parts were here. It was going to be hard to explain this door.

I saw a gap. A space on the shelves, where none should be. I was missing some arms. Not in the good way.

I EXITED, STOPPED, AND WENT BACK IN. I COULDN'T LEAVE PARTS HERE. Who knew where they would be by the time I got back? I grabbed some fingers and a forearm, then I saw a hand I liked better. I tried to rearrange things and fingers scattered across the floor. I had to get out of here. I had to be gone before security arrived. I didn't know where I would go but it had to be somewhere. I suddenly remembered Lola's heart, the one I was making. I dumped the parts on the nearest horizontal surface and left for Lab 3. I swiped my finger across the security panel, just in case, but it gave me red, so I stepped back and kicked the door. I tried to be more gentle this time but it blew off its hinges and smashed through a mounted spotlight. Glass rained to the floor. This noise would draw assistants like osmosis. They couldn't stay away from the sound of something breaking. I thudded inside and pulled black cloth off Lola's heart. I stared in dismay. It was spread across the steel workbench in thirty pieces. I'd forgotten: I was tinkering with valves. It would take hours to put together. I couldn't even gather the pieces without scratching contacts and bending circuitry. I heard the elevator. I thought it was the elevator. It could have been anything. I needed better ears. I left the disman-tled heart and stuck my head into the corridor. No one. But it was only a matter of time. An elevator stood open, empty, and I couldn't delay any longer. I ran, the Contours thumping the floor. Inside I pressed for G and of course nothing happened. I swiped my finger. The panel emitted a regretful tone and said: CONTACT MANAGEMENT. I stepped out of the car and kicked the stairwell door. I was panicking and didn't control the force at all and the door bounced off the stair banister and flew back at me. I threw up my hands and it ricocheted off the doorway, eight inches away from decapitating me, and went skidding down the concrete steps. "Whoa," said someone behind me. Assistants were coming. *Up up up,* I told the Contours, and they began cantilevering up the steps. On the third turn they froze in mid-step. I thought: *Oh God, they have turned me off.* But I could feel frigid stairwell air on my metal legs' mesh array and that meant I had power. I triggered a soft reset by imagining my left knee rising three times. The hooves rose and came together. A bug. Some kind of regression. I would have to look at that. I set off again and two levels later froze again. I reset the legs. It must be the steps. Finally I reached a door marked GROUND. I leaned against it rather than kicking, and it groaned and popped open. A man in a suit gave me a surprised look. Not security. That was lucky, because I was agitated and not making completely logical decisions. If someone tried to stop me I didn't know what would happen. I had to find Lola. I didn't know what it would accomplish but I felt confident that together we could figure something out. The Contours took this idea and ran with it. They cracked every tile on the back route to Building A and nudged open the stairwell door. It took five minutes and ten soft resets to ascend eight floors. This was terrible. This was sloppy unit testing. But I made it and thumped past potted plants and banged a metal fist on Lola's door. "Lola! Lola!" I couldn't wait. I popped open her door. I was getting the hang of this. I pistoned into her suite but it was empty. She wasn't in the bathroom. She wasn't anywhere. This didn't seem possible. Lola was always here. I didn't know where to go.

The Contours started moving. I had to backtrack my thoughts to figure out where they were headed. The recovery room: where Lola had been before they brought her here. I had no idea why she might be there but it was the only place I could think of. The Contours cantilevered easily down five floors and I thought I must be figuring out the particular configuration of terrain that locked them up when they completely missed a step and hit the next one like a mallet. Cracks shot through the concrete all the way to the opposite wall. I gasped and clutched at the sides of the bucket seat. My thighs were drenched in sweat. I had never tested what happened when water pooled around the nerve interface needles. It couldn't be good. I had to get off these stairs. I focused manually on each step to override the automatic pathfinding. My teeth hurt. I was grinding them. When I finally popped the door on the medical level, my body was shaking. I had never done anything so physically demanding. I stepped into the corridor and four Better Future security guards were waiting for me.

"Dr. Neumann," said one. Not Carl. "I would very much appreciate it if you could calm down a second."

All four guards had a hand resting on a gun holster. They were telling me that this didn't have to get serious but it could. I wondered whether I could get past them on the Contours before they could draw their weapons. Probably yes. They were underestimating my acceleration. Of course, it would be a temporary solution. But it was something. I decided to do it. Lola emerged from a doorway. "Charlie!" She shouldered her way between the guards. "You look terrible. What's wrong?"

"They . . ." I said. "What are . . . why are you here?"

"There's a man. He had an accident. They asked if I could help him." She tried to push hair out of my eyes. "Charlie, you look like you're having a heart attack."

"What man?"

"Through here. Come on. I'll show you."

"What accident?"

She pulled me by the hand. I followed and the guards moved aside. "He's a security guard. He's . . . you know, he's that security guard."

Which security guard, I wanted to say. But I couldn't, because I already knew.

"His name is Carl." She stopped outside the recovery room and turned to me. I saw a terrible light in her eyes, like love. "He doesn't have any arms."

AND THERE HE WAS: CARL, SITTING ON THE EDGE OF THE BED, NAKED but for boxer shorts, flexing one arm. My arm. It was a Beta prototype: thin, hollow bands of delicate al-titanium alloy foil rods on ball joints with independent axes of rotation. Its main advantage was it could reach in any direction, including backward, and it weighed ten pounds, which was ideal for the user who hadn't upgraded the load-bearing capacity of his spine. The nerve interface was first generation, good only for motor function. It was essentially a trainer arm. But this did not change the fact that Carl should not have it.

To his credit, he looked mildly ashamed. He stopped flexing. His eyes shifted. His lips twitched, as if he wanted to smile but thought maybe that would piss me off. This was a good call. Because in this moment, it was everything I could do not to kick Carl through the wall.

"He had an accident," Lola said. She saw something

about the way the arm was strapped around Carl's shoulder she didn't like and began fooling with it. "He's not allowed to talk about it, but . . . well, obviously it was traumatic. And it's so lucky, because you have these amazing units. I was just telling Carl." Her fingers continued to fiddle around bulging muscles. The guy was like an anatomy textbook. It made no sense that someone who put this much work into his body would want to remove part of it. Except for the burned fiancée thing. *You can never be too strong.* "I'm so glad you're here, Charlie, because what you've gone through, how you turned your amputation into a positive, it's what Carl needs to hear right now." She smiled, one hand resting lightly on Carl's shoulder.

I said, "I need to talk to you."

Her eyebrows rose. "Well . . . okay." She walked around Carl. "Keep practicing those lifts."

"Okay," said Carl.

"HE *SHOT* YOU," I WHISPERED. "IN THE *HEART.*"

Lola scowled. She had a hell of a scowl. I had never seen it before. Her eyebrows rotated thirty degrees. "You think I don't know that?"

"Then why—"

"Because he's *hurt.*"

"This . . ." Down the corridor, a guard coughed into his hand. I forced myself to lower my voice. "This was not an accident."

Lola's eyebrows flipped. "Why would you say that?"

"Because nothing that happens here is an accident. Cassandra Cautery said—"

"*Your* first transfemoral was an accident. You got caught in a clamp."

"That was different. That's not the point. The point is—"

"What's the point?" She put her hands on her hips. These emotional cues were distracting. I was used to arguing with scientists, who would explain with perfectly bland faces why you were wrong and stupid. "Tell me the point."

"The point is they're my parts."

Lola went still. When she spoke, her voice was low and dangerous. "You didn't just say that."

"I built these. He took them without asking. Or *someone* took them. How would you feel if you saw someone else wearing parts of your body?"

She screwed up her face. "What?"

"He's got a piece of *me* in his *body*." I felt panic. "I'm not explaining this very well."

"It's a prosthesis. A prosthesis, Charlie."

"My prosthesis."

"He's lost both arms!" Her voice echoed up the corridor. I glanced over my shoulder. The security guards avoided my eyes.

I swallowed. "I can . . . I'll make something. Something just for him."

Lola stared at me. "I'm surprised at you."

"They're going to give him the big arms. The ones I made for me. They're not going to let me have them." I tried to touch her arm but she shook me off. "Let's go to your suite. You shouldn't be here. You just had heart surgery."

"That was two months ago," she said, which surprised me, but I guess it was true. "I'm fine. *That* man . . ." She pointed at the recovery room. "Is not."

"Lola," I said. "Wait. Don't go in there." But she did.

"I UNDERSTAND," SAID CASSANDRA CAUTERY. "THEY'RE YOUR PARTS." She spread her arms. "What's to get? They're your parts."

I nodded. "My parts."

"I had a sister once. She used to borrow my clothes. I'd be looking everywhere for this one particular belt and she'd walk in wearing it. Drove me insane." She put an elbow on the arm of the sofa. Her legs were tucked beneath her, as if she might be about to curl up for a nap. It was not a particularly nice sofa. It looked like one from the lobby they had been going to throw out. "And that was just clothes."

"Right."

"I should have thought this through. I blame myself for forgetting your feelings in all this."

"I wasn't going to chop off my arms. Not today."

"Of course you weren't. Right? Of course you weren't. That was just me . . ." Her hand danced in the air. "Getting obsessive about control again. You have to understand this project is forcing me to go beyond my comfort zone in a lot of ways. Like I told the Manager, Charlie, I relish challenge. I relish it. But, wow, it's hard for me to sit back and let things happen. I have to force myself to do that. And what happened today, Charlie, was I panicked and reacted on instinct." She took a breath. "I promise to work on trusting you, Charlie. If I do that, can you trust me?"

I hesitated. She seemed convincing. But then again, I was an extraordinarily poor judge of people.

"You want the arms. I know that. I will fight to get you those arms. What can I do to make you feel comfortable, Charlie? Tell me."

A thought occurred. "Uh . . ."

"Anything."

"Well . . ." I cleared my throat. "About Carl . . ." I paused, in case Cassandra Cautery wanted to leap ahead. "He says he had an accident."

"Not quite true. He volunteered. We needed someone to test arms and he came forward. Don't ask me why. But he did." She held up her palms. "I couldn't tell you. I knew how you'd react. But there was a scheduling issue. Your department produces more prototype-stage products than you can field test. You were blocking the funnel. But forget that. That's resolved. What's the problem with Carl?"

"I'm not comfortable with him."

Her eyes held mine. "Would you like me to do something about that?"

"Can you?"

"Whatever you want."

I did not feel proud of myself. But I remembered Lola's eyes when she had said: *He doesn't have any arms.* "Can you get rid of Carl?"

"It's done."

"Really?"

"It's done. Forget about it."

"I feel bad for him, but—"

She waved a hand. "I get it. He's a distraction. He impairs your ability to work."

"Yes. Exactly. He impairs."

"Don't spare him another thought," she said.

THE ELEVATORS WORKED. I HAD RENEWED ACCESS. WHEN I EXITED AT the labs, I passed a closed, pristine stairwell door. It had been two hours and already they had erased everything I had done.

I shouldn't be here. I had been awake for twenty hours and could feel an adrenaline crash coming. But I didn't want to lie in that bunk room with a dead potted plant. I didn't want to stare at the ceiling and think about what I'd asked Cassandra Cautery to do.

I swiped into Lab 3. The lights flared like supernovas. On the steel workbench gleamed tiny valves and switches. I closed the door and made my way to the bench. I retracted the Contours to a comfortable height, picked up my Z-specs, and began to work on Lola's heart.

I EMERGED SO TIRED I COULD BARELY KEEP MY HEAD UP. THE CONTOURS bore me along, not minding that I nodded off once or twice. They were good legs.

Lola leaned against the wall outside my bunk room, fingering the hem of her polo shirt. Over the heart was stitched a Better Future logo. "Hi."

"Oh," I said. "Hi."

"I'm sorry about before. The argument."

"Okay." Now she was here, I couldn't even remember why we'd fought.

"I'm a yeller. I should have warned you. It comes with growing up fighting with your mom. I was thinking that to you, maybe it came across more angry than I meant. Because you have a different baseline."

That made sense. I nodded.

"So, Charlie, I'm kind of scared you don't like me anymore."

"Oh," I said. "No. That's not true."

"Are you sure?"

"Yes."

She held out her arms and we hugged. She turned her head and kissed my neck. "You're the best. I don't mean that like an expression." She stepped back and kicked my Contours. They tingled, as if I were outside in a thunderstorm. "I should let you sleep. You look beat."

"Okay."

"What you said about making parts for Carl . . . I realize that's a big thing. It's really sweet. It's like the best thing you could ever do for someone."

"Um."

"Sleep. I'll talk to you when you can think straight."

"Okay." I went inside and closed the door and stood there.

I COULDN'T SLEEP. NOT BECAUSE OF PHANTOM PAIN. BECAUSE OF CARL. He crawled into my mind and I couldn't get him out. I woke sticky with sweat, from dreams of Carl following me. He stood in the Clamp, looking at me armlessly as the plates closed in. His eyes said: *How could you do this? You know I need parts.*

I sat up. Carl was bad, wasn't he? He had shot Lola and stolen my arms. Or if not stolen, at least used them. The point was he was a destroyer of relationships. He was dangerous to an important thing I had.

But he had no arms. Without my help, he would get hospital prosthetics. He would live a terrible life.

I woke the Contours and levered upright and headed to the Glass Room. I would call Cassandra Cautery. I didn't know her home number but I would leave a message on her voice mail. Then I would be able to sleep.

But with the dial tone in my ear I hesitated. My brain whispered new scenarios. Carl doing physical therapy with Lola. Her standing behind him, encircling his torso with her arms, showing him how to move. Her breath tickling his ear.

I saw movement beyond the green glass. Jason, working late. I thought: *Maybe there's another way.*

I LAY STILL WHILE THE fMRI MACHINE THRUMMED AROUND ME. IT WAS unsettling, because I had to lie back and with my head poked into a small hole in a large machine. The issue was the hole looked like a mouth. It was also difficult to forget that the unit generated enough magnetic force to pull a pin clean through my body. I was glad I had thought of this. If things progressed like I planned, it would soon be difficult to MRI myself nonfatally. The *whoomp-whoomp-whoomp* was comfortingly rhythmic.

"That's good," said Jason's disembodied voice. "Now regret. Something you wish you could change."

"An uncle of mine died from colon cancer. I was twelve. I remember thinking how ridiculous that was, a failure in one small body part being fatal. I didn't understand why they couldn't give him a new colon."

"Sorry. I'm not seeing much. Can you try again? Something more . . . emotional?"

"Well . . . once in junior high I didn't go to a school dance, because I thought nobody would want to go with me. Then afterward I heard this girl I liked would have." Isabella. She had been good at chess. Always underdeveloped her rooks, though.

"Still not definitive."

I almost said, *Let's skip regret.* Because, really, how important was that? It was a social emotion. Group survival was maximized if all members felt an emotional obligation to treat one another fairly. But you personally wanted to be able to cheat and steal without remorse. I'm not saying that's a great set of values. I'm just saying logically.

"I fell out of a tree as a kid," I said. "I cut my leg open and had to get stitches. It left a scar. A little white line. Now it's gone I kind of miss it. It was a physical connection to my past. Not an important part. But still. I'm disconnected in a way I didn't anticipate. My body maps space to time. It has an embedded history." Jason was silent. "Of course, human tissue completely regenerates every seven years. It's unlikely that scar was composed of the same molecules. Do you think it's really appropriate to consider people to be the same entity they were seven years earlier? Because, physically, they're not. They're connected but every part has changed. Like a renovated house. It seems like after seven years you shouldn't be liable for things you did before. Why should a man be imprisoned for a crime committed by a different physical entity? Should we expect a couple to stay married when they barely share a molecule with the people who said, 'I do'? I don't think so. I know it's not that simple but that's my feeling."

Silence. I had wandered off topic. "I think that's as close as we're going to get," Jason said. "Let's try longing."

"THERE." JASON POINTED TO HIS MONITOR. WE HAD BEEN MAPPING MY brain for six hours. In the darkened observation room, his eyes were pits. "Activity in the ventromedial prefrontal cortex. Highly localized."

I looked up from wiring myself into the Contours. It was the first time I had done this in a while. It hurt. But not in a completely bad way. "That's guilt?"

"Yes." Jason paged down. "According to Krajbich et al., patients with damage to the VMPFC are quantifiably less sensitive to guilt. Regular people have a guilt quotient of two hundred. But VMPFC-impaired people average twenty-seven. That means they feel an amount of guilt that's negligible compared to the norm."

I activated the Contours. Sensation spread down my metal legs. I wouldn't say it was worth losing both legs just for this, but it was a good feeling. "Interesting."

"On every other measurable emotion, the two groups scored the same. Oh. Wait." He peered at the screen. "Envy's up."

"Envy?"

"Actually, that's within the margin of error. Probably meaningless."

"So if my VMPFC were suppressed, I'd feel less guilt, but otherwise be the same."

"A lot less guilt."

"Right. A lot less guilt."

"And/or regret. They both lit up the VMPFC."

I pondered this. "Is there a difference between guilt and regret?"

Jason stared blankly. "I don't . . . think . . . so."

"I guess one is . . ." I shook my head. "Lost it."

"Emotions aren't really my . . . area of expertise."

"Let's assume they're the same."

"Okay." He looked at the screen. "I'm not sure how you'd suppress the VMPFC, though. I mean . . . without actually . . . cutting it out."

An awkward silence descended. I had crushed my right leg in front of Jason. He had tried to stop me. Then I crushed my hand in front of him. He possibly had unresolved feelings. "I guess that would be kind of drastic."

"Kind of irreversible."

"Although I wouldn't regret it." This was a joke. Jason stared at me. "Because of the lack of a functioning ventromedial prefrontal cortex."

"Oh. Yes."

I tried again. "It's what people aspire to, isn't it? A life lived without regret? That's a saying."

"But doesn't that mean you should be bold? Take risks? Not surgically excise the capacity for regret from your brain."

"Hmm," I said. "I suppose so, yes."

"One thing that surprises me about this place," said Jason. "No one ever says *shouldn't*. As in, you shouldn't do that. They'll tell you something's impossible, or too expen-

sive. But never *wrong*. And I know we're builders, not phi-
losophers. I read the mission statement. But sometimes I
wish we had some ethical documentation. I kind of want
someone very wise to tell me there are some things I
shouldn't do even though they can be done. Is that stupid?
It's probably because my family, you know, they're Chinese,
and growing up they were very strict. Very moral. I fought
them. But now I'm free, I'm floating, like I've lost my feet.
Do you know what I mean?"

"Not really."

"No?"

"I don't worry about religion."

"It's not necessarily—"

"Anyway," I said, because Jason was getting seriously off
track, "what about a *helmet*. Fixed needles, each capable of
delivering a measured dose of tetrodotoxin to various areas
of the brain. Press a button: bam, take out the VMPFC." I
gestured to the screen. "Or whatever area needs suppressing
for a few hours."

"Uh . . ."

"And not just tetrodotoxin. Adenosine, for alertness. Any
chemical, primed for delivery to the right spot at the right
time. *That's* interesting."

"I don't know if . . . I mean, there's a lot that could go
wrong."

It was a fair point. I needed my brain. It was one of the
few parts I couldn't replace. I shouldn't rush in. On the other
hand, injecting localized neurodoses of tetrodotoxin for guilt
suppression was a really good idea. "Let's just do one."

"One?"

"Injection. For testing."

"I'm not sure I should do that."

"Sure you should. I'm telling you to."

"Uh."

"Just position my hand in the right place and give me a little drill," I said, because my machine fingers were steadier anyway.

I HAD NEVER BEEN VERY INTERESTED IN HACKING MY HEAD BEFORE. You would think so, but no. I had tried things: coffee, energy drinks, alcohol, caffeine pills. But I had never been enthused. As I watched a screen showing myself sliding a needle through my skull, I thought I understood why. Swallowing something gave control to the pill. Drug addicts were called *users,* and now I realized how appropriate that was. Pills made you a passenger. To control your own experience, you needed to build it. You couldn't ever truly own anything you couldn't modify. I had always thought that.

I retracted the needle. Jason taped a small cotton patch over the entry wound. It was on the top of my head; when I straighted in the Contours, it should be invisible. He stepped back. "Do you feel anything?"

I opened my mouth to say no, then realized maybe yes. Because when I thought about Carl, that situation seemed pretty okay. Not great for Carl. It was a bad result for him, due to me. But those were just facts. They carried no emotional connotation. I nodded. "Yes," I said. "Good."

I WENT TO SEE LOLA. DAWN WAS BREAKING, SHEDDING SOFT YELLOW light along the corridor, and I had about four hours of near-zero capacity for guilt. When I knocked she cracked open the door and squinted at me with sleep-bleary eyes. "Charlie?"

"I know it's early. Can I come in?"

"Um. Yeah." She rubbed her hair. I had thought it was

out of control before. Overnight it staged a full-scale rebellion. She swung open the door and I clomped inside. She was wearing an oversized yellow sweater and no visible pants. The sweater said: VISION + DARING = BETTER FUTURE. Her legs were very beautiful. You had to give it to biology sometimes.

"I've been working. I wanted to see you."

She dropped onto the sofa. "That's nice."

I looked around. "Where's that nurse?"

Lola's eyes widened. "Charlie. You broke the pattern."

I couldn't believe it. I had forced myself to stop thinking about how to get rid of the nurse, because it was consuming all my waking hours. Now she was gone. It was a miracle.

Lola rose from the sofa. My heart thumped. Her hand closed on my shirt and pulled me closer. A delicious feeling shot through my body. I thought: *I should map that for the helmet.*

"She could turn up any moment," said Lola. She leaned upward. We kissed. We had kissed before. But not like this. Not without external observation. I felt anxious, because one thing that nurse had been good for was covering the fact that I was not a good kisser. I was enthusiastic. I was interested. But I had no technique. I was all over the place. I got hair in my mouth and Lola put a hand on my cheek and guided me back to her lips. She did not seem upset or exasperated. She was prepared to tolerate mistakes. She had realistic expectations. I relaxed. I grew more confident. Lola pressed against me. I was doing this. I was some kind of superman. I kissed her and her tongue touched my lips and I gulped audibly and she sniggered into my mouth. It was hotter than it sounds. Her hand found the back of my head and pushed me closer. I fell into her. She was a gravity well. An irresistible attractor. She took hold of my metal hand and guided it to her Better Future sweater, where DARING rose and fell across one breast. I felt softness and warmth and violet harmonics around five gigahertz. "Not so hard," she whispered. I opened my eyes because I wasn't the one pressing there. She was. Except she wasn't even touching my hand.

I tried to pull my hand off her chest. It resisted, then came away. Lola's eyes popped open.

"Stop. Wait." I backed away. "You're attracting me."

"It's mutual."

"Not like that."

She looked confused. Then her eyes widened and she stepped back. As she did, I felt a slight release, as if I had been bracing myself against a force too subtle to notice until it was gone.

"Did you feel that?"

"What is it?"

"I'm not sure."

"Charlie?"

"It's okay," I said, although I didn't know if that was true. "There's something . . . maybe some kind of magnetic field."

"Field?"

"Wait here. I need to get a scanner."

"It's my heart," she whispered. "Isn't it?"

"I don't know. I'll find out."

"What did they put in me?"

"Please," I said. "Don't cry, Lola, because I don't think I can come any closer without damaging one of us."

She nodded. "Please hurry."

I EXITED ON THE GROUND FLOOR AND HEADED FOR THE ELEVATORS to take me to the labs. Halfway there a young woman fell into step alongside me. This was no mean feat because I was really moving. I glanced down. It was Elaine, my ex-assistant who had had nightmares. She was shorter than I remembered. No, I was taller. She clutched a clipboard to her chest. Her white coat flapped around her legs. Her acne had not improved. "Dr. Neumann. Are you busy?"

"Yes." We rounded a corner and passed the atrium. Inside, early-rising suits strategized over bowls of muesli.

"I've been trying to reach you. I sent e-mails."

"I don't read e-mails."

"Well . . ." She broke into a run. "I've been following your work and, well, actually, I wasn't at first because I wanted to make a clean break. Because of the trauma. But you're using so many people and everyone's talking about it and I saw projects going into limited testing. And of course you can't get into them because everyone who knew has already signed up for slots and now the waiting list is a month long and there's no way to get in. Is there?"

We reached the elevator bank. I pressed DOWN. "I don't know what you're talking about."

She came around in front of me. "I want to be a test subject for Better Skin."

I tried not to look at the spots on her forehead but couldn't help it. "I don't actually select test subjects."

"But you could. You could get me in."

"Um . . ."

"I'd follow protocol. I would be an extremely good test subject."

"I know you would, Elaine." At last, the elevator arrived.

"I wash my face eight times a day. I use aloe vera. I use methylhydroxide. I sleep with a face mask. It wakes me up but I use it. Please."

"I'll see what I can do." I entered the elevator and pressed for the labs. Elaine stayed where she was, her hands pressed together.

"Thanks," she said. "Thank you."

. . .

I SWIPED MY WAY INTO LAB 5 AND INTERRUPTED A BUNCH OF LAB assistants shaving off Mirka's hair. The floor was littered with dark filaments. In a bald head, Mirka's cat eyes looked enormous, like a Japanese cartoon. We all stared at one another and then I clomped across the lab and began searching for the hand scanner.

"We're, ah . . ." said Jason. "I guess you're wondering what we're doing."

"No." Half-dissected electronics lay all over the workbench. "Where's the scanner?"

"There," said several cats at once. I couldn't see where they meant until I followed their pointing fingers and shifted a schematic. A tiny part of it must have been poking out, too small for me to notice. A cat said, "Why aren't you wearing your Eyes, Dr. Neumann?"

One of the assistants held a surgical drill, I noticed. That couldn't be good. But I didn't have time for this. "Don't do anything stupid," I said, and left.

I RODE THE ELEVATOR UP TO GROUND, TURNING THE SCANNER OVER IN my hands. It was very basic, with a narrow electromagnetic range. But that should be enough to tell what was happening inside Lola. Right now I couldn't imagine why her heart would start emitting a magnetic field. It was a pump.

The elevator doors opened. For a second I expected Elaine. Can I have the Skin? But the area was empty. It was very empty. I thumped along the corridor and past the atrium and now its tables were empty, the muesli-eating suits vanished. When I reached the elevators for Building C and went to press the call button, it was dark. All the panels above the elevators were blank but one, which ticked downward from 18. I waited. When it opened, it had Cassandra Cautery in it. "Charlie. We need to talk."

"Something's wrong with Lola."

"It's taken care of. Come here."

I hesitated, then entered the elevator. Cassandra Cautery swiped her ID tag. The doors closed.

"We have a little situation." She touched her palms together, as if praying, and put the fingers to her lips. "It's all right. Everything is fine. But we do have a problem we need to deal with."

"Is her heart malfunctioning?"

"Let me just lay something on the table. The company has made a significant investment in Lola Shanks. That life-saving operation, that did not come cheap." This did not strike me as a very fair assessment, since the operation was life-saving only because she was shot by Carl, but I kept silent because I wanted to get to the part where Cassandra Cautery explained what was wrong with Lola. "You can debate whether the right decision was made. I know I had concerns. But that was not my call." Her eyes flicked to the floor numbers ticking upward. "I've always tried to do the right thing, Charlie. You understand that, don't you?"

I said nothing.

Her tone sharpened. "When you asked me to dispose of Carl, did I quibble? Did I say, 'Gee, Charlie, that's a little heartless, he's a ten-year employee with no arms?' No. I didn't."

"Fire."

"What?"

"I asked you to *fire* Carl."

"You said *get rid of*."

"That's the same thing."

She hesitated. "Of course it is. The point is, I've tried to provide you with a supportive environment. I've sheltered you from the harsher realities." She stuck a thumb in her mouth and gnawed at it. Then she pulled it out and stared at it like it had betrayed her. "No one appreciates the middle manager. Upstairs, they've forgotten what it's like. They think you tell employees to do something and they do it. But it's not called *telling*. It's called *managing*. The only reason this company functions is because people like me keep them and you apart."

The elevator doors opened. We were not on Lola's floor. We were somewhere else.

"But no, no, no," said Cassandra Cautery. "You and Lola Shanks couldn't keep your hands off each other, and everything's gone to shit."

I saw myself in a huge silver mirror hanging on the opposite wall. Beside it sat a little table with a lamp and a vase of white flowers. On the other side was a life-sized statue of a woman with an outstretched arm and blank eyes. Some kind of goddess. Cassandra Cautery exited the elevator.

A beautiful girl appeared, smiling like a sunburst. Beside her, the goddess seemed plain. "Hello! You must be Dr. Neumann. And Cassandra! How *are* you? What is that shirt, by the way? I always mean to ask."

"I don't remember."

"Well, I love you in it." The girl put her hands on her hips. "Is he ready?"

The girl turned solemn. "He'll be two minutes. But if you come with me, I will get you completely set up with whatever you need. Is that okay?"

The girl sashayed away down the corridor. Cassandra Cautery stared after her with loathing. I felt out of my depth, like a deep-sea fish hauled to the surface. I was not compatible with this environment. I did not possess the parts necessary to survive in it. "Where's Lola?"

"Being looked after." Her voice was flat. She didn't look at me. "You need to stay away from her, Charlie. At this point you would do her more harm than good." She walked after the girl.

I looked at the scanner in my hands. Then I put it on the carpet beside the elevator and followed.

THE GIRL TOOK US TO A SITTING ROOM. I SAY THIS AS SOMEONE WHO IS not totally sure what a sitting room is. I mean something from an eighteenth-century mansion: drapes, busy wall-paper, chairs with curving, detailed legs. *Turned,* I think is the word. I straightened my posture. It just felt necessary.

"You know who we're meeting," said Cassandra Cautery, once the girl had closed the door on us. This was not posed as a question, although I didn't know the answer. "The Manager."

"Which manager?"

"*The* Manager."

"Who?"

"The Manager," she said. "The Manager. You know. The Manager."

"That's his title?"

Cassandra Cautery stared at me. "Of course not. He's the chief executive officer. But everyone calls him the Manager. That's what he does. He manages. You know when Congress wanted to shut us down after the Boston VL38s turned out to be not so nonlethal? Of course you don't. Because he managed it. How can you not know the Manager?"

Now she mentioned it, *The Manager* did sound familiar. He might have signed off on a few company-wide e-mails that I skimmed through. There might have been a few inspirational quotes from him on the cafeteria notice board.

When people told stories about employees who vanished, projects that evaporated overnight, lab fires that were never officially reported and accidents that never happened, they might have said: *Then The Manager came.* "The Manager."

"Exactly." Her thumb slipped into her mouth again. "The Manager."

THE DOOR HANDLE CLACKED OPEN. I WAS DISAPPOINTED. THE WAY Cassandra Cautery had been acting, I expected lightning crackling around the shoulders of his tailored suit. And he was in a suit, and I guess it was tailored, but otherwise he looked normal. If I had been buying a car and this guy walked out of the salesroom, I would not have been surprised.

"Dr. Neumann." He came at me with his hand outstretched and his teeth exposed. His hair was extremely neat. I wouldn't have thought you could get hair to sit like that. Not with consumer-grade chemicals. "Can I get you anything? Water? Coffee? Something to eat?"

"No." I shook his hand. This lasted a while and he smiled the whole time.

"Now." He looked at my legs. "What's protocol here? Do I offer you a seat?"

"I'm comfortable."

"Of course you are. You know what? Let's all stand." Cassandra Cautery, who had popped out of her chair when the Manager walked in and was now in the process of lowering herself, arrested her descent. "Okay with you, Cassie?"

"Of course," she said. Cassie. I would never look at her the same again.

The Manager walked to the window and drew back the drapes. I squinted against the glare. I could barely make out his face. "It's a thrill to meet you, Dr. Neumann. I'm sin-

cerely disappointed it's taken this long." He did not look at
Cassandra Cautery, but in my peripheral vision she tensed.
This was some kind of silent, manager-level communica-
tion. "I've taken a personal interest in your project. We have
our fingers in many pies, of course, a large number of speculative pies, but yours captures my imagination. So much
of what we do, Dr. Neumann, is about incremental
improvement. It's about doing what we did the year before,
only slightly better. Products that are a little lighter. A little
cheaper. A little more reliable. You people in the labs, you
come up with an incapacitating sound wave that's like
nothing anyone's ever seen, but the police departments
don't want sound guns. They want Tasers. In fact, they
want the Tasers they're used to, which have been through
committee and achieved sign-off from relevant stakehold-
ers, only a little lighter, cheaper, and more reliable. So we
take this wonderful innovation that comes from the labs
and crush it down to incremental improvement. And I find
that depressing. I really do. It's less than we all deserve.
Sometimes when I drive in to work, Dr. Neumann, and I
see the buildings coming toward me, I think: *Why aren't we
doing more? Why aren't we changing the game? Why aren't we
running the world?*" He chuckled. "That's an expression.
But you see my point. We have the brains. We have the
production capacity. We have the network. Yet we're a mere
company. An extremely well-respected company with an
unparalleled history of technical achievement. We should
all be proud of that. But we should also strive to be more.
More than just a company that builds what its customers
want. What I've been thinking is: *What if we could tell
them?* What if we could say, 'Hey, you know what? You're
getting a fucking sound gun. Because it's a seriously great
technology, and you'll figure that out if you just take it.
You'll get over the sonic leakage and the reverb and bone

damage and all that. Just take the fucking gun.' And I truly believe, Dr. Neumann, if we do that, people will start to realize, Hey, these guys at Better Future know what they're talking about. Hey, we don't need to figure out our own requirements. We don't need to write up a spec that says each Taser should come with a strap exactly twenty-eight-point-one inches long, and if it's thirty, my God, there must be half a dozen meetings and phone calls and maybe the whole order should be canceled. They can just sit down with us and ask, 'What can you give me?' And we'll tell them. We'll tell them." The Manager put a hand on my shoulder. It felt fatherly. "That's what excites me about your project. It's a game changer. We don't need a demand analysis on Better Eyes. We don't need to run around asking our customers what kind of quantity of Better Skin they might consider and under what specs. These products are self-marketing. They put us in the driver's seat. And the best part, Dr. Neumann, the terrific irony, is that it happened because *you* changed *our* game. Did anybody ask you to do this? No. You took it upon yourself. I look at you, Dr. Neumann, and I see a man controlling his own destiny. A man who refuses to let others define him. Nature dealt you a hand, you tossed it back. You said, '*I'll* decide who I am. I'll choose the limit of my capabilities. I will be not what I was made, but what I make.' "

I blinked. "Yes. That's it exactly." I wondered why Cassandra Cautery had been so concerned about letting me talk to the Manager. He was fantastic. He was just like me.

"I could not be prouder to count myself as one of your supporters." He smiled. I smiled back. "Now. Let's talk supersoldiers."

The Manager turned to the window and gazed into the distance. There was nothing out there but sky. I struggled to rearrange his last sentence so that it made sense. I thought: *Did he mean super solder?*

"The equipment carried by the average modern-day soldier weighs a hundred fifty pounds." He turned and spread his palms. The light flooding in behind him made this vaguely messianic. "That's a standard, what-do-you-call-them, grunt. The specialists lug half that again. The primary limitation of today's soldier is simply that he can't carry everything. War has become a load-bearing exercise. A logistics puzzle. And, sure, tell me it's never been any different. Tell me that throughout history, battles have been won on the back of resource coordination. I'll agree with you. To a point. That point is when the gap between what's possible and what's practical to carry becomes a canyon. And that's what we have today. Imagine weight wasn't an issue. We'd have soldiers who run at fifty miles per hour, leap twenty feet into the air, fire fifty-millimeter chain guns, shrug off enemy fire like it's rain. We'd have Better Soldiers. And let me tell you, Dr. Neumann, as tickled as I am by the consumer-level products your people are producing, the Better Eyes and Better Skin and so forth, they're nothing compared to what we can do with the military." He held up a finger. "Let me correct that. What we can do with the *militaries*. I won't bore you with business details, but there is a protocol for developing military products. The first step is you go to Defense and say, 'Hello, just letting you know, we're thinking about making a mobile combat exoskeleton.' And they say thank you very much and here is a set of papers legally compelling every employee within a hundred-foot radius of our building to be cleared through military intelligence, a four-star general to be in the room whenever we utter the project's name, and so on. Ten years later, when they allow us to build a crippled, simplified version of the product we originally designed, they give us

another set of papers saying how many units we will produce, how much they'll pay us for each one, and how many
years we'll serve in prison if we sell a single piece of related
technology to another sovereign nation. And you know
what? That sucks, Dr. Neumann. That is what keeps us
small. So this time, I want to try it another way. Try it in-
house. And I'm not saying we'll sell these things to North
Korea. I don't think anyone wants North Korea with an
army of, you know, unkillable Better Soldiers. But it's not a
bad thing for that possibility to be out there. It's not a bad
thing if we can go to DOD and say, 'Whoops, mea culpa,
turns out some of our people went ahead and developed
human war machines, and they're already on the ground in
various poorly governed countries across the world.' They'll
rant and scream and threaten, of course. But then we'll do a
deal. On our terms. Because we have the tech."

I said, "I don't want to be a supersoldier."

Cassandra Cautery smiled. The Manager laughed. "Of
course you don't! Good God, Dr. Neumann, perish the
thought. You're a thinker."

"You're the brain," said Cassandra Cautery.

"Exactly. Your role is hands-off." His eyes flicked to my
metal hand. "Excuse the expression. I mean there's no need
to put yourself through QA for every Better Part. We have
people for that. Cassie must have talked you through this."

"The thing with Charlie," said Cassandra Cautery, "and I
hope this doesn't offend you, Charlie, but the thing is, he's
an artist. He has that mentality. I've been extremely,
extremely cautious about bothering Charlie with the practical applications of his work, because for him it's a personal
project. Very personal. That's what inspires him."

The Manager was silent. "I'm not sure I understand. He's
an employee, isn't he?"

"Of course, but—"

MACHINE MAN ■ 173

"Are you an employee, Dr. Neumann?"

"Yes."

"You're paid to perform work for Better Future, correct?"

I hadn't checked my bank account for a very long time. But I assumed so. "Yes."

"Then I think we've established your role." He nodded. "I understand there are at least half a dozen people now capable of original part design. You should be proud of the way you've passed on your skills, Dr. Neumann. No employee should be irreplaceable."

I said, "I want to make parts for myself."

"Let me tell you what I want," said the Manager. "I want you to assist our test subjects. Help them adapt to life with Better Parts. That's your specialty now. Not design. Look at you. If I'm booking in for some hard-core surgery to become a Better Soldier, you're the guy I want to talk to. You're the guy I want beside my bed when I wake up, telling me it's okay, it's great on the other side. It's Better. I'm not saying this has been the problem. Cassie, I'm not blaming you for the issues we've had with test subjects. I'm just saying, the last thing we need is Better Soldiers having psychotic breaks."

I said, "What test subjects?" I look at Cassandra Cautery, then back to the Manager. "You mean Carl?"

"Dr. Neumann, I can't believe you don't know this. You are not the only recipient of Better Parts." He glanced at Cassandra Cautery. "Honestly."

"Who else has . . . has . . ."

"There's you, those in your department, and the volunteers."

"Which volunteers?" I felt myself shaking. "Does Lola Shanks have a Better Part?"

"Of course. Well. That was an early one. Before we had the volunteer program up and running. We had to make a leap of faith. I know you can appreciate that. When you crushed your leg, did you know how it would turn out? Did you know for sure you would even survive? No. But you did it. Because great achievements require great courage. And it was obvious from the beginning that it would be easier to recruit volunteers for some Better Parts than others. The Eyes, the Skin, sure, they're lining up. But who wants a military-grade spine? Who wants a satellite-linked eardrum? Don't say you. We've been through that. The world is not full of Carl LaRussos. We will not stumble across a group of people eager to replace vital organs. So we seized the opportunity that presented itself."

"What's in Lola?" My throat burned. All I could think about was her on the operating table, her hand limp and helpless. "Her heart. What is it?"

"Well," he said. "Something better."

A jolt of rage burst through my body. I did not usually get angry. I had never felt like this in my life. Certainly at no point while connected to the nerve interface, painstak-ingly teaching the Contours the language of my electrical neuroimpulses. They had no idea what I was telling them. That's my explanation, anyway, for why my legs twitched, and I kicked the Manager through the window.

EARLIER, I HADN'T PAID MUCH ATTENTION TO WHICH FLOOR WE WERE on. But as I moved to the shattered window and pushed aside the flapping drapes, I realized: we were really high up.

9

"YOU'VE KILLED HIM." CASSANDRA CAUTERY STEPPED CAREFULLY OVER the broken glass and braced herself against what was left of the window frame. "Look. He's just lying there."

I tried to say, *I didn't mean to.* But my chest was locked tight around my lungs.

"That guy is dead." There was a touch of awe in her voice. "He is definitely dead."

Against my better judgment, I looked down. Most of the space between Better Future and the road was occupied by a wide, healthy lawn. But it was bisected by a narrow concrete path, and on this lay the Manager. I'm tempted to claim this as bad luck. But from the way his legs were bent over his head, it didn't matter.

The Contours took an unexpected step forward, as if they wanted to look at what they had done. I teetered.

"Charlie . . ." Cassandra Cautery murmured. Her eyes didn't move from the Manager's tiny, broken body. "You are in so very much trouble."

The Contours tensed. Four sections contracted two inches. I wasn't making them do this. It must be a fear reaction: my terrified brain barfing out static. But that's not what it felt like. It felt like they were making their own decisions.

Behind me, someone gasped. The Manager's beautiful assistant stood with one hand on the door handle, the other flying to her mouth, her eyes shocked wide. What would happen next became clear: the alarm call, the security guards. My legs were right, I realized. They had figured this out before I had. I looked at the drop, took a breath, and jumped.

AS I FELL THROUGH THE AIR, THE CONTOURS EXTENDED TO THEIR FULL length. The hooves splayed into three toes, maximizing their surface area. The Better Future lawn rushed at me and I closed my eyes. My spine tried to impale my skull. When I could see again, the Contours were three feet long and had no hooves. I thought they had snapped. Then they began to reextend, and I remembered this was what they did on impact: retracted, to soak up deceleration. The hooves had sunk into the earth. I pulled one free, then the other, and shook off clods of soil.

The Manager lay a few yards away. He didn't look any better up close. I felt sick, then angry, because if the Manager had had some Better Parts, he would be fine right now. He would be walking around on machine legs and I would not be in this situation. What kind of CEO organized a project to manufacture artificial parts and had none himself? It was ridiculous. I stared at his biological mess and was furious. It was not my finest moment.

Ahead of me, the lobby doors slid open. I thought, *Maybe it won't be guards,* and was wrong. Then I thought, *Maybe they don't know this was me,* and they drew their guns, and I thought, *They won't shoot unless I run,* and was wrong again.

THE FIRST SHOT THUMPED INTO MY LEFT BICEPS. I FELT IT NOT SO much as physical pain as an insult. I hadn't realized how deeply offensive it was to have someone deliberately injure you. I shouted, "Hey!" My voice was thick with outrage. I was going to march up to this guard and explain I was a human being, dammit, with a brain and rights and an ID card, and you can't just *shoot* people. You can't just *kill* them. Which was a little hypocritical, given I was standing next to the Manager's folded-up body, but that didn't occur to me. I was indignant about my violated biceps. The only thing that drove this plan from my mind was the realization that this bullet was not the last of today's insults: that more insults were heading my way unless I got out of there.

So I did. My legs fired. My neck snapped back. Something passed by my head so close it sucked hair into its wake. I grabbed at the sides of the bucket seat, afraid of falling out, which was more or less impossible but that's not what it felt like. With each step my legs stretched out before me and my hooves drove into the lawn. They slipped on a slick patch of grass, then we reached the sidewalk and I felt them settle. They liked concrete. We both did. I clung on and cars and trees blurred past me until the security guards were far, far behind and I was safe and I realized I had left behind something important.

I DON'T PLAY THE LOTTERY. I DON'T CARE WHAT MY HOROSCOPE SAYS. I think most things about the world could be improved if people thought more about what they're doing. When someone gets upset with their computer, I tend to side with the computer. I think art is overrated, and bridges are underrated. In fact, I don't understand why bridges aren't art. It seems to me they're penalized for having a use. If I make a bridge that ends in midair, that's a sculpture. But put it between two landmasses and let it ferry two hundred thousand cars per day and it's infrastructure. That makes no sense.

I mention this because what I did next was not completely logical. And I know if I heard about this from somebody else, I would lose a little respect for that person. I would think, *Well, that's just stupid.* But I would be failing to appreciate the difficulty of performing an emergency situational assessment from the middle of one. When someone shoots at you, your hypothalamus sends a lightning bolt into your neuroendocrine cells, which dump cortisol and adrenaline and norepinephrine into your bloodstream, and then you are no longer a very good decision-making machine. You are a quick decision-making machine. And I don't want to hide behind my biology, because at some point you have to take ownership of your neurochemistry, but I do want to point out that I didn't decide to go flight-or-fight; my body did.

I SLOWED. I STOPPED. ON THE SIDEWALK AHEAD, AN ELDERLY LATINO woman struggled along with bags of groceries. She saw my hooves and her eyes bulged. *"Diablo."*

Lola was back there. She had who-knew-what in her chest cavity. Cassandra Cautery said they were taking care of her but that could be a lie. They had installed a device in Lola without her knowledge.

"Diablo!" cried the woman.

Maybe I should go to the police. Tell them there was a

woman with a malfunctioning Better Heart she hadn't
asked for. That had to be some kind of crime. And guards
had shot at me and that was wrong so the police should be
on my side. I had metal legs but they would get over that.
Although I had killed the Manager. Possibly from their
point of view I was a violent criminal. Had Better Future
already reported me?

"*Diablo!*"

"Quiet," I said, because that was making it hard to think.
My wounded biceps began transiting from comfortably
numb to distractingly sore with hints of impending agony. I
tried to concentrate. My legs shivered. That was weird. I
hadn't known they could do that. I wished Lola was here.
She would know what to do. It was my weakness: I could
not predict people. Lola could. Maybe there was a back
entrance. A way into Better Future not protected by security guards with guns they weren't shy about using. I mentally scanned floor plans. There wasn't.

"*Diablo!*" the woman shrieked. She dropped her groceries
and clapped her hands to her cheeks. "*Diablo!*"

"Then why am I going back?" I shouted. I wasn't angry
with her. I was just emotional about my own likely death.
The Contours began to hammer the sidewalk, bearing me
back toward Lola.

I WASN'T AN IDIOT. I DIDN'T APPROACH FROM THE FRONT. ADJACENT TO
Better Future was a small industrial plant, and I positioned
one hoof on its chain-link fence and pushed. The metal
jangled and shrieked and tore from its frame. I ran between
building-sized vats and emerged to discover not one but
two fences between me and Better Future, because neither
company trusted the other. The Better Future fence was
higher, stronger, and more likely to automatically notify

somebody upon being breached. I raised a hoof and tore down the first fence, crossed eight feet of no-man's-land, and positioned a hoof against Better Future's fence. Every muscle in my body contracted. My teeth gouged my tongue. *"Farg!"* I said. I backed up, my nerves trembling. I didn't know why I hadn't realized it would be electrified. It was lucky my electronics were insulated or this would have been a humiliating ending. I looked around for something helpful, like maybe a tall tree I could push over, but saw only struts and scaffolding and other excellent electrical conductors. I looked at the fence again. Maybe twelve feet high. I could possibly jump that. I had never gotten around to testing the Contours' vertical leap capability under controlled conditions but that one time they had leaped sixty feet in the air. I looked at the Better Future building. I concentrated on a patch of perfect grass on the other side of the fence. I thought, *Take me there.*

The legs settled. I tensed, as if there were anything my muscles could do, and the legs sprang. My torso compressed like an accordion. I bit my tongue again. As I passed over the fence I let go of the seat and flailed my arms in the air, because my body still couldn't come to grips with the fact that it was attached to two tons of titanium. The Contours thumped into soil. I rocked forward in the seat. I breathed. I was okay. That was actually not so bad. That was the least terrifying and physically damaging leap I had performed in the Contours so far. I thought, *I'm getting the hang of this,* and looked at the Better Future building, and thought, *Oh, shit.* The Contours were not good on stairs. I wouldn't be able to run between floors. Why hadn't I fixed that? Why hadn't this occurred to me before I was standing on the lawn? I could see what I thought was Lola's balcony and thought, *Jump,* and, *Are you crazy, that's like fifty feet.* I began to walk toward the building but without enthusiasm.

I didn't know if I could do this. I couldn't think of any logical reason why not but it was incredibly high and would kill me if I got it wrong. I thought, *Is that even the right balcony?* I thought, *I don't even know if she's in there.* I stopped. I felt relief, then shame. I thought, *Fuck it, I'll do it,* and changed my mind again. Sweat tickled my ribs. My biceps throbbed. I thought, *That needs medical attention. I should have it seen to before I do anything to make it worse.* Lola's balcony was high. It was really high.

A Better Future Hummer skidded around the corner, its engine screaming. Its tires tore up chunks of turf and spat them across the grass. It fishtailed one way, then the other. Its grille centered on me. I stood frozen. Then I put up my hands. I did not want to get shot. The Hummer accelerated and a part of my brain informed me that it was doing so well beyond its need to reach me in a hurry. I ignored this information because surely that couldn't be right, until it was incontrovertible and too late to address.

There is an expression: *When all you have is a hammer, everything looks like a nail.* I had a hammer. I had a servo-magnetic lithium-powered titanium hammer. So when the Hummer fell upon me, I kicked it. It went up on two wheels. The other two passed over my head. It sailed a drunken twenty meters, teetering on the brink of tipping over, like it was in a circus. As it wobbled toward the Better Future building I realized the driver faced two mutually exclusive objectives: to bring the car down onto four wheels or to not ram a ground-floor meeting room. This was really an either/or decision but the driver tried to accomplish both and the Hummer hit the building at a thirty-degree angle and disappeared halfway inside. Glass and brick dust burst across the lawn.

Arguably, I deserve no credit for this. My input was limited to being very sure that I did not want to be run over.

The Contours took care of the rest: bracing of one leg against the ground, timing of the swing, delivery of the correct amount of force. But then again, that was my code. I had written it without this particular situation in mind, but the fact remained, they were my instructions. From this perspective, I deserved plenty of credit, even more than someone whose body was grown for them. So I looked up. I located Lola's balcony. I jumped.

Glass flashed past my face. Wind pulled at my clothes. I squeezed shut my eyes and gritted my teeth and tried not to die. It felt like I might. The g-force eased and I opened my eyes to see whether I was anywhere near where I needed to be to survive and saw my hooves clear a balcony railing by two inches. I landed as gently as if I had just stepped off the lowest rung of a ladder. I understood the physics, but still. I sucked in air. I was alive. I looked at my Contours and had never felt so much love for an object.

The balcony door slid back. "Charlie!" Lola came out of the suite. I was on the right balcony. Spatial skills: I had them. She threw herself at me. Inside, through the glass, I saw cats in lab coats everywhere. Jason and Mirka among them. I saw the nurse. They began to hastily empty the room. "Did you feel that? I think it was an earthquake!"

"That was me."

Lola leaned over the balcony. "How did you get here? Did you jump? Did you *jump?*"

"We need to get out."

"What's that smoke?"

"Lola. It's important we get out of here as fast as possible."

"Okay." She took my hand, the biological one. "I knew you'd come back. I knew it."

I threw a glance at the suite. It had cleared out. Those damn cats. Then I realized I couldn't jump out of here. Not with Lola. The moment my legs touched the ground and I began to decelerate, Lola would weigh the equivalent of two thousand pounds. "Oh. We have a problem."

"What? Let's go."

"I can't hold you."

"Sure you can." She held out her arms. "I'm little."

"When we land, you'll weigh as much as a car." To her expression, I added, "That's not me. That's physics." I looked at my metal fingers. If I'd had the arms, this might have been doable.

"Are you bleeding?"

"Oh. Yes." I showed her my biceps. "I got damaged."

"You mean injured."

"What did I say?"

"You . . ." She shook her head. "What happened?"

"They shot me."

"Who shot you?"

"The company. Guards."

"No!"

"Yes."

"Why would they do that? Charlie?"

"I kicked the CEO."

Lola's eyebrows leaped. "Oh, no."

"It was an accident."

"What kind of accident?"

"I'll explain later."

"How badly hurt is he?"

"Um . . ."

"They have really good doctors here. Maybe—"

"He's dead."

"Oh, Charlie."

"I'm sorry." I meant for upsetting Lola. The Manager I was still mad at.

"And now they want to kill you?"

"I don't know. They shot at me."

"They must think you're dangerous. It's a misunderstanding."

"Should I try to talk to them?"

Lola frowned. "What did you mean before, 'That was me'? How did you make that smoke?"

"I kicked a car. It tried to run me over. I had to kick it. Into the building."

"Oh. Oh."

"That's bad, isn't it?"

"I think that's really bad."

"They're putting parts in people. Military parts. They gave you a military heart."

"A what?"

"A military—"

"What does that mean? What the fuck is a *military heart*?"

"I don't—" Something went *dink*. "Was that the elevator?"

"We have to get out of here," said Lola.

"Yes."

"Pick me up and run. We can go down the stairs."

"The Contours aren't good on stairs."

"What does that mean?"

"A bug, I guess. I haven't had a chance to go through the software—"

"What does that mean for *us*?"

"It means we can't take the stairs."

"Okay. We can . . . let's try to sneak down in the elevators."

"The elevators won't work unless . . ." Footsteps. Lola squeezed my hand. I felt that strange attractive force stir, trying to pull my fingers toward her chest.

"Charlie . . ."

It was a puzzle, I realized. Like having a bag of corn, a chicken, a fox, and a boat that could bear only one object across the river at a time. I could jump out of here, but Lola couldn't. She couldn't open the stairwell doors, assuming security had locked everything down, but she could walk down stairs, which I couldn't.

"Can you stomp through the floor?"

"What? It's reinforced concrete."

"Is that a no?"

"Obviously it's a no!"

"Don't look at me like that!"

"I just . . ." I had it. It was simple. I would accompany Lola to a stairwell. Kick open the door. Jump down to ground level. Reenter the building. Kick open the door at ground level. Grab her. Run away. It was a good plan. Simple. It made a few assumptions about my likelihood of being shot. But it was a solution. I took her hand and entered the suite.

A man appeared in the doorway. A guard. And I stood there, my plan forgotten, because the guard was Carl.

HE LOOKED DIFFERENT. AT FIRST I COULDN'T PUT MY FINGER ON IT. I was distracted by other thoughts, like why he was here. I had thought he was gone. Terminated, one way or another. But here he was, blocking the only exit that didn't require falling eighty feet.

"Hi, Carl." The light from the corridor made it hard to see his face. "How are you?"

He didn't move. Lola peeked around me.

Still nothing. He was wearing his security uniform, although that looked different, too. "There has been a strange series of events," I said. "I don't know which side of the story you heard, but . . ."

Carl stepped into the room. What was different about him became clear. I hadn't clicked earlier because Carl had always been big. But not this big. Not so big he had to turn sideways to fit through a door.

His arms were concealed beneath his uniform. But where his hands protruded from his sleeves they were thick blocks of gray metal. They looked like sledgehammers. I had never seen these before.

"Miss Shanks," Carl said. "You were always very kind to me."

His eyes moved to mine. In that moment it was clear to me that Carl knew I had asked Cassandra Cautery to get rid of him.

"In appreciation of that," he said, "I will give you a head start."

CARL'S PANT LEGS JUTTED IN ODD PLACES. WHEN HE STEPPED, STEEL gleamed between his pants and boots. He did not have metal legs. But he had something on his legs. A kind of exoskeleton, like scaffolding. It made sense. You couldn't weld titanium to a man's shoulders. It would crush him. But this annoyed me. An exoskeleton was a hack. It was layering technology on top of a broken system. It was a failure to address the root problem.

Carl stopped at a service elevator and swiped his ID card. This was interesting because a moment ago Carl's hands had been blocks of stone. Now they had split into fingers supple enough to grasp the tag. It seemed they could separate into at least four digits, then come together to deliver a punching force. That wasn't a bad idea, for security guard hands.

"This will open in the garage. Then you're on your own. I advise you to run."

Lola and I shuffled inside. Lola said, "Thank you, Carl."

"I'm not doing you a favor. I'm repaying a debt."

Lola looked at me. "Um," I said. "Thank you. And I'm sorry."

The elevator doors began to close. Carl raised a hand to block them. His fist was a block again. "Pardon me?"

"I'm sorry."

"For asking them to get rid of me? Is that what you mean? For having them take away my arms because you didn't want to share your parts? Is that what you're talking about? The time I spent in a bed with a button to push with my foot when I needed someone to help me go to the bathroom? That?"

He lowered his arm. I heard the thin whine of servomagnetics. The elevator door began to close.

"Don't apologize," Carl said. "I have my own parts now."

LOLA WAS SILENT AS THE ELEVATOR DESCENDED. I RISKED A GLANCE AT her: she stared straight ahead, her arms stiff. I said, "Do you think this elevator really takes us to the garage, or is it a trap?"

"Did you take Carl's arms away?"

"I don't think it's the best time to discuss this."

"Did you make them take away his arms?"

"They weren't *his* arms," I said, but Lola's lips thinned to a dramatic slash and I decided to drop this argument. "Let's talk later."

"I'm disappointed, Charlie."

I felt bad. My tetrodotoxin had worn off. I knew it wasn't my top priority but I wished Lola wouldn't be disappointed. The elevator thumped to a stop. The doors seemed to take a long time to open. I held out my arms. "Come here." Her eyebrows dived like submarines. "I need to carry you."

The doors slid apart. At first I couldn't see anything. There was too much contrast: the bright elevator, the dark garage, the brilliant rectangle where the ramp led to sunshine. I should have been wearing Eyes. But the shouting was clear. I heard phrases like *there he is* and *take him.*

Lola jumped into my arms. I wrapped them around her and accelerated into the darkness. The Contours punched the concrete like rifle shots. Lola slipped out of my grasp and slid around my side. I hadn't realized how much I'd adapted to the Contours: how I leaned with them as they moved, how a tiny click near the hip meant they were about to jag, and I should compensate. These things were far more difficult with another human being in my arms. Lola's fingers clawed at me. I got hold of her, then the Contours sidestepped a guard I hadn't even seen and Lola yelped and slipped all the way onto my back. Her legs locked around my waist. Her arms gripped my neck in a choke hold. My eyes watered. There was a noise like a metal waterfall breaking on concrete that sounded like a spark gun I had seen in the previous year's prototype demos and I was pretty sure it was neither noncrippling nor nonlethal. We burst into sunlight. Lola bounced around to my front. The top of her skull popped me on the nose. We hit the road, clinging to each other like lovers, who were very angry with each other. *Safe,* I willed the Contours. *Take me somewhere safe.*

AT SOME POINT WE STOPPED. LOLA CLIMBED OFF ME, SLOWLY AND painfully. I saw a leafy suburban street. It looked odd, like something from a TV show, and I realized why: I had grown up here. The Contours had brought me back to my childhood.

"You have blood on your chin," said Lola.

I wiped it with my sleeve. There was a lot. Most seemed to be from my biceps. Where I had been shot. Where I had been *shot*. I knew this already but felt shocked all over again. I shivered. I was cold and hot and dizzy. "I think I'm going into shock," I said. I didn't know the technical definition but this felt like it.

Lola walked a few feet away and sat on the grass. She seemed to be watching her shoes.

I put my arms around myself and squeezed. I wondered who lived in that house now. Maybe if I knocked on the door they would invite me in for chocolate milk and let me watch TV.

"You're selfish," said Lola.

I looked at her. That seemed unfair.

"I didn't think the idea was to be better than everyone else. I didn't think this was *competitive*."

I wondered what would happen to the Contours if I fainted. They would probably just stand here, with me slumped over.

"Is it about getting revenge on jocks who were mean to you in high school? Is that what you're doing?"

I squinted. It seemed odd that Lola could have such a wrong idea about me. She didn't seem to understand me as well as the Contours did.

"We are supposed to help people," Lola told her shoes.

The tetrodotoxin had definitely worn off. I decided to argue. It would be my first fight with a girl since elementary school.

"I'm a prosthetist," said Lola. "I *give* parts to people."

"Just say you love Carl."

Her head turned toward me. In the dusk, her face looked slightly unreal. "What?"

"You love him. Him and his new arms."

"I love Carl?"

"Sssssuh," I said, which was going to be the start of something but I forgot what.

"What?"

"Go and marry him, then."

"Are you crazy?"

"Nung," I said. My head lolled. I felt dizzy. Something passed overhead; a bird or spaceship. The world was getting heavy. It was darkening at the edges. I tried to calculate the chemical reactions of everything sloshing around in my veins, the adrenaline and beta blockers and analgesics, but the equations slipped away and merged with one another. What did you get if you dissolved one chemical equation in another? It was a good question.

Charlie, said Lola. I peered at her because her lips were moving but making no sound. Then I realized they were but I was listening to the wrong frequency, in my head. I was lolled back in the Contours, looking at sky. Lola was trying to keep me upright. "Charlie!"

"What," I said.

"We need to get you to a hospital." She looked around. "Shit. Not a hospital. They'll find us."

"Who."

"The . . . Better Future. The people who will kill us to cover up their illegal human trials of artificial body parts. Remember?"

"I need . . . to sit . . . down."

"You are sitting down."

I looked at the Contours. That was right.

"Charlie. Stay with me."

Somewhere, a dog barked. Strands of Lola's brown hair floated on the breeze.

"I know somewhere. A friend from the hospital. She lives near here."

"A friend?"

"Yeah. Charlie. Charlie."

"What?"

"You need to walk a little farther."

I looked at her. I guessed our fight was over. "Okay."

"Okay?"

"Okay."

WE CLIMBED STEPS TO A NEAT SUBURBAN HOUSE AND STOOD ON ITS darkened porch. Lola raised her hand to ring the bell, then hesitated. "One thing. Don't criticize her dogs."

"Why would I criticize her dogs?"

"I'm not saying you would. Just don't."

The logical inconsistency temporarily overwhelmed my pain and exhaustion. I was that kind of guy. "You must feel I would. Otherwise why mention it?"

"Forget it."

"Is something wrong with her dogs?"

"No, but she loves them, and if you say something, it will be awkward."

"Okay." Pain rising. "I won't mention the dogs."

"*Do* mention them. Just say nice things."

"I'll say she has very attractive dogs."

"Don't say that! That sounds creepy."

"What should I say? Lola! Tell me what to say!"

She rang the doorbell. "Say you like their outfits."

The yapping began. Lola had not mentioned how many dogs: clearly there were many. And they were small. I could tell.

The porch light flicked on. I was mildly shocked at Lola's appearance: her eyes were sunken shadows, her Better Future sweater stained with dust and blood. We would not make a great first impression.

The door opened and a woman stood framed in the

doorway in a satin dressing gown, holding what I thought was a purse until it barked. Additional small dogs stood behind each of her ankles, barking. They were clad in little red-and-green tunics. The woman threw an arm around Lola. Lola burst into tears. Over Lola's shoulder, the woman took in my face, body, legs. I knew her, I realized. It was Dr. Angelica Austin.

"Can we come in?"

Dr. Angelica hesitated. She had tried to get me classified as a psych case. That seemed rich, now I knew she kept a house full of tiny dressed dogs. "Of course. Of course." She held open the door. For a moment I thought she was going to close it before I could follow Lola. Possibly she thought that as well. But her lips twitched and she let me pass. As I entered the hallway a dog darted between my legs and I almost stood on it. I had to manually instruct the Contours to halt. The dog was too small to trigger my automatic collision avoidance. I thought, *That could be a problem.*

Dr. Angelica closed the door. "I shouldn't be surprised." The dog in her arms stared at me. I didn't know what it was thinking. But it was something.

"We're in trouble," Lola said. "We need help."

I closed my eyes. I was done. I saw the Manager fly backward out the window. His eyes stayed on me the whole time.

"Charlie."

I opened my eyes. Cassandra Cautery was there, shoulder-to-shoulder with Lola. "Sorry," I croaked.

"He goes in and out," said Lola.

Cassandra Cautery nodded. It wasn't Cassandra Cautery. It was Dr. Angelica. They didn't look anything alike. "Let me take a look at that arm."

"Don't take my arms." Dr. Angelica's deep brown eyes were like her dog's. They had similar expressions, too. Now I knew what that dog was thinking: *This guy is trouble.*

. . .

I DIPPED IN AND OUT OF CONSCIOUSNESS. I BECAME AWARE OF LOLA and Dr. Angelica unstitching me from the nerve interface as if receiving telegrams about it. It was data without information.

"I warned you," said Dr. Angelica.

"I know," said Lola.

"This is exactly like that transtibial."

"It's not. He loves me. You don't know, Angelica. He risked his life for me."

"You're the first person to treat him like a human being since he lost a limb. Of course he loves you. They all love you, at first."

"Let's not do this."

I opened my eyes because there was a tugging sensation on my arm. Dr. Angelica was sewing up my skin with surgical thread.

Lola stroked my hair. "It's okay, Charlie." I was lying in her lap. "She's fixing you."

I closed my eyes.

"What's wrong with this guy, I doubt I can fix."

"Stop it."

"He's a self-injurer. I didn't even want to release him."

"You don't understand."

"That's what you said last time. And the time before that. And don't say, 'It's different.' I've heard that before, too. I heard it before that footless wonder tried to beat you to death with a chair."

"He had problems."

"It's always a man with something missing, it's always you trying to put him back together, and it always ends badly. Tell me, Lola. Look at me and tell me what attracted you to this guy. It was the fact that he was short a leg."

"Okay. It was. Of course it was. But so what? Can't that turn into something else? Something good?"

"It's weird, Lola. I love you, but this thing you have for amputees, it's not good for you."

"You like guys with good arms. You're attracted to . . . to muscle fiber. Isn't that weird? Liking a guy because of his bone structure, or the color of his eyes? Aren't those weird things? I love Charlie. And maybe when it started it was weird, but it's *all* weird. This whole process of trying to find a person who fits you is weird. Why does how he smells make a difference to how I feel about him? The sound of his voice? The shape of his face? I don't know. But I don't think there's a way for people to fall in love that isn't weird."

A thin pain penetrated my bubble world. *"Urk,"* I said.

"Be careful with him."

"It's a scratch," said Dr. Angelica. "The bullet barely nicked him." But she sounded mollified. "I'm being gentle."

"Thank you," said Lola.

10

I WOKE HAPPY. IT WAS DARK. I DIDN'T KNOW WHERE I WAS. BUT I HAD come from a wonderful dream, in which I held Lola close and was safe. I lay still, not wanting to disturb it, but reality filtered in, bringing complications like the fact that I was being pursued by a vengeful security guard with multifunction sledgehammer arms. Still, it wasn't so bad. All problems were insignificant compared to Lola saying, "I love him." With Lola, everything was solvable. She was my independent variable.

On the ceiling above my head was a poster of a dinosaur. I turned my head. There were dinosaur pictures everywhere. In one corner, toy trucks overflowed from a basket. This was a kid's room. In fact, now I looked at it, this was a small bed. Very small. I raised my head. I was not wearing legs.

My toes spasmed. My foot curled. My calves turned to

screaming steel and the fact that none of this was real made no difference. I threw back the covers and massaged the space where my shrieking muscles would be but I knew it would do no good without the Contours and was right. Tears streamed from my eyes. *When was the last time you took painkillers?* my brain asked. *Twelve hours ago? Sixteen? Everything will hurt so much worse now.*

"*Legs!*" I screamed. "*I need my legs!*"

"TOAST?" SAID LOLA. "THERE'S PEANUT BUTTER. I COULD MAKE YOU peanut butter toast."

On TV, a nurse with remarkable cleavage stared out a window. The handsome doctor behind her said she would never get away with this.

"What's that?" said Lola. "Yes or no?"

"Coffee."

"You've had enough coffee." She came out of the kitchen. I was standing in my Contours in the middle of the living room, watching TV. To make room, I had hoofed the sofa out of the way. It now sat against the wall, occupied by three aggrieved dogs. One wore a little faux-leather jacket. I hoped that dog was not supposed to be Elvis.

"Why don't you have some water?"

"I don't want water." The TV doctor wrapped the nurse into a passionate embrace. That was an unexpected development.

Lola came over. "Charlie, I know you're coming down. But water will help."

I gestured at my bandaged arm. "Will it help this?"

"Angelica says that's a scratch."

"I think it's infected."

Lola fell silent. "Well, she can look again tonight."

Dr. Angelica had gone to work. She would, allegedly,

bring home painkillers. In the meantime I had to survive on over-the-counter drugs. It was a major pharmacological decrease from my regular level of medication. Every yap from those dressed-up rats was a knife in my brain.

"I'll make you toast," said Lola. "And bring water."

She went into the kitchen. I didn't want to be irritable. It was my body, punishing me for the lack of painkillers. *Lola took your parts,* said my body. *She took your legs while you slept.* I ignored this. I was not going to get into a debate with my body. I would give it what it wanted. But one day, it would pay for this. Better Future was not the only research lab in the world. I would figure something out. This was not over, and I knew that was true because it had to be.

DR. ANGELICA ARRIVED HOME AT 6:18. EVERY MUSCLE IN MY BODY WAS made of glass. My bowels were panicked and my nerves easily startled. I had nearly trodden on tiny scampering dogs so many times that I was ready to do it on purpose.

They heard Dr. Angelica's approach before I did and went into a barking frenzy, throwing themselves down the corridor and pawing at the door. I had a moment of terror that maybe it was Carl, then Dr. Angelica dropped to her knees and scooped up as many as she could, laughing as they squirmed and licked her face. It was kind of disgraceful. I mean, I understand it's nice to see each other, but have some dignity. You don't need to roll over and expose your genitals. I don't know how anyone can appreciate devotion that slavish. It's not objective. I have a similar issue with religion.

Dr. Angelica set a bag on the floorboards. This was one of those rare situations where the social rules were obvious: I should give Angelica a minute with her dogs before asking if that bag had painkillers in it. I waited silently at the end of the hall, not making anything of the fact that every organ in my body was weeping. Finally she looked up. "Meds?"

My teeth were chattering. "Yes, please."

"YOU SHOULD HAVE BEEN TAPERING THE DRUGS." DR. ANGELICA DREW clear liquid from a vial. "There's no reason to still be on such a high level. Who's your doctor at the company?"

"I am." I smiled at my reflection in the bathroom mirror. I was high on anticipation. My body and I were in the roller-coaster car, ratcheting up the slope.

"That's not right. These are addictive."

"Addiction. That's, what, low levels of dopamine in the brain? Fixable."

"What?"

"I can fix my brain." I trailed off, because Dr. Angelica was no longer looking like she was about to inject me. "Are you . . ."

She moved to the bathroom door and shut it. She stood there. My brain began to suggest ways of getting that syringe out of her hand without breaking it.

"You're not done. You want to replace more parts with prostheses."

I hesitated. "I don't like the word *prosthesis*. It implies a poor substitute. I'm improving. Did you know I can just think of a destination and these legs will take me there?" I threw this in because Dr. Angelica, as a surgeon, was supposedly a woman of science. I didn't expect everyone to be on board for a totally artificial body. But pathfinding legs, come on.

"Last night you woke screaming because you couldn't sleep without your prosthesis. That's not improvement. You're getting worse."

My legs stepped forward. Dr. Angelica's eyes widened. So

did mine, because I hadn't quite intended that. I had just been thinking about getting that syringe.

"The biological part of me is having trouble adjusting," I said. "That's not an argument against the technology." Dr. Angelica's arm moved. I thought, *Oh God, she is going to smash the syringe.* "Wait! I appreciate your concern. But this is my body. I can make my own decisions."

"I don't care about you. You can dice yourself into bite-sized pieces, for all I care. I care about Lola."

"Well, Lola's fine. She's safe now."

"Is she?"

"Yes!" I was beginning to panic. That syringe was right there. "What do you want me to say?"

"I want you to say that Lola's perfect just the way she is."

I hesitated. Is anyone really perfect? You can't be mostly perfect. You can't be perfect some of the time. You are either perfect or not. And I don't think biology does perfect. Biology is about efficient approximation. It's about *good enough*. A vacuum is perfect. Pi is perfect. Life is not.

But I saw this would be a tough sell to Angelica, who anyway was not really asking if I thought Lola was perfect-perfect but rather biological-perfect, that is, good enough. And the answer to that was clear. "Lola is perfect the way she is."

"You hesitated."

"What?"

"What's to think about? You either want to cut her up or you don't."

"No. Wait. I had to translate your definition of *perfect*." Medicine. They called it a science, but it was more like arts and crafts with Latin names. "I don't want to cut up Lola."

"I don't believe you."

"You don't even understand what I'm doing. This isn't about cutting. Cutting is an unfortunate prerequisite for enhancing functionality."

"Does Lola know you want to enhance her functionality?"

"I don't want to enhance Lola!"

"Bullshit." Angelica raised the syringe. This time I was sure she was going to smash it. My legs hiccuped forward.

"I swear to God—"

"I can tell you're lying!"

"I'm not!" My legs took another step, a big one. Dr. Angelica backed up against the door. My legs were going to kick her. They were going to kick her right through the door. "Wait!" I yelped. "Stop! There's no problem! I promise, everything is okay, I swear, I swear it!" The legs did not move. I closed my eyes. Happy thoughts. I was relaxing here in the bathroom, by myself. I did not want to go anywhere. I did not want to move, definitely not.

Dr. Angelica sniffed. This was going to hurt me, losing control of my legs. I wasn't sure how to put a positive spin on that. But when I opened my eyes, her expression was softer. "Well," she said. "That was sincere, at least." She looked at the syringe, then set it on the sink. "Clean yourself up when you're done. You smell." She opened the bathroom door and left.

It took me a moment to figure out. Dr. Angelica thought I'd been talking to her.

"THEY'RE ASKING EVERYONE ABOUT YOU," SAID DR. ANGELICA. SHE reached across the kitchen table and speared a potato. "At the hospital."

Lola froze, a forkful of lettuce halfway to her mouth. "Who is?"

"Better Future," said Dr. Angelica. "They're all through the place, telling us to report any contact."

I was not paying attention. I was talking to my legs. *Hello?* I said. *Can you hear me?*

"What did you tell them?"

"Nothing."

Lola glanced at me. I remembered I was supposed to be eating, and stabbed a carrot. "What should we do?"

"I already told you." Dr. Angelica bent down and scooped up a dog that was whining at her feet. Its bright eyes fixed on me across the tablecloth. "Go to the feds. Say they're conducting illegal medical trials. That takes care of Better Future, I guarantee it."

Give me a sign. A twitch. Something.

Dr. Angelica stroked her dog's ears. "He'll be in trouble, but that's unavoidable. He killed a man. The point is it gets the company off your back. And they're the threat. You don't know what they're capable of. Get the authorities involved before they destroy evidence. While there's still something for the feds to confiscate." Her eyes flicked at me.

My right Contour bounced up and hit the underside of the table. The setting jumped an inch into the air and clattered back down. The dog bolted from Angelica's lap and took shelter in the doorway and stared balefully at me.

"Charlie?" said Lola.

"Sorry," I said. "Yes. I'm fine."

I STOOD IN THE BATHROOM, BRUSHING MY TEETH AND LOOKING AT myself in the mirror. My legs were not conscious. That wasn't possible. I would believe they could think for themselves when I opened them up to find them powered by tiny elves. You didn't combine a bunch of inert materials and get personality.

And yet. Something was going on. A glitch I hadn't anticipated.

Lola came in, smiled, and fished around the sink for a toothbrush. Her hip brushed mine. She came up with a

202 ■ MAX BARRY

short blue one, eyed it, and squeezed on toothpaste. "Did you know there's a condition where you find your own saliva disgusting?" She poked the toothbrush into her mouth and spoke around it. "Imagine that."

"Mrph," I said.

"Ah had to schlee on the schofa las nigh." She shook her head.

"Schlee?"

"Schlee." She angled the toothbrush and tilted her chin. An ocean of toothpaste sloshed inside her mouth. "Sleep."

I felt a subtle, invisible tugging.

She leaned forward and spat. "Let's pull that mattress off Harrison's bed. I can sleep next to you." Harrison was Angelica's son. He visited two weekends per month. Lola had told me this earlier, her eyes hot with outrage, before launching into a story about people I didn't know doing things I was supposed to care about. I always have trouble with those kinds of stories because they contain no useful information. I was sorry to hear that Rod prioritized his own career over Dr. Angelica's. But I didn't know Rod. I didn't understand what I was supposed to do with that information. "Maybe we can . . . get to know each other."

I went to spit into the sink but the Contours didn't move. They were rigid. I thought, *Tilt.*

Lola's fingers addressed a wrinkle on my shirt. "Come to bed."

A thought whispered inside my brain: *The legs don't like Lola.* That was silly. But it fit available evidence. *They're jealous.*

"Come." Lola's fingers found mine. She opened the door and peeked out into the corridor. I followed her to Angelica's kid's bedroom. Her back looked small and vulnerable and I had the sudden thought that the Contours were going to kick her. I stopped. Lola turned around and beckoned. I felt dismay. I had spent a lot of time thinking about going to bed with Lola. A lot of time. But I did not want to kill her. "Come on, Charlie." She came back and pulled me into the bedroom and closed the door. Her arms snaked around my waist. Her face tilted.

"Just a minute."

"Mmm," said Lola. She rose up on her toes, her lips seeking mine.

"I'm not sure—"

Our lips met. I forgot about self-aware legs. Or, at least, they seemed less relevant. The important thing was to get closer to Lola. Then I realized I *was* getting closer to Lola. The attractive force was rising, tugging my metal fingers toward her heart. Lola's eyes sprang open. Her hands pushed against me. "Charlie!" For a second, she couldn't separate herself. Then she took two stumbling steps backward. Her chest rose and fell. "It's back!"

I had three data points now. One: in her suite, when we had first found ourselves alone. The second, when I had rescued her. And now. "It happens when your heart rate increases."

"What?" Lola clutched at her chest. "What does?"

"Oh. Wait. Don't get scared. That will make it worse."

"What is it doing?"

"Try to think about something else. How about those dogs of Angelica's? They're so cute." At this moment, they all began howling. A set of paws came scampering up the corridor, baying. Those useless fur sacks. "Okay. Let's think about this."

"It's a bomb. Oh God. They put a bomb in me."

"Maybe," I said. Lola blanched. "No. That wouldn't be cost-effective."

"What?"

I had to raise my voice to be heard over the dogs. "You

want to blow something up, is the best way to do it really to go to all the trouble of surgically installing—"

"*It's shaking!*" Lola's teeth chattered. I became aware of a tone: a whine so high-pitched it was only just entering my detectable range. That explained the dogs. "Charlie . . . I think . . . you should . . . run."

"We just need to lower your heart rate. Concentrate on putting yourself into a calm state."

"I can't!"

"You can. Lola. You control your body."

"Run, Charlie!"

The whine became so loud it was difficult to hear anything else. "I'm not running. What we have here is a technical problem. And we can solve it. Together—" There was more to this sentence. I was going to say we were two rational people and logic could move mountains. This would either reassure Lola or bore her; either way would reduce her heart rate. I still think this was a good idea. But before I could get it out, Lola exploded.

SOMETHING BLEW THROUGH ME IN A GUST, LIKE A WIND MADE OF needles. My legs twitched. My ears rang.

The house fell silent. I looked at Lola and she looked at me and we both seemed okay. Lola said, "Are you . . ." and so did I. She took a step forward and nothing bad happened. We smiled. Lola fell into my arms. "That was scary. What was it?"

"Something that didn't work, I guess."

"I thought we were going to die." She shuddered. "I thought I was going to kill you."

A moment passed. There was an odd scent in the air: something acrid.

Lola looked up. "The dogs are quiet."

We listened.

Lola reached for the door handle. I went to step out of the way, but didn't. I tried that again.

"Charlie?"

That scent was familiar. It was what you got when you plugged a circuit into a power supply it wasn't designed for. The smell of fused transistors.

The digital clock radio on the bedside table had gone dark. On a shelf, a small stereo that normally glowed red from a power button: nothing.

"Are you okay?" Angelica's voice floated toward us. "The power's out!"

"No," I said. "No, no, no."

Lola touched my arm. "What is it?"

I opened my mouth and closed it again.

"Are you hurt?"

"Yes. Yes."

"Where?"

"My legs."

"Your . . ."

"EMP. Electromagnetic. Pulse."

"What does that mean?"

"You killed my legs," I said.

THERE ARE FIVE STAGES OF GRIEF. THE FIRST IS DENIAL. FOR EXAMPLE: *My legs can't be dead. They can't be.* Next is anger: *You killed my legs, get out, get your hands off me,* et cetera. There is some screaming and raging in this stage. Some unfair accusations. Tears and bruised feelings.

Then bargaining. Quieter. *Just let the battery be all right. Please let the battery be functional.* Fourth, depression. *They're dead. I'm dead.* This is a kind of wallowing. A shutdown. The final stage is acceptance. I include no example because I was a long, long way from acceptance.

. . .

ON THE FOURTH DAY LOLA ENTERED MY ROOM. UNTIL THEN SHE HAD been leaving trays of food outside. I learned to wait until her footsteps receded, pull myself to the door, and drag in the food before the dogs descended.

But this day she opened the door. She wore a green blouse and an air of quiet misery. I was on the carpet, surrounded by my parts. Parts of my parts. I had disassembled them and arranged the pieces in concentric circles. It looked as if I had suffered the world's neatest explosion. Which I had. What had come out of Lola had killed no one, disturbed nothing, hurt no body but mine.

"I think . . ." she said.

These disassembled components, they didn't mean I was fixing them. I had taken the Contours apart because I couldn't think of anything else. I was trying to break my problem down until I reached something fixable. That was how you solved anything: you divided it.

Lola said, "I think it's unfair to act like this is my fault."

"It's not your fault." I did not look at her as I said this because I did not really believe it.

"They put it in me." She took a step forward and her foot landed beside a three-foot-long section of titanium that had once controlled plane stabilization. My issue was so many sections were machine-welded. I couldn't open them with domestic tools. "They put that thing in my chest and didn't even *tell* me."

I almost didn't say it. "You could have calmed down."

"I could have calmed down."

"Yes."

"Charlie. I *tried*."

I picked up a radial bolt. I wasn't sure where this had

come from. I had made notes, in the beginning. I should have kept that up.

"My heart wouldn't slow down. It—"

"People are very selective about their bodies," I told the bolt. "Anytime their bodies do something good, they claim it. They say *I* did this. But something goes wrong, it's not *I* anymore. It's a problem with their foot. Their skin. Suddenly it's not them anymore. It's the body they're stuck in."

"What are you saying?"

"Nothing." I rolled the bolt around in my hand. "I'm just making an observation."

Silence. The door closed with a *click*.

I FOUND A SKATEBOARD BENEATH THE BED AND HEAVED MYSELF ONTO it. With one functional hand and one half-useless one I could wobble along at extremely low speed. It was difficult and degrading but I could do it. When I was sure nobody was around I opened the door and edged into the corridor. Halfway to the bathroom a dog trotted up and sat on the tiles. I knew it couldn't have helped me if it wanted to but it still felt rude. I dragged myself into the bathroom and shut the door. My breathing was harsh and ragged. I had become incredibly unfit. I put my half-hand on the toilet seat and my full hand (my *good* hand, now) on the nearby bench and strained. The muscles in my arm trembled like frightened girls. I flopped over the toilet seat and my lips kissed porcelain and I didn't care because at least it was progress. I wrestled myself upright. As I began to urinate I felt proud.

When I emerged, three dogs were sitting on the floor outside. They didn't look scared or curious. They were just there. "Shoo." I pretended to lunge at them. One stood, looked at the other two, and sat down again, as if faintly embarrassed.

They were communicating telepathically. As individuals they were stupid but together they formed a single intelligence. A pack mind. And it was planning something. It was gathering observational data for later use. As I rolled toward my bedroom, I felt Dog's many eyes burning into my back.

I TALKED TO MY PARTS AS I WORKED. FOR EXAMPLE, I WOULD PICK UP A mirror plate and say, "And what's your problem?" Or, when contemplating a radiation shield: "You need an arc welder. That's what you need." They didn't answer. I wasn't crazy. It was just a way to focus. But sometimes I heard footsteps outside the door and realized this might not be obvious to anyone else.

I regretted what I'd said to Lola. I told the Contours that. "She tried to calm down." This was late one night, after a frustrating few hours prying apart transistors. "She didn't want you to die." Then I wrapped my arms around my chest and cried, because I was really tired.

The next day, I decided to apologize. I would make things right. I didn't want to wallow here, a filthy, stinking, grieving thing, dragging itself around. I didn't want to make Lola sad. Then I sat up and parts of the Contours fell everywhere. I had slept with them to stave off phantom pain. Don't ask me why that worked. It just did. I thought, *I'll just fix one thing.* If I could do that, take one step toward restoring functionality, the Contours wouldn't be dead. They would only be temporarily disabled.

So I crawled off the bed and began hunting for one fixable thing. But I couldn't find it. Weeks passed.

I HAD AN EPIPHANY. I WAS ON MY STOMACH, STRAINING TO REACH some titanium pieces that had somehow wound up under the bed, and thought, *These are just metal*. I guess that doesn't sound very revelatory. But it was. I stared at these pieces, which had once been the core of my fingers, and they didn't look like part of me.

I sat up. I would never put the Contours back together: I knew that now. Previously, this had been a paralyzing fear, but I mostly felt relief. Part of me still wanted to fix them, to try one more time, but it was a small, receding part. I looked down and thought, *I'm a mess*.

I had damaged Lola. Maybe she had left. Someone was bringing me food and listening outside the door, but that could have been Dr. Angelica. I pulled open the door. Fresh air hit me like a slap. A piece of paper lay in the corridor: a clipping from a trade supplies catalog. It was an advertisement for an arc welder. On it was Lola's handwriting: *For you, in the garage.*

I was still there when she appeared at the top of the corridor. "Oh," she said. "You . . . well, I heard you needed one. It took me a while to get." She shifted from one foot to the other. "I hope it's the right kind."

I croaked: a low, pathetic sound. "I'm sorry."

"It's all right," Lola said. "It's okay, Charlie."

AS I ENTERED THE BATH, A FILM OF GREASE PEELED AWAY FROM MY skin, forming a swirling Mandelbrot slick. I was the center of a galaxy of sweat and dissolving dirt. I hadn't realized how badly I stank. You could get used to anything. Your brain complained only about change.

Lola began to wash me. I could not really believe the lack of vindictiveness. I hadn't known this about love: that you did not need to deserve it. I thought there was a set of criteria, like a good sense of humor and looks and wealth. You could compensate deficiencies in one area with excellence in another, hence rich, ugly men with beautiful wives. But there was an algorithm involved. That was why I thought I was unloved: I didn't score highly enough. I had made some attempts to improve my score and also told myself I didn't care because if that was what women wanted, something fake and temporary, I would rather be alone. And sometimes I was just lazy and would rather code things. But here I was soaking in a bath of my own filth with Lola scrubbing my shoulders, and what algorithm could explain that? That problem was nonhalting.

Lola left and came back with a set of prosthetic legs, like the day we'd first met. She rested them against the wall. "Now, these are nothing special . . ." They had crutchlike poles and plastic buckets. They were prosthetics for war veterans abandoned by their government. "They were all Angelica could get without arousing suspicion."

"Oh," I said.

"They're basic, I know. They're not like . . . they're really basic. But they're something."

"Thanks."

She smiled. "Want to try them on?"

The straps were frayed and worn, dark in patches. A lot of amputated thighs had sweated into these. The sockets were loose in some places and strangling tight in others. When I slid the plastic around my thighs, my tissue wailed. I was used to nanoneedles, not gross pressure. It felt like fitting a glove onto my eyeball. I belted the strap around my hips. I slung an arm over Lola's shoulder and she helped lever me upright. I couldn't sit in the sockets, like the Contours: I had to move them, as if they were stilts. They were stilts. I took a step, hanging off Lola, and sideswiped the wall with a rubber toe, leaving a black mark. "That's okay," she said. "Keep trying." The sockets were filling with blood, I was sure.

By the fourth step I noticed my body liked it. My thighs

didn't like it. My thighs hated me. But my brain was feeding me endorphins, pleased to be moving. *This is what you're supposed to do.* My brain was not an intellectual. It took pleasure in simple things like long walks and hard work. Maybe it had a point. It was probably just the endorphins, but suddenly it seemed possible to live like this. Perhaps Lola and I could build anonymous lives in some tiny Canadian snow town. Lola could bake pies. I could grow vegetables. I would be the man with no legs and the half-hand who was a scientist once. The townspeople would find me aloof but grow to respect me. They would call me Doc.

Lola lowered me to the toilet seat. "That was awesome, Charlie. That was an insanely good first effort." She reached for a buckle.

"Again."

Her eyebrows jumped. "Are you sure?" She clapped her hands. "That's the spirit, Charlie! That's the spirit!"

NIGHT FELL. I WON'T RECOUNT THE WHOLE SWEATING, GROANING ordeal. I'll just say it was one of the most horrible experiences of my life. I speak as someone who crushed his legs in an industrial clamp. The problem was I went to bed with no parts. It was just me and Lola curled inside my arm and this seemed doable with the lights on, but as soon as silence fell, I knew it was a mistake. I lay there staring at the ceiling. I felt a crawling. Not painful. But there.

I tried to ride it out. I thought about other things, like whether Carl would find me, and what he might do if he did. The crawling escalated to pangs. I twitched and Lola's head came up. Her eyes glittered in the darkness. "It's okay," I said, but I wanted her to know I was lying.

"Do you want to put your legs on?"

212 ■ MAX BARRY

I shook my head. I chewed my teeth. At midnight we switched on the light and strapped me into the war veteran legs. The relief was immediate. I massaged their stark poles with shaking fingers and felt invisible muscles loosening. Lola snuggled into me. I closed my eyes.

I woke screaming. My legs were inflating, stretching. My thighs were on fire. It was unlike anything I had ever felt. Lola scrambled for the light. I grabbed at the poles, willing my brain to realize they were there. But that wasn't the problem. I knew it immediately. It wasn't that I didn't have legs. It was that I didn't have Contours. My baseline had changed. I needed my *real* artificial legs.

"I'll get the nerve interface mat," said Lola.

"No," I whimpered. "Not yet."

MORNING WAS BETTER. LOLA PADDED OFF TO THE SHOWER, CLAD IN A borrowed T-shirt that said DINO-ROAR! I tried walking in the war veteran legs by myself. I staggered into the corridor, taking huge, toddlerlike steps, bouncing off the walls. There were no dogs around. I should have noticed that.

"He *has*." It was Lola. She had detoured to the living room for some reason. "You'll see."

"You bought him a frickin' welder. You're enabling him!" Dr. Angelica, of course. "I swear to God, Lola! This ends with you in pieces."

"He's trying. You'll see."

"Trying to get to the garage, I bet."

"He's using those, those *stupid* legs. He's changed."

"He hasn't. They never do."

I formed a smug little plan. I would totter out there on my pole legs. Dr. Angelica would be surprised. Lola would glance at her like *See?* And I would be all *What?*

I got one pole in front of the other. As I reached the end

of the corridor, I attained balance and entered the living room walking, actually walking, albeit stiff-backed and goggle-eyed, like a zombie. Lola and Dr. Angelica turned. It was perfect. Then I stepped on a dog.

"Biggles!"

I had never heard a more piercing sound, and I've worked in metals fabrication. Dr. Angelica rushed at me, her fingers hooked into claws. I looked down and saw a dog, Biggles, I guess, trapped under the rubber toe of the pole. Mostly it seemed to be Biggles's blue vest, but he was making a hell of a noise, so maybe some of Biggles was there, too. I tried to raise my leg but snagged on his coat. Then I was off balance and could do nothing but pivot. Dr. Angelica's shriek reached a new pitch of outrage. It possibly looked like I was grinding on the dog. She banged into me with her shoulder and I hit the floor in a tangle of poles. When I levered myself up, Dr. Angelica was cradling Biggles in her arms. Biggles licked her face, whimpering.

I realized they had planned this. Dog, the pack mind, had sent Biggles to throw himself under my poles. He was a suicide bomber. I looked around for the furry faces I knew would be watching from a dark doorway somewhere. "It's a setup." In retrospect, I should have kept this theory to myself. "Biggles did it on purpose."

Dr. Angelica hit me. You would think a surgeon would be careful about using her hands as blunt instruments. But she let me have it. Her nails raked my cheek. On all sides came yapping and shrieking. Dogs streamed out of the walls. Biggles bit my finger. *"Get out!"* Dr. Angelica screamed. *"Get out you asshole you asshole get out!"*

"Stop hitting him!" said Lola. The dogs' yowling melded with Dr. Angelica's enraged screams and Lola's shrieks until I couldn't tell one from another. At Better Future I once attended a demonstration of sonics-based nonlethal weaponry and what came out of that gun did not sound as bad as this. I wrapped my arms around my head. Pain exploded in my kidney. I looked up. Dr. Angelica had kicked me. She stared down and in this moment I was glad she did not have a scalpel. Lola grabbed a fistful of hair. Dr. Angelica shrieked. She swung a looping punch at Lola and Lola ducked and they stood a few feet apart, shocked at each other, or themselves. Dr. Angelica clutched Biggles tight and ran out of the room. A train of little dogs trotted after her. One looked back at me before he disappeared and I sensed him gloating. The bedroom door slammed.

"God," said Lola. She looked at me, then the closed door. "God."

I began levering myself up. "That was an accident."

Lola blinked. "Of course." She came over and helped me onto the sofa. "You're scratched. Let me see that finger."

"Biggles can't be too hurt, if he can bite like that."

"Shh."

I shushed. In the silence I heard Dr. Angelica muttering to her dogs. "She's going to kick us out, isn't she?"

"I don't know."

Dr. Angelica's voice rose. It sounded strident. I had never heard her talk to the dogs like that.

"How could she think you would deliberately step on Biggles?" I said nothing. "Nobody understands you," Lola said.

Dr. Angelica said, "Svvn nmm hrr nww."

"Is she on the phone?"

We listened. Now there was silence. But I knew what Dr. Angelica had done. I could almost hear it: the white van with the Better Future logo on its side.

I struggled to my feet. My poles, I mean. A standing position. I got upright. "Where are Angelica's car keys?"

"What?"

"Her car keys." I managed a step, then another, and made it to the kitchen doorway.

"Why do you want Angelica's car keys?"

This was a difficult question to answer without elevating Lola's heart rate. Elevating Lola's heart rate would be bad. It could lead to an electromagnetic pulse, a dead car, and no way out. I had to execute the world's calmest escape. "I just . . ." I spotted them on the counter, and scooped them up. "Let's go to the garage."

"Why?"

"I feel like a drive."

Lola stared. "You want the welder."

"What? No!"

"Angelica was right." She put her hands on her forehead. "I'm so stupid." Her eyes popped open. "Do you love me? I mean, even a little?"

"What?"

"You've never said it."

I felt surprised. But she was right. I guess I assumed it was obvious. "Oh."

" 'Oh'?"

"I mean, I love you." It sounded bad, even to me. "You know."

"How am I supposed to know that?"

"From observation!" I tried to spread my arms, but I was holding crutches. "I almost died trying to get you out of that building! What other hypothesis better fits available evidence? Schizophrenia?" I bit my lip, because that was workable.

Lola stared.

"We are going to walk past the welder and get in the car. Come see."

"Then why—"

"Just come. Please. Now."

11

THE CAR WAS A HYBRID, LIKE ME. LOLA CLIMBED INTO THE DRIVER'S
seat and adjusted the mirror. "I'm not sure we should be
doing this."

My pole legs snagged on the passenger door somehow.
They were so ungainly. I had to do everything. In frustration I ripped off the straps and pulled at the sockets. They
resisted, the plastic sucking on my skin, then popped off
with a slurp. I threw them into the backseat.

"I don't even know where we're going."

"Anywhere." I pulled shut the car door. Through the
window, I saw it: the arc welder. My breath caught. It was a
gray refrigerator on wheels. That thing had to be 200 amps.

"I should leave a note . . ." She reached for the door.

"No! Stop!"

"Charlie, what the hell? You're not making any—"

"Quiet."

"What?"

"Shh."

"What?"

"Stop talking."

"You stop talking! Asshole!"

I hunted between the seats until I found a remote control. The garage door began to rattle upward. "You need to turn off your brain."

"You want me to be a machine!" Her face flushed. This was not good. None of this was good. "You want to switch me on and off whenever you want!"

"Lola, you remember that EMP weapon in your chest." The garage door retracted into the ceiling. Beyond lay a concrete driveway, flanked by garden beds and an inviting empty road. "The one that activates at high heart rates."

"I remember, Charlie."

"Well, the thing with that is you need to stay calm. You understand? You need to be isolated from stress."

"Is something happening?"

"No. But please drive."

Lola stared at me. Then she leaned forward and pressed a button. The car started, near silently.

"Thank you." I began to relax. She put the car in gear. She seemed focused. She was being a machine. Then a white Better Future van jumped the curb, engine shrieking, and slewed across the driveway in front of us.

THE VAN'S REAR DOORS BANGED OPEN. CARL WAS IN THERE. I DIDN'T SEE him. But I knew. We would try to squeeze past and Carl's metal arm would shoot out and grab our bumper. Our little hybrid wheels would smoke, the engine would scream, and I would turn to see vengeance burning in his eyes.

"Drive!"

I braced myself against the impending acceleration. But there was no acceleration. I looked at Lola. Her eyes were closed.

"Zero, one, one, two, three. Five. Eight. Thirteen."

"What are you doing? Is that Fibonacci?"

"Twenty-one. Thirty-four. Fifty-five." Guards emerged from the van, armed and grim-faced. "Eighty-nine. One hundred thirty-four."

"One hundred *forty*-four."

"*Shut up!*" Her eyes opened, took in the guards, and squeezed shut again. "*Oh God!*"

"It's just, if you're going to do Fibonacci . . ." I forced myself to stop. "Okay. You recite arbitrary numbers." Five guards. But still no Carl. I had to figure out how to operate a motor vehicle when one of us couldn't see and the other couldn't reach the pedals.

"Tibialis anterior. Extensor hallucis longus. Extensor digitorum longus. Fibularis tertius."

She was reciting muscles I didn't have. But this gave me an idea. I shouldn't think of us as two people. We were a collection of body parts. We had one pair of eyes, two feet, three hands, two brains; everything we needed. It was a matter of resource allocation.

I took hold of the steering wheel. "I'll steer. You keep your eyes closed and work the pedals when I tell you."

"Triceps surae."

"Depress the accelerator as far as it will go."

The guards began to close in. "Plantaris," said Lola, and stepped on the gas. The car leaped forward. I aimed for a guard to the left of the van: an older guy with a mustache. He stepped professionally out of the way. He didn't look scared, which was a little insulting. Although it was hard to tell. It was a bushy mustache. As we passed, he unloaded his pistol into our tires. The car rang with flat impacts, as if we were being attacked by a baseball-bat-wielding gang. This would have been an improvement on reality, now I think about it, so maybe I should have tried to sell that to Lola. We bumped onto the road. I hauled on the wheel, which was not easy with one hand from the passenger seat. "Less acceleration!" I said, but not quickly enough, and we thumped against a 'parked wagon. I was thrown against Lola. Her head rebounded from the side window. She said something that sounded like *guk* but probably wasn't. I got my hand back on the wheel. "More acceleration!"

We didn't move. I looked at Lola and her eyes were wide open and fixed on me. She looked pale. "You're . . . okay."

"I'm fine." I threw a glance out the rear window. Better Future guards jogged after us. Still no Carl! I couldn't think where he could be. But we weren't moving, and that was more urgent. "Let's go."

"Maybe that was a mistake. Closing my eyes."

The car dash was dark. There was a smell in the air, sharp and hot.

Lola leaned forward until her forehead touched the steering wheel.

"Did you . . ." I couldn't think of a word for it. "Discharge?"

"I thought we . . . hit something. I thought you might be hurt."

"Put your hands on the dash! Do it now!"

Better Future guards encircled the car, pointing weapons at us. *"Let me see your hands!"* one yelled, and another said, *"Now! Do it!"* in case there was any confusion. They seemed more nervous than when I had been trying to drive a car through them. A guard pulled open my door and leaped back, as if I might bite. *"He's moving!"*

"No legs!" said the older guy with the mustache. "He's not wearing the legs!"

"Confirm that! Subject has no legs!"

Guns disappeared into holsters.

"Get them into the van," said Mustache. "Double time."

Hands reached for me. "Go away," I said, and was ignored. Two guys got me under the armpits and pulled me out of the car. "At least bring my legs!" I twisted around and caught a glimpse of guards dragging Lola out of the driver's seat. Another was peering through the side window.

"Here . . . no, they're not the legs! They're just crutches!"

"Where are the Contours?" said a guard carrying me. He spoke with no strain.

A black town car drew to a halt in front of us. All its doors popped open at the same time. From the rear emerged Cassandra Cautery. Her gaze flicked over me and settled on Mustache. She seemed eerily calm, her face expressionless. It made me nervous because I had no idea what she was thinking. "The legs?"

"We haven't—"

"Find them."

"Yes, ma'am."

"And put him in the car. We have time, I think."

"Yes, ma'am." They carried me toward the town car. Then there was a noise, a kind of crunch from somewhere far away, and everybody stopped. A siren wailed; a car or a house alarm.

"Screw," said Cassandra Cautery. "He's coming."

She looked at the guards and snapped her fingers. They bundled me into the backseat of the town car and slammed the door. I noticed it wasn't locked, so I opened it again. A guard looked down at me and pushed it closed. This repeated twice more.

"Stop that," the driver said. My door locked with a

thunk. I saw his eyes in the rearview mirror: condescension, from a guy with one foot resting on the accelerator of a 200-horsepower vehicle.

The opposite door opened. Cassandra Cautery slid her gray-skirted butt onto the leather seat. "Go," she told the driver. As the car pulled out, she turned to look out the rear window.

"Where's Lola?" I got no reply, so twisted to see for myself. The white van doors were pushed closed by guards, then the vehicle peeled onto the road behind us. A few remaining gray uniforms scuttled toward Angelica's open garage. "Who's coming?"

Cassandra Cautery looked at my thighs. This whole time, she was yet to have an expression. "She toasted the Contours, I assume."

"Yes."

"Good." She glanced out the back window again. "Do you know what my life has been like the last five weeksh?"

I peered at her, because it sounded like she said *weeksh.*

"Oh, you want to see? Have a good old look." She leaned toward me and pulled out her lip. Among her gleaming white teeth was a gap. Not like before. It was a chasm. She released her lip with a *plop.* "They said they could fix it. They ground the tooth all the way down and you know what? They were wrong. I can't feel half my fache. *I can't feel my fache.*" She stabbed her forehead with her finger. "It's like *stone.*" She noticed the driver watching us in the rearview mirror. "What are you looking at?" His eyes flicked back to the road. "Science is bullshit, Charlie. It's bullshit. You want super legs and lab assistants with eyes like headlights and *that's* possible, oh sure, you can turn a lab technician who looks like a *horse* into a supermodel. But when it comes to a perfectly shimple thing like diastema you *paralyze her fache.* I'm married. Did you know that? He's a litigator. And he expects me to have *expresshions*. He expects *reshponses*. What's going to happen when he notices this?" She stared at me. "I want to drop a bomb on your department. I don't care about revenue projections. I don't care about schtrategic vision. What *they*"—she jabbed a finger at the car ceiling— "never appreciate is that mesh breeds. It eatsh organization. And your department is nothing but mesh, creating more mesh, and so help me, it's going to eat the company. No one gets it. You breathe a word of this and you'll regret it." This was directed at the driver, whose eyes were drifting to the rearview mirror again. "We have a new shee ee oh. You should appreciate this. You can't kill a manager. They just replace that part and restart the machine. He even looks similar. *You'll* never meet him." She stabbed a finger at me. "You will never be in the same room as a listed corporate officer again. But they want to use you. Leverage the investment. But, Charlie, I'm dying to end this. I'm looking for an excuse. One twitsch in the wrong direction and I'm bringing down the curtain on this shorry enterprise. Understand?" Before I could answer, she waved her hand in my face. "Don't answer. It doesn't matter what you think." She turned and stared out the window. She put her elbow on the sill and her hand on her forehead. Her fingers probed. It reminded me of how I massaged the Contours.

"Who's coming?"

"Hmm?"

"You said—"

"Carl's coming." She turned back. "This is what I mean. Did I want to rush into expanded testing? No. Did I want to weaponize Lola Shanksh? No. But we're an engineering company. I say, 'Let's stop and consolidate a minute before rushing into new products,' everybody jumps up and down, bleating about processhesh. But a man wants his limbs removed and that's fine. No one sees a problem. You people have thish mentality that the world is all hard science or hocush-pocush. Nothing matters but numbers. Well, we needed psychologists. But we didn't get any because we're full of engineers, and engineers think psychologists are witch doctors."

I didn't say anything. Psychologists are witch doctors.

"So Carl went under the knife. We gave him those, you know, little arms to practice on. Then you found him and hit the roof, asked me to dishpose of him—"

"I meant *fire.*"

"Let's not get into a thing, Charlie, because it's incredibly cold either way. I couldn't do that to Carl. The kind of legal liability it would have opened up . . . so I hid him from you. But of course we had to take away his arms and he didn't like that. He didn't like that at all. We made him a new pair as fast as we could—your team did—but, like I said, we had no psychologists. We didn't see the cracksh. It seems obvious now. You look at the tapes. He's talking about his arms like they're alive. Like they've got a mind of their own. Then he split. Shtole some things. Now he's trying to find you. He wants your partsh." Behind her, the streetscape grew industrial: we were closing in on Better Future. "Some kind of revenge fantasy, I asshume."

"He wants my parts? You mean he wants to kill me?"

"I don't know what's running through his head. But the way we get through this, Charlie, is by ensuring there are no more Carls. No more major body alterations to people who can't handle it. Testing confined to test subjects who have a proven psychological detachment from their own physical form." She eyed me. "That's just you, if you haven't guessed."

I wasn't ready to depart the topic of Carl wanting to kill me, but this got my attention. "You're going to give me parts?"

"Your legs didn't start talking to you, did they?"

"Um," I said. "No."

"Then yes. Whatever you want. Carte blanche. It's like a dream come true for you, isn't it? You get everything you want, because I'm running along behind you, cleaning up. I'm resigned to it. It would just be nice if someone stopped for one moment to say, 'Hey, Cashandra, just letting you know, we couldn't do this without you.' I'm too capable. Anyone else in my situation would be insane from the stress. Do you know how old I am? Thirty-four. I'm only thirty-four."

I licked my lips. When Cassandra Cautery had said, "They want to give you parts," something in me had lit up. It began sending out pulses. *Parts. Parts.* "I can really have parts?"

"Yup." The Better Future complex rose ahead. They had installed searchlights on the roof, which shone in the dusk light. "The building's been repaired, in case you're interested. The entire wing had to be checked out for structural damage. People worked out of the cafeteria for weeksh. It was a nightmare." She twisted to look out the back window. "Carl's tracking us. Once he gets here, we'll . . ." She glanced at me. "Give him the medical care and attention he needsh."

The drumbeat in my head became almost painful. *Parts. Parts.* I tried to push it down, because I needed to establish something. "Are you sure I can actually have whatever parts I want?"

"Yes."

"For myself."

"No one else can handle them."

"I can design and build my own parts."

"In between testing military-grade Better Products, absolutely. Charlie. Trust me. There's no catch."

I wished I was better at reading faces. Whenever someone looks me in the eye and speaks earnestly, I believe them. I have no siblings.

The car descended the ramp to the underground garage. Yellow lights flicked past the windows. I tasted oil. I remembered that fantasy I'd briefly entertained at Dr. Angelica's about escaping to a snow town and living out my life as a hermit, free from technology. What had I been thinking? That was really dumb.

"Welcome home," said Cassandra Cautery. I didn't look at her because I didn't want her to see how excited I was.

I HAVE A STRONG FOCUS. WHEN SOMETHING GETS MY ATTENTION I FOR-get about everything else, like who I was talking to or where I was going. When I was six I got distracted at my birthday party by the washing machine, which was new, and sat in the laundry room watching it tick through cycles until my father came in and asked what the hell was I doing, every-body was leaving. In high school I was crossing the road and a beautiful girl walked by and I didn't realize I was standing there gaping until she turned to see why everyone was honking. The look she gave me still makes my ears burn.

It's a useful trait. I'm not sure I could have advanced far in science without it. But it's not always appropriate. Sometimes this doesn't bother me, because that washing machine really was more interesting than the birthday party, but other times I wish afterward that the shutters hadn't closed. I wish I'd retained enough self-awareness to realize I was standing in the middle of the road like an idiot. I wish that when the town car drew up beside the parking lot elevator, my brain left room for thoughts besides *Will I get parts now* and *I wonder what they've done on legs*. Because the door opened and I saw a guard with a wheelchair and I did not once think about Lola.

· · ·

CASSANDRA CAUTERY RODE IN THE ELEVATOR WITH ME. THE DOORS
opened on the ground level and a guard wheeled me into
the corridor. Three white coats stood facing the wall with
their hands neatly folded behind their backs. When we
passed the atrium, all the chairs were turned away. I saw the
backs of suit jackets. A year or two earlier, I had been in the
cafeteria when a guard asked everyone to please turn and
face the wall because they had to bring through some classified material, and I had faced the wall.

As we descended, Cassandra Cautery said, "Your department has been busy in your absence, of course."

The doors slid apart. At the end of the long corridor was
a kid in a green T-shirt and ripped jeans. I did not recognize
him because we did not employ anyone who had the time
to put in three hours a day at the gym. His eyebrows
ratcheted up. He slapped his forehead like he couldn't
believe it. In the process, muscles rippled and bulged. "Dr.
Neumann!" He turned and cupped his hands around his
mouth. "Neumann's back!"

"Better Mushles," said Cassandra Cautery. She sounded
disgusted. "They grow while you shleep, apparently."

Cats emerged. Few wore lab coats. Instead they had short
dresses, sleeveless tops, miniskirts, heels, shirts with the top
buttons undone. The boys were huge and the girls were
reeds. They began to clap. Jason elbowed his way to the
front and grinned. He was no longer skinny. His teeth
shone like stars. I felt ugly.

"What's annoying," said Cassandra Cautery, "is they *look*
like this, but they *act* like assholes."

"I heard that," said Jason. There was laughter. "With my
Better Ears."

"Move out of the way," said Cassandra Cautery. The lab
assistants parted. As I drew closer, I smelled a cloying mix-
ture of musk and sweat, like entering a bad dorm room. I

coughed. "Sorry. It's the Better Muscles," said Jason. He shuffled alongside, threading his way through other cats. "They produce a few nasty by-products. But we're working on Better Scent."

A familiar-looking girl smiled with her lips pressed together, then gave in and showed teeth. "Hello, Dr. Neumann." She was Elaine, my old lab assistant, with Better Skin.

Cassandra Cautery turned. "Get lost. This part is private." They began to disperse. Cassandra Cautery swiped open the lab door, juggled cards to swipe again for me, then it was the guard's turn. The door closed behind us with a *smack*. The room was full of parts: metal and wire spilling from stainless steel shelves, themselves jammed together. I saw joints. Fingers. Baglike organs. They had been busy. Very busy.

We squeezed between the shelves. "There." She gestured, with distaste. For a moment I thought my Contours had come back to life. But they were black, not silver. They had larger hooves. They stood on a black rubber mat, held in place with metal cords that dropped from the ceiling. "They're calling these Contours Mark Three. Don't ask what happened to the Twos. You don't want to know. They're a revishion of the original Contours, upgraded for strength, bug fixes, et cetera."

I wheeled myself forward and touched the Contour Threes. Their metal skin was mottled, covered in a billion tiny bumps. I didn't know why. But I was intrigued. I ran my fingers down the legs and was surprised by their slimness. "Where's the battery?"

"Relocated."

"What?"

"They draw more power. The battery got too big. And there were concerns about safety. It's not a good idea to store a masshive energy source in a limb exposed to impacts." She held up her hands. "Don't argue. You weren't here for the Twos."

"So where's the power source?"

"Here." She moved to a shelf on which sat a steel object the size of a vacuum cleaner. On one side was stamped the international symbol for radiation. "Pocket reactor."

"But . . . the legs aren't modular? They're not self-sufficient?"

"I don't know what to tell you, Charlie. It's the direction the team took after you ran off."

"So to wear the legs I need the abdomen?"

"Yes."

I chewed my lip.

"Also, the abdomen requires a shpine upgrade."

"A what?"

"It weighs eight hundred kilograms. It'd fall right out of you."

I eyed the abdomen.

"And if we're doing the shpine . . . well, you can stop there. It's just . . ." She shrugged. "It's hard to make work without the upgraded torso."

"The what?"

"I thought you would be totally into this," she said. "Isn't it what you always wanted?"

"Yes . . ." I said. "No. I don't like using other people's technology. I like to build my own."

"Oh. Well, that's going to be something of a tough sell to management, Charlie, with thirty tons of military equipment waiting around for you to field-test." She opened her mouth like she was about to laugh, then snapped it closed. "I'm kidding. You can take it as slow as you like."

I touched the Threes. I wondered what that rough surface was for.

"Where does this end for you, Charlie? New legs. New

arms. Just out of curiosity. When do you say, okay, now I'm happy?"

I blinked, because that was an odd question. You didn't stop improving things. Reaching a point where everything was as good as it could be, that would be terrible. You might as well die.

"You know what? Forget the abdomen. We'll get you a really long cord, we'll plug your Threes into the generator, you can figure it out from there. How does that sound? Just dip your toe in the water."

"Okay."

"Okay!" She clapped her hands, took a breath. "Let's get you into shurgery."

"Surgery?"

"I forgot to mention. The, ah, the nerve interface or whatever on the Threes . . . the part that plugs into you? It's a different configuration. Or something." She waved her hands. "I don't know. But they need to take another inch or two off your thighs." Her cell phone trilled. She studied the screen. "We can't dither all day, Charlie. What's it to be? Shurgery?"

Part of me wanted to say *Wait*. Because did I really need to rush into the Contours? The rest of me said *Yes*.

"We'll get you on a gurney, somebody can explain it all on the way. How's that? Okay?" she said. "Okay?"

THE CEILING OF BETTER FUTURE WAS A CHECKERBOARD. THE LIGHTER squares were actually lights: they glowed uniformly, as bright in the corners as the middle. I had never appreciated this until I lay on a gurney and watched them pass over my head. "These lights are neat."

"Can we get him sedated?" This was Cassandra Cautery, walking alongside. Cats were accumulating, and people in green scrubs. "We have a time presshure."

"I'll find out."

I felt thrilled, and nervous, and like I had forgotten something. I wondered what that was. I jumped. *Where's Lola?*

"Being treated," said Cassandra Cautery. "They wanted to check her over, make sure she was okay."

"I want to see her!"

"Would you like me to make a call? I can have her meet us in surgery."

"Yes."

"Okay. Done."

"Are you sure?" I felt light-headed, even though I hadn't had any drugs yet. "You're not just saying that?"

"Gas here." A plastic mask approached. "Head forward, Dr. Neumann."

"Can you make the call right now?" Hands took hold of my head. The mask snapped around my mouth and nose.

"Will do, Charlie. I have the phone right here." She wiggled it. But she did not use it. We passed through a doorway. The glowing checkerboard ceiling was replaced by white sheetrock and surgical lights. I saw many people in green and thought, *Do you need that many people for an inch or two of thigh?* They grew fuzzy. Fuzzy and warm. My head was heavy.

"Did you," I said. The rest of this was *give me a general.* I tried to push out the words but couldn't feel my mouth. My head lolled. I got it up and saw people laying a green sheet across my body. *Why do I need general anesthetic,* I said. My eyes closed.

"He's out. Go."

I heard a click, then an electrical noise, like someone was testing it: *vnnnnn . . . vnnnn.* A man said, "How much are we doing?"

"Everything," said Cassandra Cautery.

12

I BECAME AWARE OF SMOKE. I FELT ALARMED, IN A SMALL, SECTIONED-off part of my brain. In my line of work, smoke means someone made a mistake. Somebody forgot to check a tolerance. Convert from imperial. This smoke curled along the ceiling above me. I wasn't sure whose mistake it was. But it was pretty.

Get up, said the part that was worried about the smoke. Another part said, *Lie here a little longer,* and that felt more persuasive. I was doped. I was relaxed. I would never feel this peaceful again, not without chemical assistance.

Something slooshed. Something went *sssssss,* like an old man easing into a favorite chair. I felt wet. But also safe, and warm, and protected. I closed my eyes.

Someone coughed. I opened my eyes, because that was disconcerting. I waited, hoping it might go away. *Cark.*

Cark. It sounded perfunctory. Like the owner didn't expect it to do much good.

I pondered its implications. Or I floated along on its implications. I let its implications surround me without penetrating. I might have done this for a while, but water began falling on my body. I thought maybe rain but then probably not because I could see the ceiling. I felt my dream state dissolving, and was sad. But it was also good, because I could feel myself coming back. My thoughts began to organize themselves. I raised my head.

I was in an operating theater. Of course I was: I had been brought here for surgery. But things lay scattered and over-turned: a gurney, drip stands, equipment that looked like somebody should be keeping it sterile. Surgical blades glimmered from the floor tiles in rapidly pooling water like coins in a wishing well. A long crack ran up the wall. I thought, *Earthquake?*

Cark.

I saw a man slumped against the wall. His green scrubs were speckled dark down the front. His lips were red. He stared dully at his legs, which jutted out on the tiles. His eyes rose to mine and he blinked once, slowly.

"Help," I said. He didn't react. I felt a little bad, because obviously this guy needed some help, too. I planted my right hand on the table and levered myself up on my left elbow, or tried to. It didn't work. I looked down to see what the problem was.

A tide of blood washed from a gash in my left shoulder. Or not a *gash:* the opposite of that. *Gash* implied a cut in something otherwise whole. I had ropy strings of skin and muscle connecting me to an arm that was otherwise severed. On the tiles, discarded, was something I first mistook for a drill. But it wasn't. It had a long, flat blade. Liquid red ribbons threaded the water around it. It was an electric saw.

I looked at the guy on the tiles. "Did you . . ." I said. Because this guy looked like a surgeon. I thought maybe he had started to amputate my arm but not finished. "Can you . . ." My voice was a croak. My throat felt abused. The man stared at me without expression. His head bobbed with each beat of his heart. "Why . . ."

Cark, went the surgeon, and he made a fresh dark spatter down his scrubs. He was not going to help. He was going to lie there and die. Or lie there and watch me die and then die himself. I felt panic. It was not a good time to panic. It was time for objective, clinical assessment. But an ocean of blood was draining out of a canyon in my flesh and my brain gibbered, *That's fatal, you're going to lose consciousness.* I lifted my right arm—I had a right arm—without any real plan and saw bright red. I was lying in a red bath. Blood ran over the sides of the table and pattered on the tiles below. I was a bloody water feature. There was too much blood here. I should be dead.

My legs looked odd. As in, I had some. Beneath the saturated green surgical cloth was a definite leg shape. Tubes ran between layers of the cloth to nearby devices: a black box on a trolley, four different drips. The box was making the slooshing sounds. With each sloosh, the tubes connected to it bucked, dark fluid moving through them. I decided this was keeping me alive. At this moment, the box stopped slooshing and started slurping like an enthusiastic child chasing the last of a milk shake. Beige spots appeared where the tube was connected to the box and raced toward my body.

I grabbed at my mostly severed arm and tried to mash it back on. It was like handling a steak. The sounds—it wasn't the squishing that got me. The sucking or squelching. It was the rasping. I almost couldn't do it. But I didn't want to die. So I did.

Blood squirted. I couldn't seal it properly. "Help!" I said. Before I'd been prepared to cut the dying guy some slack, but now I really needed him. "Help me, you shit!" I flopped to the edge of the table so I could see him while holding my arm. His eyes were empty. He had died. The fucking guy had died. I felt rage. I wanted to go over there and cut off his arm and die in front of him and see how he liked it. I felt terror and dizziness and regret. I so very much didn't want to die. I felt cheated and angry at someone or something. I whipped my head around, in case there was something useful nearby I hadn't noticed, like maybe a surgeon who wasn't dead. My eyes fell on the electric saw.

It was a long way away. I didn't know if I could reach it. And maybe this was just as well, because was it such a bad thing to lie back, close my eyes, and not saw off my arm? No one would blame me for that. But it would mean dying and I did not want to die, I was more sure of that the closer I got to it. So I strained and stretched and looped my fingers around the saw's cord. I put the cord in my mouth to change my grip and pulled again. It was a long cord. I pulled and bit and pulled and got the idea that maybe this cord had no end, because wouldn't that be hilarious. It could be like string theory. I could be quantumly entangled. The saw clanked onto the metal table. I remembered what I was doing and groped for the power button.

One time in a mall I saw a guy demonstrating an electric carving knife. He was showing a silver-haired couple how easily the knife could whir through a roast chicken, slicing off strips of steaming meat with a noise like *vrrrreeeee*.

For some reason I expected this to sound different.

WITH MY EXCESS ARM OUT OF THE WAY, I CLAMPED SHUT THE ARTERY. I'll spare you the specifics. Let's just say it was a temporary

solution involving my fingers. I needed to buy enough time
to get off the table and find medical assistance. I didn't even
care that those assholes had sawed off my arm. I would for-
give them that if they helped me live. I leaned forward and
took the green surgical cloth in my teeth. I pulled it back,
then leaned forward for another bite. Each time I dragged
the cloth a few inches closer. I was hoping to reveal a set of
Contour Threes down there, because otherwise I was essentially stuck on this table. I tugged the cloth and it bunched
up around my face. I tried to nose it aside. I was tempted to
take my hand off my artery, because that would be so much
quicker, but I didn't, because it would also be fatal. I caught
a glimpse of black titanium and thought, *Oh, thank God.*
The cloth's center of gravity passed the edge of the table
and began to slide to the floor by itself. I saw more metal,
and more, and as the cloth passed my thighs I thought,
What is that? because there was metal where my thighs
should be. And there was metal instead of hips and a metal
stomach and my belly button was a logo, a circular design
that even upside down I recognized as Better Future's, and
still the cloth slid and I was metal all the way up, a titanium
landscape. Tubes led from a gap somewhere beneath my
chin, carrying fluids to and from the metal, and I was connected to the metal by tubes and nothing else. I sucked in
breath to scream and two of the tubes rose slightly, feeding
me air, and I lost it all in a sound like a deflating tire. I had
an arm. I had a shoulder. I had a head. I wasn't sure what
else.

A face appeared. Its hair was matted with blood. It
belonged to a boy. One of his eyes was the deepest brown
and the other was regular brown. He said, "Dr. Neumann.
Oh. Dr. Neumann." He disappeared. "He's alive!" He
returned. Water fell into his hair and down his nose. His
mismatched eyes swam with concern. "It's going to be all

right. Everything's going to be all right." He touched my hair, hesitant, then with confidence. "You can do it. Hold on. Hold on."

The room filled with noise. Someone took hold of my head from behind and people in green scrubs moved in to mess with my tubes. No one looked at my face. Something clicked. I heard a high-pitched whine and a deep hum. I felt a sharp pain in my neck and spreading warmth and I twisted to see who was doing that. The hands on my head tightened. "Blood," someone said, and someone else said, "Got it." Hands pried my fingers away. I resisted but they were firm. I began to feel heavy. Someone said, "He's alive?" in a tone that suggested she did not really want to hear the answer. Cassandra Cautery's face hovered. She held a hand towel to her ear, stained red. Her hair was the color of ash. Her jaw muscles reminded me of insects that could bear food many times their own weight. But she had no expression. "Charlie? You woke in the middle of a bad dream, is all." I tried to hold my eyelids open. "Back to sleep, now. We'll finish up here and everything will be fine." I began to cry a little, because now I was going to live.

I REGAINED CONSCIOUSNESS ALL AT ONCE, LIKE TURNING ON. I WAS standing. I was surrounded by light. The operating theater was clean. It was not raining. It was full of cats and people in green scrubs and all of them were looking at me.

"Got him." Jason had a small laptop balanced on one hand and poked at it with the other. A cord came out of the laptop and ran into a mess of other cords going in all directions. Something was wrapped around my head. Something hummed.

A young woman stepped in front of me. Elaine, I

remembered. Her eyes were orange. "Dr. Neumann, can you hear me?"

I nodded. I tried to touch my neck to see what was there and something went *whnn-hnn, whnn-hnn.*

"He's trying to move his arm."

"Leg now."

"Lots of motion requests."

I looked down. My legs were Contour Threes, black titanium. My hips were conjoined ring sections. Metal crawled up my chest. I had arms. They hung from insulated chains from the ceiling. One was silver and ended in a three-pronged claw, each prong a long, multiarticulated digit. The other was black with a thin, tubular biceps with a bulbous forearm. It had no hand I could see. I gagged. I did not feel sick. Not physically. I felt strong and alert and a little cold. But my brain vomited, *Wrong wrong wrong.*

"Dr. Neumann?" Jason slid closer. "You're probably feeling strange right now but when you calm down you're going to realize this is really cool."

"Bringing up tactile."

A lightning storm of pins and needles ran through my body. My metal parts stopped being objects and started being me. I had been able to feel before but not like this. Nothing like this. I remembered their bumped surface, which I'd felt in Lab 2. *Help me,* I said.

"Enhanced sensory feedback. It's like a million times better, isn't it? We use it ourselves. Because the point at which Better Feelings could reproduce the full spectrum and fidelity of biology-based sensation, we passed that a while ago."

"Registering with core," said Mirka.

"Seeing that."

"We're talking out loud," said Jason, "so you can follow along."

238 ■ MAX BARRY

Hunger roared through me, as an idea rather than a feeling: I was suddenly very sure I needed food. "Whoa," said a girl with yellow eyes.

"Dampen that."

"We'll hook you into Better Voice in a minute," said Jason. "You can initiate chats and save contacts in an address book and everything."

I thought, *Lola, Lola.* Tears splashed on my chest with a sound like *punk, punk.*

"You're making him cry," said Mirka.

"Correcting."

"Bridging waveforms."

Mirka said, "He's still crying."

"Levels look okay, though."

"Maybe he's really sad."

Jason went away and came back with a tissue. He wiped one of my cheeks, then the other. "Dr. Neumann?"

I opened my mouth but there was no air. I manually inhaled in a gasp. "Where. Is. My. Body."

"You mean . . . do you mean your old organic parts? Well . . . incinerated. There's not really . . . there's not really anything else you can do with them."

"Still really sad," said Mirka.

"Active correction?"

"Yes."

Stars burst inside my head, wild and brilliant, full of suggestion.

Jason said, "Do you remember when I asked you about ethics? You wanted to suppress your guilt and I said maybe we shouldn't and you said there was no such thing as *shouldn't.* Actually, you didn't even understand the question. Well, I get that now. I totally get it. Because sometimes you feel a kind of biological revulsion against an idea but it's only because you're not used to it, right? It's just a matter of baselines."

"Improving. Approaching sync."

"I mean, it's not like there's any fundamental integrity of emotions, am I right? Everything's chemicals, when you get down to it."

My teeth chattered. Elaine said, "That's a sawtooth, can we do anything about that?" Two cats, male, approached with power drills and positioned themselves against my abdomen. The drills went *whreeeee.*

"So, the thing is," Jason said, "while you were away, we made a lot of military parts. I mean, a lot. And management has been really, really anxious to get them into testing. Only we figured out that sticking them into random volunteers and seeing what happened, that wasn't such a great idea. So we've been waiting. For you. And once we got you . . . I don't think management was ever going to wait around until you were, you know, completely comfortable. Because, like I mentioned, there's an awful lot of stuff bottlenecked. Very valuable stuff. Also, the government seems to have been probing this area a little more closely than they like lately. So management is super-focused on getting some results of labs ASAP. And that's why, uh . . . why you're a little more advanced along the whole body replacement path than you might have anticipated." He swallowed. "But there's good news. You get to go out."

"What," I said.

"I'll be honest. What they were planning was pretty bad. They wanted you attached to the parts but not able to control them. We'd move them for you and read your sensory feedback. They said it was the quickest way to test. Which, you know, I guess it is. But still. That's a little inhumane, in our opinion. Being connected to tech but not able to control what it does. That's like the ultimate user. Anyway, Carl ruined everyone's plans. So now they let us activate you. It's actually a great opportunity, because if you show them you can be trusted, they might let you stay active."

"Little angry, now," said Mirka.

"Uh," said Jason. "Let me explain the Carl situation. Do you know Carl? Of course you do. I forgot, because we weren't allowed to tell you about him. But we were working with Carl. Before he went crazy. So what happened was Carl came back. He turned up on the front lawn. Which was a surprise to security, because, well, they expected him, but not at the front door. There are plenty of entrances and a guard knows them all. Of course, they had people in the lobby. They put snipers on the roof, guys in mounted Hummers, prototype weaponry from Speculative Military Products. There was a sonics gun in the garage, the back lawn was sown with EMP mines, and the lobby guys had . . . well, an electroshock cannon. Like a Taser, firing a couple hundred darts a minute. And the problem was no one asked our opinion. If they had, things would have been different. But you know users. They never spend the time to properly understand the technology. They only want to learn the bare minimum. Enough to make it work. And that's just not viable when the technology is this powerful. We're really at the point where users in that sense are becoming obsolete, I think. I don't think the world can be adequately navigated by someone who doesn't understand tech anymore. But anyway. So Carl turns up. I don't know if anyone told you, but when he left, Carl took some stuff. He took a Fiber Shield. Did you go to the Fiber Shield presentation? It's a bomb, but it throws out tiny fiber strips, a fog of microribbons. They float in the air, tens of millions of them, and their ends are sticky. They're harmless, but a high-speed projectile moving through that fog hits a ribbon and gets pulled off course. Gets unbalanced. It might go left, right, who knows. The point is it diverts. In the presentation, they set up a target behind the fog and did a bunch of test shots and every one missed. By a lot. It was kind of awesome. It's not exactly guaranteed protection, you know, like I wouldn't want to stake my life on it, because the amount of diversion depends on how many ribbons the bullet hits, the angle at each collision, all these random variables. The project leader, that's Abeline Knudsen, who did that paper on disruptive resonances in inner ear fluid . . . well, she said, fire enough bullets and eventually one will go straight. Or straight enough. So, actually thinking about it now, maybe the security guys knew that. Maybe that was their plan: if he uses the Fiber Shield, pour bullets into it.

"Well, Carl appeared on the lawn. We were in the labs, watching on CCTV. Carl—and you know, we liked Carl. We liked him a lot. We were sad he ran off. Anyway, Carl sets off the Fiber Shield, and boom, disappears in fog. Everyone starts shooting. So much gunfire, we could actually feel it. And you know how far down we were.

"The guys in the lobby with their electroshock cannon, they open fire. They spray these million-volt darts, which are a lot lighter than bullets, of course, and when they hit the fog they go *everywhere.* Left, right, up in the air, back at the security guys. They hit guards, they land on the roof, they spam the lobby, and everywhere they're sparking and starting fires. It's already chaos and then a Hummer takes one in the fuel tank. Then it's nothing but fire and smoke and people screaming, and Carl comes in and does what he likes.

"So now everyone's really keen to recapture Carl," said Jason. He frowned at something on my chest, tapped it, and looked at another cat, who approached. "Since public exposure at this point would not be good for the company.

Of course they sent security guys off after him, and of course that didn't work, because Carl is, well, Better. So now it's your turn to go. After Carl."

The chains around my arms rattled to the floor. Both limbs moved smoothly into a loose resting position. From this angle, I could see that my left arm definitely did not have a hand. It had a hole.

"Arms online in ten."

I said, "Why. Does—"

"Five. Four. Three. Two."

"Stand by," said Jason. "This might feel weird."

"Arms online."

I felt a distant prickling, like somebody telling me a story about my childhood. My right arm, the one with tripod fingers, twitched. I realized I had done that, and was immediately struck with a bolt of agonizing phantom pain. I screamed and tried to grab the arm, to unbend the muscles. My other arm swung in an arc. Jason ducked. My metal limbs clanged together. I tried to cry out but had no breath. Jason shouted. Lab assistants attacked laptops. The bulbous arm made a rapid clicking noise, like a nine-year-old riding a bike downhill with playing cards stuck in the spokes. I had seen a boy cruising like that once, when I was a kid. I had thought it the coolest thing ever.

"Dr. Neumann! Stop that! You'll damage the hammers!"

"Dampening! Full spectrum!"

The pain subsided. I whimpered soundlessly against its return.

"Sorry," said Jason. "We're still feeling our way around here. Don't clench your left fist. That's a mental command for firing."

My teeth chattered. "Firing. What."

"Aha. You have an MAC-701 rotary cannon in that arm." He grinned. "Nice, huh?"

I began to shake. "Take. Them. Off."

"Dr. Neumann—"

"Don't. Want! This!" The gun arm rattled, stopped, rattled.

"Dr. Neumann! Dr. Neumann!"

A window opened in my head. Through it poured Jason, and his desire for me to calm down. I felt his compassion and excitement and awe, and when I did calm down, I felt his gratitude. It was extraordinary. What had Jason called it? Better Voice. That was underselling it. That was like calling sex Better Hugging.

"Thank you," he said. "Thank you."

"THERE'S A LOT OF AMMUNITION IN THAT ARM. BUT IT'S NOT unlocked. That was one of Cautery's conditions. We can enable it when you're clear of the building. And just so you know, we can remotely disable it. That was another condition. Which sucks, I know, but we won't need to do that. Just try to, you know, not shoot anything except Carl."

"Connecting subsystems."

Muscle spasms ran through my legs. Before I could inhale, the pain was gone.

"Better," said a boy in a white T-shirt. "We're getting this."

"Responses verified. We have a solid feedback loop."

"Screen is green."

I found the window in my head, the one Jason had climbed through. I pictured his face in it and poured a message through: *No no not doing this.*

"Uh," said Jason. The window closed. He turned to Mirka. They eyed each other silently.

"Fine," said Mirka. She handed off a laptop and approached. "Dr. Neumann . . ." She brushed a hair from my forehead. "The thing Jason has not told you is that once

Carl gained entry to the building he came here, to this room. He stood beside you. You were unconscious. Your arm was detached. It seems to us that Carl thought you dead. Or that your death was imminent. He left. He located your friend. Lola. And he took her. I am sorry."

"It's highly likely she's still alive," said Jason. "I mean, we don't think he took her to cannibalize her parts. We think it's more an affection thing. We spent time with Carl during recuperation and he talked about her a lot." He looked at Mirka, then back at me. "Okay! Well . . . I think that's everything. Do . . . do you have any questions?"

"Any," I said. "Questions."

"Yeah."

My lips stretched. I exposed teeth. I felt dizzy. The Contour Threes bent and the hoof came forward and met the ground and fired locking pins into it: *snack-snack.* Jason and Mirka hopped back. I stared at my foot. The hoof. I raised it and swiveled it. I wiggled a flat metal toe and it did as I meant. I had not made this but still it was interesting. I watched the toe move back and forth. Jason cleared his throat. Mirka put her hand on his arm. I kept moving the toe. I lowered it and raised the other hoof and set it back down. I looked around at the cables and tubes coming out of my body. I swung my pronged claw arm in an arc and swept half a dozen cables off me. One sparked and I felt a temporary heaviness in my parts followed by a lifting warmth emanating from my abdomen. I stepped forward. Cords popped from my metal skin. Lab assistants yelped and scrambled out of the way. "Shut him down!" someone said, and Jason said, "No. Wait."

In the steel finish of a cabinet I saw my reflection. I saw it with Better Eyes. My head was metal. Black bands ran across the bridge of my nose, my forehead, and my chin. These glimpses of skin were all I had. Everything else was metal.

I said, "Am. I. Wrong."

Jason crept forward. "No, Dr. Neumann. You're not wrong. You are not wrong."

I nodded. Servos in my neck whispered. I felt scared. But okay. I said, "Where."

I CLOMPED THROUGH THE BETTER FUTURE CORRIDORS ESCORTED BY cats and security 'guards. From the expressions of the guards, I was either an awe-inspiring technological miracle or the worst thing they had ever seen. I was not quite sure myself. They led me to stairs and I hesitated but the Threes took the steps easily, cantilevering to maintain a solid footing. There is something deeply satisfying about a system that works exactly like it's supposed to. I'm not sure everyone feels this way. It might be an engineering thing. But by the time we reached the bottom of the stairs, I was kind of in love.

They led me to the underground garage. This was to avoid being seen by emergency services people who were crawling around aboveground. I didn't understand how the garage was supposed to make any difference, since it exited in the same general area, but that wasn't my problem. The garage had its own generator and halogen lights making everything blindingly bright or lost in impenetrable shadow. Better Future vans and Hummers idled in the dark, chrome reflecting like supernovas, tailpipes belching fumes. I blinked and the scene normalized, my Eyes adding information from infrared and ultraviolet, filling in fields and illuminating motion.

"Hold here a second," said Jason. The cats swarmed. I was interfaced with. I felt impatient and my legs hiccuped forward. "Whoa," said Jason. "Wait up."

He thought it was me. But it wasn't. I remembered Cassandra Cautery asking: *Your legs didn't start talking to you, did they?* But that wasn't anything to do with me. That was a software glitch. Maybe these Threes had the same software. It wouldn't have been rewritten from scratch. The glitch could still be there. It could be in everything.

"Dr. Neumann." Mirka approached. "Just while we are running through the final checks, there is one thing I must raise. There is potentially an issue with Lola's Better Heart. The military function. The EMP draws a great deal of power. There is a safety margin, of course. Even after EMP, the battery has much power to maintain heart function. And the EMP will not fire unless the battery is full. Except . . . that part is perhaps not fully functional. We do not think it anything to be concerned about. But . . . well, management said there was a woman on the table who needed an install and we were forced to act before we were ready. The EMP should not have fired twice. It definitely should not have done that. I saw the subject, that is, Miss Shanks, and . . . perhaps this was the light, but her skin looked gray. Which to me suggests the battery has drained to the point where it impacts heart function. And please do not look so worried, because the Heart needs only a little power to pump. It will definitely not stop, we think. But if the safety mechanism is nonfunctional and her heart rate rises above the trigger threshold then the EMP might fire. Again. Which would be bad. The battery does not have that capacity. So, again, this is just a precaution. I do not want to make your life harder and I know you have a lot on your plate. But if you do find Lola Shanks it would be extremely good to avoid making her scared or excited or engage in any kind of exercise."

"ALL CLEAR," SAID JASON.

A van door opened and a woman climbed out. I had seen her outline in infrared but not realized who it was. A neat rectangle of plaster covered her left ear. Her hair was gray. A thin rivulet of dried blood traced a curve from her hairline past her cheekbone.

"Charlie. Before you go . . ." Cassandra Cautery stopped. She stared at my crotch, where Elaine was kneeling, studying a device jacked into a flip-up port. "What is that?"

"It's a simple way to interface with—"

"You put a port in the dick?"

"The main transport bus—"

"Shut up," said Cassandra Cautery. "I went to Yale. Did any of you freaks know that? My advanced antitrust lecturer said I had a *relentlesh deshire to organize. Her words. She said she would follow my career with interest.*" Her voice shook. "And look at thish shit!"

No one spoke. Elaine unplugged her device from my groin with a *pop.*

Cassandra Cautery shook her head. I felt awkward, because unless something happened soon, there was a real risk I might run through her. "Charlie . . ." She inhaled. "I just wanted to say, please be careful."

She walked back to the van. Doors slammed. The cats shuffled away. It was time.

I FOLLOWED THE BLACK VAN UP THE RAMP. IT MOVED SLOWLY, AS IF afraid of leaving me behind. I felt insulted. Didn't they know what I was? *Kick it,* suggested my legs. Not in words. But I could feel their desire.

The window in my head opened. I thought I could close that window, if I wanted. I was developing a feel for the interface. *Dr. Neumann, we're almost at the top. Are you ready for some acceleration?*

Yes, I thought.

The van sprang ahead. I didn't need to instruct the

Threes: they shifted into a lope by themselves. The first time I'd run on artificial legs they had tried to shake every bone out through the top of my head, but this was a river cruise. Improvements to the gait model, shock absorption through the torso . . . and, of course, I had fewer bones.

A rectangle of light appeared. As the ramp broadened, Hummers slid up on either side. Fresh air slapped my face. I was outside. The cars turned onto the road and the Threes followed. I got too close to a Hummer and my gun arm clanged against its side. The Hummer rocked. Its tires squealed.

I thought, *Was that deliberate?* I was talking to my parts. They couldn't hear me. They weren't conscious. But it was the best model I had for this behavior, so I was going with it until I figured out something better. *Okay, then.*

I veered left. My gun arm kissed the Hummer's door. I pushed, gentle but firm. The Hummer fought back. White smoke streamed from its tires. The Jason in my head radiated alarm, and I gently closed the window on him. I pushed the Hummer until it popped out of formation and spun in a smoking half-circle. Then I accelerated through the gap and left them behind. Wind blasted by, tearing at my eyes. For the first time since I had gained consciousness I felt glad to be alive.

13

ONCE AT UNIVERSITY I FED A DOLLAR INTO A VENDING MACHINE, pressed C and 4, and nothing happened. So I pressed the buttons again, with more authority, then CANCEL, then many buttons at the same time. I cursed and slapped it, because I was nineteen and someone was coming down the corridor, and I said, "Fuckin' machine."

Later I saw another guy staring at it. I opened my mouth to tell him it was busted, but before I could, he slapped its side, the exact place I had, and said, "Fuckin' machine."

I guess it's always uncomfortable to discover you're not as individual as you thought. But it really bothered me. From one perspective, I was an independent animal, exercising free will in order to elicit predictable reactions from an inert vending machine. But from another, the vending machine was choosing to withhold snacks in order to extract predictable, mechanical reactions from young men. I couldn't figure out any objective reason to consider one scenario more likely than the other.

I tried to raise this with a philosophy major at a floor party. She said, "Oh, you're a determinist." Her tone implied that this was naïve and funny. I knew what the word meant when applied to algorithms but not people. "You don't believe in free will," she said. "You think everything's gears and levers." She had a lollipop and at this point she sucked it. I didn't think I disbelieved in free will but as we talked I learned she thought brains were magical consciousness fairylands so maybe I did. Before we got anywhere she went off and made out with a guy I didn't know. I felt lonely and unsatisfied and went downstairs and sat on the floor in front of the vending machine. I didn't know why, exactly. I just felt we had something in common.

THE STREET TURNED TO MEET THE MAIN ROAD AND I FOLLOWED IT, moving between cars. A horn blared. A yellow sedan was in the lane ahead and I saw the driver's eyes flick into the rearview mirror. Then the car leaped into the SUV beside it. Glass popped. I pounded past. I was supposed to be keeping a low profile, but that wasn't my priority. My priority was finding Lola before her heart stopped.

Something went *clunk* in my gun arm. I thought, *Oh-oh,* because maybe this was how they remotely shut me down. Then I remembered what Jason had said about unlocking my ammunition. I felt an urge to test this hypothesis. I should wait. I shouldn't start shooting things on a major roadway. But on the other hand, it was really tempting. The day I bought my phone, I had a major report due and tried hard to resist playing with it. I held out until nightfall but by six a.m. was still awake and discovering new features and

I had to call in sick. This was like that, only attached to me, and with bullets. *I should test it now,* I thought. I couldn't wait to learn how it worked until Carl was running at me, swinging sledgehammer arms. That would be really poor planning. I looked around. Coming up on the right was a giant billboard. On it an attractive family in bright clothes laughed and draped themselves around a game console. I thought, *That.*

I raised my gun arm. I clenched my mental fist. The arm barked like a chain saw. It sounded angry. The billboard burst apart. Shell casings jingled across the asphalt beside me, jettisoning from my arm in a flume of white gas. Pieces of billboard fluttered to the ground. As I ran through them, I thought, *I am a Lola-rescuing machine.* And something inside me replied, *I am a Lola-rescuing machine.* I smiled, because if that wasn't an echo, it was pretty clever.

ON OCCASION JASON APPEARED AT THE WINDOW INSIDE MY HEAD. Each time he imparted an impression of location and I accepted this and closed the window again. I didn't need to plot a route. My legs could do that. It left me free to consider what I would do when I encountered Carl. Although, after the billboard, maybe I was overthinking it. The facts were I had speed, strength, smarts, and a gun. Carl had arms. What was he going to do, punch me in the head? Actually, maybe yes. I should be wary of that. But that was surely the extent of the danger. All I had to do was keep my distance.

The Contours left the roadway and leaped nimbly over the railing. I flinched, but they knew what they were doing. My hooves dug into a concrete embankment and I heard the locking pins fire. Twin jets of concrete dust spat by my face. I was damaging a lot of city infrastructure here. The

Threes tensed and sprang across a wide concrete storm drain. I braced but it was like landing on a sofa. We ran beneath a bridge. I heard a helicopter and wondered if it was for me. Ahead was a storm tunnel, big enough to drive a car through, but its face was protected by an iron grate. My legs slowed. They felt hesitant. *Oh,* I thought. *Sorry.* I raised my gun arm and clenched and the grate disintegrated. The Threes picked up speed. My abdomen rotated in three ringed sections and I passed through the remains of the grate sideways, then swiveled to face forward again.

My hooves slapped through low water. It was black in the tunnels but on the electromagnetic spectrum the walls were edged in fluorescent blue and the water flared motion white. The tunnel turned, forked, and forked again. Finally I stopped. I looked around. I didn't see what was so special about this section of tunnel. Then I noticed a hatch twenty feet above my head. A ladder ran up the wall. But I wouldn't be needing that. I raised my gun arm.

Then I reconsidered. Carl was close. I shouldn't alert him. I lowered the gun arm and studied the other one, the one with the triple prong of claw fingers. I hadn't tested this yet. I wondered what it could do. I pointed at the hatch and thought, *Remove that.*

The claw fired out of my arm, trailing metal cable. It popped the hatch out of its housing, bent it in two, and pulled it back down into the tunnel. The cable ratcheted back into my arm but before I could flinch at the sight of a folded metal hatch rocketing toward me I was holding it. I looked at it a moment. That was pretty good. I placed the hatch on the ground and looked up. The access hole was not wide. I wasn't sure I could fit through there. But of course this wasn't something I needed to figure out. At least, not with my brain. I had parts for that.

The Threes settled and sprang. My arms folded tight

against my body. We scraped against concrete and a constellation of sparks blossomed near my face. Then we were through. The Threes spread and my hooves locked on to solid concrete floor. The crack of the firing pins echoed like gunshots. That was a shame.

I was in a multilevel parking garage. Cars filled the bays. From my last contact with Jason, Carl was here somewhere, but I didn't know where. I chose up. As I rounded the first level, I began to feel nervous. This was not a great environment for spotting Carl. The concrete shielded EM and infrared was polluted with recently active car engines. I slowed. I decided to abandon my surprise plan. I was feeling pretty unstoppable, at this point. I sucked in air and shouted: *"Lola!"*

My voice bounced back at me. Nothing. I inhaled again. *"Charlie!"*

I ran. Two levels up, a brown sedan backed out in front of me, its red brake lights steaming, and I pushed it aside with my gun arm. I didn't mean to hit it hard but the Contours braced automatically and the sedan bounced into the wall. I rounded another corner and stopped because there was Carl.

He was bigger than I expected. He hadn't grown. I had just forgotten. He was shirtless, which allowed me to see the metal support structure around his torso. His arms were huge, much larger than my own. He was built for strength. It was a moment before I realized he had Lola in front of him, his hands gripping her shoulders. She was so small by comparison that I had missed her. She stared at me with her mouth open. I looked different, of course.

"Hold it," said Carl. "No closer."

This was pretty stupid. Carl had clearly not thought through our relative strengths and weaknesses. If anything, he should be trying to lure me closer. This was why I was going to beat him: the intelligence differential. I raised my arm. He didn't even know I had a gun. This was going to end really quickly.

I thought, *Is Carl such a bad guy?* Maybe he wasn't. Maybe I could talk him into releasing Lola and he could get the psychiatric help he needed. Now I had him at my mercy, I felt a little bad. He had only wanted new arms. You couldn't blame him for that.

"Charlie," said Lola. "Please listen to Carl."

Her tone was odd. She didn't sound terrified. And why would Lola say that? Was she confused? I realized the way Carl's hands were hovering near Lola's shoulders, that wasn't to hold her. That was protective.

"Carl wants to help," said Lola. "He didn't kidnap me. He rescued me."

I said, "What?"

Carl cleared his throat. "Dr. Neumann, this might be hard to hear."

I thought, *Just shoot him.* A part answered, *Yes.*

"I thought I wanted to be strong. I knew I couldn't go back. You know. For my fiancée. But I wanted to be prepared. In case I needed to be strong again. So I wanted the arms. You understand."

Stockholm syndrome? That was when kidnap victims sympathized with their abductors. It was a psychological condition.

"The thing is, after I got the arms, they started talking. Took me a while to believe it. Thought I was going crazy."

I hoped Lola was hearing this. And drawing the logical conclusion: that Carl was insane.

"They wanted to crush things. To smash. I tried to tell people. But no one would listen. Not management, not the scientists, those kids. They only cared about the arms. I started sleeping with them, because it hurt to take them off, and one time I woke up and they were bending the bed in half. When I got irritated, they grabbed things. Then they threw a guy against a wall. I thought I'd killed him. That was when I knew I had to take off. I had to find you, and warn you." His eyes moved to Lola. She tilted her head to look up at him. I did not like that. I didn't like either of them. "Sorry about leaving you behind. I thought you were dead."

"Lola," I said. "Come. Here. A minute."

"I hoped Lola could help me figure out what was going on. That's why I saved her. I carried her right out through the flames. I was strong enough this time. And I was right. She's helped a lot."

"Lola," I said. "Really. Come here."

She said, "Charlie, can you talk to your parts?"

This was irrelevant. "Carl. This is a gun. This arm. It shoots. So let go. Of Lola."

"Oh, Charlie," said Lola. "Charlie, no."

"It's all right. Just. Ahead. Of schedule."

"We have to get rid of your parts."

I said, "Pardon?"

"You told me once you don't need to think about where you step: that the legs figure it out. That's clever, Charlie, that's the kind of thing you do, but it created a problem. Because brains are plastic. They adapt. When you lose a limb, the parts of your brain in charge of it, the neurons, they don't just sit there. They look for new jobs. There was a woman with a transtibial earlier this year, and I know how this sounds, but her eyesight improved. One man got better at math. We try to get people into prosthetics quickly so that we can capture those neurons for motor function before they wind up somewhere else. And what I think, Charlie, is your machine parts are too easy. They didn't give your neurons anything to do. So they wound up all over.

Can you talk to your parts, Charlie? Do they have a mind of their own? Because I think that's you. Your subconscious, being no longer so sub. But it's okay. Over time, we can retrain your brain. With physical therapy, we can move your neurons elsewhere. We can—"

"Let me. Stop you. There." I drew in breath for an entire sentence. "I'm not sure you appreciate that at this point I am a head."

"Charlie—"

"There is no. Getting rid of. The parts. I *am* the parts. Look. I passed that point. I sawed off. My arm. Sawed it off. So let's calm down. And forget crazy ideas that. Can never happen."

"The id is supposed to stay underwater, Charlie. It's not supposed to be conscious."

"The *id*. That's psychology! A soft science!"

Carl said, "Dr. Neumann, I understand—"

"Shut up. You don't understand. You have parts. I *am* parts. I'm technology. You're a man with help. You are *nothing* like me." *Shoot him,* suggested a part of me. It was a solid idea.

"I should have realized earlier," said Lola. "I should have stopped you."

"You shouldn't. *Move away from Carl.*"

"Charlie, we need to get you out of those parts before you go crazy."

"You're crazy," I said. It was not a very good argument. I was panicking because Lola was supposed to be on my side. "The thing is, Lola. The person I was. Nobody liked him. Then I did this. And people got interested. People like you. So how is. This bad? It's not. It's . . . a lot of parts. I'm still getting. Used to them. But let's not talk about. *Going back.* There's no back. I'm better now. Yes, the parts talk. But that's okay. It's like having company. And nothing works perfectly. The first time. You don't scrap a project. Every hitch. You look for. Iterative improvement. The point is. On balance. Am I not better?" I could see from Lola's expression that this was not very persuasive. "Forget that. Fact is, I need parts. To live. There's nothing I can do. My hands are tied."

"It's possible that—"

"*I don't care!* Even if I could. Survive. On some shitty life support system. I don't want to! Do you know what. This body can do? I have GPS! What are we supposed to do? Go back to *maps*?" I forced myself to calm. "What you're talking about. Is asking me to live in a cave. Like a *Neanderthal*."

"Who's 'we'?"

"I didn't say *we*." But maybe I did. "The parts and . . ." I didn't finish this sentence. *Shoot,* said the parts; they had been saying this for a while and it was increasingly hard to ignore them. My eyes moved to Carl. He was the source of trouble. He had been since day one. Shooting him would solve everything. Or not. Maybe the logic of that wasn't quite there. But the part that wanted to shoot didn't care. It just wanted him smashed. Lola would understand. Not right away. Eventually. It was the only way, because Lola wasn't going to stick around for a head. I didn't care what she said. That was not a viable long-term relationship. It was best for everyone if I shot Carl now.

Lola walked toward me. My heart leaped, because this opened up an excellent opportunity for firing on Carl. She stopped a few feet away. "Charlie . . . you never wanted to be a gun. Did you?"

"There's nothing wrong with. The gun." My legs rose up on their hooves, settled. Things were going to happen whether I wanted them to or not. It was out of my control.

"We can get through this. Somehow we will—"

"Look at Carl!" I shouted. "He's got arms! If the parts are so dangerous. *Why is. He wearing. His arms?*"

Carl looked at Lola, then back. "Well . . ." He sounded apologetic. But only a little. "Because if you won't give up your parts, I have to take them off you."

HERE'S WHAT SHOULD HAVE OCCURRED TO ME ABOUT CARL: HE HAD attacked Better Future and lived. They had deployed armed guards and serious hardware and he prevailed through clever planning and tactics. What this made clear, or should have, was that Carl was not an idiot.

HE TURNED AWAY A MOMENT. THEN HIS ARM FLICKED IN MY DIRECTION. Something dark and cubelike hurtled toward me. Even before I saw what it was, it revealed that I had seriously misread the situation. Because being stronger than Carl, and faster, and better armed, that didn't matter if he could surprise me by throwing things. The factor I had forgotten to include in my behavorial model was that I had never fought anyone in my whole life. I had almost hit a girl in elementary school. She pushed me over before I could commit. That was the extent of my hand-to-hand combat experience. Carl was trained to overpower people. It was his job.

The cube was a car battery. I flinched. The car battery ricocheted off my shoulder with a *clang*. I thought, *Wait a minute, that didn't even hurt,* then a second battery hit me in the head and I screamed, because some of that was flesh. I staggered in a circle. Red waves poured from my shoulder, not exactly pain but rather a logical outrage. My ringlike abdomen rotated. I brought the gun arm around. But Carl was already on top of me, his elephant arms swinging. His fist contracted into a solid punching block and connected

with my stomach. Lola screamed. I staggered backward and
sat down on the hood of a car. Its windshield cracked. But
the surprising thing was the weakness of his punch. I had
tried to ride what I expected to be a huge transfer of
momentum but totally overcompensated. Sitting on the
hood of a red sports car, I realized that compared with me,
Carl's arms were not very strong. Of course they weren't.
He was mostly organic. Despite his exostructure, he
couldn't carry around my kind of hardware. For that you
needed to be metal all the way through. I didn't want to let
his fists near my face. But he was not a big problem.

The Contours bent in three places, levering me upright.
I swung my claw arm, aiming for his head. Carl not only
deflected it but had time to first give me a patronizing look.
He got his other fist beneath my arms and red waves blossomed around the side of my chest. "You want her," I said.
"Don't you." His block hands began to open, splitting into
thick digits. One clamped on the forearm of my gun arm.
The other closed on the thinner biceps. He strained. Red
washed through me. I wailed, *Stop stop he is ripping me.*

"She understands me," said Carl.

My tripod claw fired and locked on to Carl's arm. His
eyes widened. I pulled. Carl's metal fingers squealed along
my titanium arm, losing grip. I could hardly feel my gun
arm. But it was there. It was functional. I tried to back up,
pushing Carl away with the claw. All I wanted in the world
was to get my gun arm on him and insert a lot more metal
into his body than he already had.

My heels hit the car I had sat on earlier. I pushed and it
shrieked, metal on concrete, folding up against the low
retaining wall behind me. I raised my gun arm and Carl
knocked it aside. The car behind me popped and banged.
Suddenly there was less resistance and I staggered momentar-
ily. I didn't know what had happened but it created a gap

between me and Carl and I swung the gun arm up. He ducked beneath it and punched the barrel upward. I kept walking backward, trying to find the distance I needed to finish this, and I discovered the reason the car was no longer pushing back on me: I had forced it completely over the retaining wall, sending it tumbling end-over-end through the air. The way I discovered this was all of a sudden so was I.

Night sky revolved. Something bright and white passed before me. I was spinning head over hooves, feeling the terrible mass of my body swell with kinetic energy. I caught a glimpse of Carl, framed by the punctured concrete wall of the garage. The next time I revolved I was ready and my claw hand fired, trailing metal cable. It snapped around Carl's exoskeleton and yanked him off his feet. Another revolution. The brightness was blotted by a shape I finally recognized as the car I had kicked backward out of the lot. It hit the brightness and broke it into a thousand winking pieces, because the brightness was a lattice of frosted windows. The world slipped by. The sky rose. Carl fell toward me. I heard but did not see the car burst against the floor of whatever building was down there. Then it became visible again as a crater of scattered glass and metal. It was a live preview of coming events. I tried to twist my body into a posture that made it less likely that I would land with the many tons of my body above my biological head. But it didn't respond. I screamed at my body's betrayal.

My ringed abdomen swiveled. My legs extended. My hooves splayed, the toes extending. I hit the car like a bomb. The Threes retracted, eating momentum. The locking pins fired. I felt my left hoof grip the floor and my right hoof slide. It had come down on the hood of the car and flipped it into the air. I staggered. I was upright. The car hood came back down and tried to cut off my head. My claw hand released Carl and the cable whipped toward me.

The Contours took a stumbling step, then another, and we almost had balance when Carl landed like a meteorite. The impact shoved us and suddenly there was a man there, a guy with a white face and horrified mouth and it was everything I could do to not stumble over the top of him. My abdomen revolved. I walked backward through a tall display case. Glass rained down. But I was balanced. I was alive. I felt like crying. I loved my body.

My claw hand completed retracting into my arm with a *thwack*. I was in a store. It was a great white cathedral of glass and air. Two dozen people cowered behind counters and display cases. The walls were lined with white flaglike posters like political propaganda and the cases were shrines built around tiny phones and computers and tablets.

Shards of glass fell from me like water. No one ran. No one screamed. I found that a little odd but then again I was in a technology store. *Carl,* said my parts, and that was a good point. I scanned the wreckage. Maybe he had bounced. He had pretty good armor but not much in the way of shock absorbency, I would have thought. I looked away then back because I had caught motion flare, and he had a tire and was ratcheting back an arm to throw it at me.

I raised the gun arm. This time I would not be distracted by minor projectiles. I squeezed my fist and as the internal barrel spun I thought, *Actually, that tire is going to make quite an elastic collision.* It hit my gun arm and bounced into my face. My head snapped back. I saw into the heart of the universe. My body sang and my brain crawled in the dark, trying to remember where the controls were. Powdered sheetrock drifted like stardust. I got my head balanced with the horizon. People in hip shirts and cargo pants jostled for the double-door exits in peer-seeking algorithmic patterns, like a school of fish. A man with sledgehammer arms and a yellow-gray exoskeleton ran toward me. He seemed familiar. I knew him from somewhere. I thought, *That's that guy, isn't it, Carl,* and he punched my legs. I jerked but did not fall. The Threes were better than that. Carl's arm wrapped around my throat. The other clamped on to my tripod arm and bent it back. *"Ag,"* I said. Red pain waves poured from my elbow. I couldn't see Carl but fired the claw hand anyway, hoping it might find a way to pull off his head on its own. Instead we tore a chunk out of the floor and hurled it across the store. It was not what I intended but maybe it was intimidating.

"I got her," Carl said. I felt his hot breath on my cheek. "I went back and got her." My arm shrieked. There was a squeal of metal. I felt separation. A part of me winked out. My forearm fell to the floor, trailing severed wiring. It did not hurt but the loss was the worst thing I had ever felt.

I rotated. I flailed my gun arm. But I could not reach Carl. His grip on my neck was unbreakable. His thick, blocky digits snapped at my gun biceps. I grieved for my arm. I did not want to be pulled apart. I told my parts, *I don't know how to do this but please just kill him somehow.*

The Contours jolted forward. They crashed through a display counter and then another. We accelerated toward a wall. A moment before impact my abdomen rotated.

We hit the wall back-first. Sheetrock burst around me. Everything was dust. *Where,* I thought, and my parts said, *I don't know,* and we took four steps backward and brought the gun arm up. We could not see Carl in the visible spectrum but in EM he was as bright as a star field. We clenched our fist and screamed fury at him through our gun.

WE WAITED. EVERYTHING WAS AWASH WITH DUST AND HEAT. THE FLOOR was littered with broken plastic and glass and electronics. The dust settled. An object coalesced into a body. The gun arm whirred like a suggestion. But we waited, to be sure. Sirens grew. The body did not move. Heat drained from infrared and motion from the microwaves. The air cleared. *I think we got him.*

Motion flared behind us. We turned and saw Lola picking her way into the store. Her eyes found Carl. He had entered the visible spectrum. His metal structure was bent and broken. Beneath it, so was Carl. Some of his metal had gone into him. I didn't want to gloat. But this was why you didn't go hybrid. "Oh, God. You killed him." Her hands flew to her mouth. Her eyes watered.

"He tried to take our parts. He ruined our arm." We showed her. "Look."

"This is wrong. This is so wrong."

Outside, tires screeched. Doors slammed. "We should leave."

Lola shook her head, looking at Carl. *She wanted him to take our parts,* we thought. It was a terrible shame because she was so very lovely. She was dear to us. But she had a bad idea, one incompatible with our existence.

Something went *clunk* within our gun arm. For a horrible second we thought it had died. Then we remembered this noise, from when Better Future had brought the gun online. We looked in our head, and on the other side of the window was Jason, watching.

WE HEARD A BEEPING. THE MAIN LOBBY DOORS BANGED OPEN TO REVEAL a second set of doors, industrial and flat-looking. These ratcheted open and we realized they belonged to a truck. A ramp clanged to the floor. Down the ramp came Cassandra Cautery and gray-uniformed security guards, who leaped off the sides, their flashlights illuminating glittering columns of dust. Behind them, the cats.

"Jeshus," said Cassandra Cautery. "Look at this." She stared at Carl without expression. If beauty really was permanence, Cassandra Cautery was more beautiful than ever.

"He wanted our parts."

"You've done a good thing, Charlie. You have." A forklift backed down the truck's ramp, orange light swirling. It completed a turn and bumped toward Carl, its prongs like a forked tongue. Driving the forklift was a boy with tan skin and rippling muscles. "Now we can clean up."

"Charlie needs help," said Lola. "His parts are destroying him."

"You calm down," said Cassandra Cautery. "You're enough trouble without working yourself up. Charlie, we have to go. Get in the truck."

"No," we said.

"No," she echoed. She sounded disappointed but not surprised. "Why are you not getting in the truck, Charlie?"

"You wanted me. Passive. Testing parts with. No control."

She pursed her lips. "Jason?" He came up behind her, gripping a tablet. "Did you tell Dr. Neumann we would be using him as a passive biological receptacle for rapid parts testing?"

"Um, it . . . kind of slipped out."

"Did it," she said. "Did it slip out."

"Yeah. Sorry." His eyes flicked at me.

She took a breath. "Charlie. I won't lie to you. We were going to do passive testing, yes. But you need to see this from the company's point of view. You're an asset. We can't have assets with feelings. We can't have assets falling in love or kicking people through windows. The only way for us to manage this situation is with complete control over everything you do. I realize that's not ideal for you. But that's the situation. Now, once things have settled down, once we've got a nice production system going, that's open for review. We can try letting you walk around by yourself for a while, in a controlled environment. You see? There's a future for you. A good future. If you get in the truck."

"Charlie," said Lola. "Listen to me. You're the most amazing person I've ever met. But not because of your body. You're more than that. You need to please remember that you never wanted to kill people. You never wanted to be controlled by your body."

We looked away. We were not finding anyone here very compelling. Cassandra Cautery wanted to put us in a cage and Lola wanted to take us apart and what we wanted was to run away and find a place to tinker. But then we looked back at Lola and remembered she was a kind of part of us, too. Not a physical part. But a key one, in the sense that we had been a different person with her. We thought, *Do we need Lola?* We felt competing desires and none felt more Charlie-like than another. We thought, *Maybe there is no core self.* Maybe it was malleable all the way down. As a kid I had felt scared a lot for no reason, and then I got older and it stopped, so which of them was me? They were separate but equally valid. I got happier when I drank coffee, bad-tempered when tired, and with a combination of stress, missing limbs, and drugs, I could kill people. And probably none of that said much about me. It was pointless to ponder who I was because I was whichever combination of chemicals happened to be sloshing around at that time. So I decided not to search for a true self. I decided to choose who I wanted to be. I liked the part that loved Lola. I decided to be that. "Okay," I said.

CASSANDRA CAUTERY HESITATED. "YOU MEAN OKAY AS IN, 'OKAY, I'LL get in the truck'?"

I shook my head. Lola edged toward me, relief spreading across her face.

Cassandra Cautery looked around. "Everybody see that? Refusing to follow orders. He's raging out of control." She gestured to Jason. "Do it." He began to peck at his tablet. The forklift rumbled toward me.

Lola gasped. I could grab her. Run. I would make maybe five steps before my body turned to stone. Then brain death. It was not a great option. I could lunge and club Cassandra Cautery into the wall. More appealing. But with the same result: me dying. Jason was a little farther. I could possibly close that gap, swat the device out of his hand. It was a temporary solution, in that this was not likely to be the only method of shutting me down. But since all other alternatives were death, I liked it.

Jason's thumb slid over the keypad. His eyes held mine. I recognized his expression from the day I'd waited for him in the lab, one leg dangling in the Clamp. He'd lunged for the Big Red Button and been too late. He seemed to have learned from his mistake.

"Quick," said Cassandra Cautery. "No time to lose."

I could stomp. Create a shock wave that would ripple through the floor and knock Jason off his feet. People would shout. Jason would scramble on hands and knees toward his computer, but I would be faster, and crush it beneath one hoof. The guards would fall back, knowing what I could do. Before they rallied, I could sweep Lola up in my arms. I could leap out through the broken ceiling and land on the roof. There would be police and ambulances, but I could run until they were all far behind, until Lola and I were beyond Better Future's digital reach. Before dawn, in another city, we could break into a factory and use their equipment to locate the part of me that transmitted. I could teach Lola to use a magnetic drill and she could straddle my chest and ensure we would never be found again.

This was a good plan.

I raised a hoof. That was as far as I got. It hung there. It did not feel different. It did not deaden. But it did not listen to me. I was a statue. I tried to turn my head to look at Lola but could only shift my eyes. Lola shrieked. I began to choke up, because now I was going to die. But I did not die, either. I just stood there.

"Congratulations," said Cassandra Cautery. "You always wanted to be a machine."

Jason poked at keys. My hoof came down. My legs jerked forward. I was not a statue. I was a puppet.

"Make him hit her," she said. "Club her or . . . punch her in the head or whatever."

"What?" said Jason.

"Make him hit her. She's no good to us alive."

"I don't think—" Jason started, and Cassandra Cautery turned and stared at him. "Okay." His head bowed over the tablet. It was typical. Technical people always talked about standing up to management, but when the moment came, they turned to water. We are not a confrontational people.

"Lola," I said.

My hoof thumped to the floor. There was a pause. My abdomen swiveled toward her. I took a step.

"My God, Jason," said Cassandra Cautery. "Can you go any slower?" He pushed sweaty hair from his forehead.

"Run," I said, but it probably didn't matter, did it? In any case, Lola did not seem to want to run. She stood still until I stopped in front of her and raised my gun arm. Then she leaned forward and hugged my metal chest. "Please. Run."

"I love you, Charlie."

I felt the stirrings of an invisible force. And I connected a few data points. The first time Lola's heart had begun to generate EM, we had been getting intimate. The second time, I had leaped in via her balcony window to rescue her. At Angelica's, we had kissed. While driving blind, we had sideswiped a car and she had said, "I thought you were hurt." And now.

I tended to be skeptical of anything that couldn't be measured, written down, and independently verified across a series of double-blind tests. But this was hard data. Lola's heart beat fastest for me.

"Lola," I said. "Kiss me." Lola jumped and wrapped her arms around my neck. "I made you a heart," I whispered. "It's at Better Future."

"Oh." Her arms squeezed me. "That's sweet."

"You'll need it. After this."

"Charlie," she said. "Charlie."

"If you kill the truck. And me. My body."

"No, Charlie."

"They can't. Get away. Then maybe cops. Medics. Save us."

"Maybe?"

"Still. Better." I felt small adjustments up my arm. It was correcting for Lola's new position. "Please," I said. "Now."

WE KISSED. THE HIGH-PITCHED WHINE THAT CAME FROM DEEP INSIDE Lola's chest could have been her singing. The electric wind that blew through me could have been her breath. The darkness that followed, it felt like her embrace.

0

"OH," SOMEONE SAID. "TERRIFIC. LOOK AT THAT."

"That's . . . what is that, second-stage?"

"No, it's . . ." Several people inhaled. There was clapping, a whoop, and laughter.

"Online." The word sounded heavy, the way you might say *We made it.*

I tried to blink. This didn't work. But I could see. There was a vase, with three yellow flowers. Daffodils? I didn't know the names of flowers. But the vase sat on a plain white surface, and behind that was a beige wall. It seemed to me that this white surface was a bedside table of some sort. I tried to turn my head to see the rest of the room and that didn't work either.

Beside the vase appeared a face. A woman, with almond eyes behind brown-rimmed glasses. "Charles Neumann?"

I swallowed, or tried to. I said, *What...?*

The woman's eyes flicked at something behind me. She was a little close for comfort. I was glad to be awake and hopefully safe but I wouldn't mind this woman backing up out of my personal space. Her eyes returned to mine, shining. For a second I thought we were about to kiss. "Response. A clear response."

Where am I? I felt panic. No part of my body was doing what I wanted.

"You're in a research and development facility. You came here as part of an asset diversification process that occurred following the hearings into the Better Future collapse. We're a joint-venture consortium of private and government interests. You..." She glanced to the side. "Should I...?"

"Go ahead," said someone.

Her eyes settled on me. "The paramedics could do nothing. By the time they got in, you were unconscious. At first... well, they thought you were inside, of course. Inside a suit. They had the jaws, tools for rescuing people from automobile wrecks, and they began to cut you out. Until they realized there was no body in there. Your companion—the woman—she presented her own challenges. Her heart had stopped, but didn't respond to compressions. At this point they didn't know what was inside her. By all rights, you should have both died there. Then the employees intervened. The... ah... the artificially enhanced employees. During the hearings, they were heavily criticized. I think, looking back, people would regret how they were demonized. It was the shock of the new. Now, of course..." She shrugged. Her eyes were beautiful. That almond color, it was very deep. "Anyway, they saved you. They knew which parts could be detached without killing you. Killing your brain. They kept you alive until you reached a hospital. You can appreciate the picture you presented. The doctors saw nothing left to save. By their definition, you weren't even a person. You were parts. But the Better People convinced them to stabilize you. They fed you oxygen, water. Then the authorities intervened. The Better People were removed. They were . . . well, as I said, it's shameful now. We had different values. They saw the Better People as wrong. Immoral." She grimaced. "They were normalized. Their enhancements removed. It was terrible. But it took us, as a society, a while to catch up. To the technology. To how it had become a part of people."

She glanced again to the side. "Several times it was ordered that you be decommissioned. There was pressure on the hospital, from within and without. Protesters camped outside. Once they broke in, and . . ." She gestured. "You couldn't remain. A compromise was brokered. You came here. At that point, you essentially became a research project. The goal was not to keep you alive, exactly. It was to . . ." She hesitated. "It's probably easiest if I show you."

She turned my head with one hand, showing no exertion. The room shifted. I saw a gray box. It looked like a piece of medical equipment. It had buttons, LEDs, about a hundred black wires. One snaked toward me, another to a monitor. I thought, *What is that?* Letters spilled across the screen:
WHAT IS THAT

In the screen's reflection, I saw daffodils. Beside them, sitting on the white benchtop, was a small black cylinder on a block of white plastic. The cylinder had a lens at the front and a wire coming out the back. I realized I was looking at myself.

"Whoa," someone said. "He's spiking."

"Load rising."

"We've got a lot of runaway processes. Core is locking."

"Shut him down. Shut him down!"

Darkness again.

. . .

A STRANGE KIND OF LIGHT. DIFFUSE. I COULDN'T FOCUS. I FELT DISORI-
entated. I had forgotten where I was.

"Holding . . . that's good. Keep that there."

"A little interplay on the message bus. Nothing serious."

"Okay . . . let him have a look. But slow."

The light lifted. Or rather, a thing draped over me was
lifted. I saw a man in a striped shirt and bow tie. The thing
was a lab coat. As it rose, its sleeve snagged and pulled me
around in a half-circle until I was facing the steel gray box.
The monitor. Words streamed across the screen: NO BOX BOX
I AM IN A BOX NN N L N OLALOLALOLALOLALOLALOLA—

"Shit!" The lab coat flopped over me again. "Take him
down!"

"You see that output?"

I felt myself shrinking, ceasing to exist in pieces.

"Maybe she's right. Maybe . . ." Before I could hear the
rest of this, I was gone.

"CHARLIE?"

I opened my eyes. No. I didn't. I had no eyes. But I saw
Lola. Her chin rested on the heel of her hand, her elbow on
the benchtop. Her hair looked as if she had pulled it into a
neat ponytail, then walked somewhere windy. "Hey." She
smiled. "There you are."

Lola, I said. *Can you hear me? I can't talk.*

"You're talking, Charlie. Here . . ." She swiveled my camera until I could see the monitor: LOLA CAN YOU HEAR ME I
CANNOT TALK. "See? You're talking."

AM I IN THERE IS MY BRAIN IN THERE

"No. Well . . . yes. But not your *brain*. You're solid state
now."

HOW AM I SOLID STATE

"I can't believe this." She wiped her eyes. "It's been so long."

HOW LONG LOLA

"It's been six years, Charlie."

SIX YEARS HOW IS IT SIX YEARS

"It feels like six minutes." She laughed. "Oh, God, Charlie, it's really you."

I AM A ROBOT, wrote the screen. I AM A BOX A DEAD BOX.

"No, Charlie. You're not a box. The box is your body. That's all."

DO NOT WANT TO BE A BOX LOLA

She stroked my camera. I couldn't feel it. But it felt comforting. "They said you were gone. But I wouldn't let them turn you off. I had to yell at a lot of people over the last six years, because they kept wanting to give up." She straightened and unbuttoned her shirt. There was a white scar across her chest, thin and faded. "Look. I got your heart."

LOLA I MISS YOU

She covered her mouth and looked away. When she looked back, her eyes gleamed. "Well, you don't have to miss me anymore, Charlie. Because let me tell you about the box. The box is special. The box has ports."

PORTS

"Yes. You can plug things in."

THINGS WHAT THINGS

"That's a good question. The answer is up to you. Because it's just an interface, Charlie. It can be configured whichever way we want. But . . . while I was waiting, I kind of went ahead and . . . it's nothing special. You can do better. But I wanted to give you something. Like you gave me the heart. I wanted you to have something I built for you myself. So I made you an arm."

AN ARM LOLA

"I'm kind of stupidly proud of it. I mean, it's so basic. But it's a start."

A START

"Yeah." She lay her head on her arm, her free hand continuing to stroke my camera. "That's what it is."

It was odd, seeing her through a lens. But not as odd as I would have thought. Perhaps people could adapt to anything. Now I thought about it, it was pretty strange that human beings felt comfortable walking around in bodies mostly made of juice. That was actually bizarre.

CAN YOU SHOW ME THE ARM, I said.

ACKNOWLEDGMENTS

One day a guy on my website took me to task for dawdling between books:

> What do you do all day? I read *Twilight* for frack sake. I'm so bored. Books! WRITE BOOKS! Short stories . . . anything.

I had been working hard, I felt. I had written lots of things. Novel openings that never went anywhere. Screenplays that were never made. Manuscripts that needed twelve months in the desk drawer before I could stand to look at them again.

I decided to prove I wasn't sitting around on my ass. Wasn't *just* sitting on my ass. I had a few pages of a story that wasn't going anywhere in long format, and wondered how it might work in lots of little parts. On March 18, 2009, I posted the first section, 200 words, to my site. This was *Machine Man,* page 1. The next day I posted another hundred; the day after, 150 more. Then the weekend. I took a break. On Monday I continued. In the early days I had a dozen or so pages up my sleeve, but pretty soon the live feed caught up to me, and I wrote most pages in the twenty-four hours before posting them. Each day I read comments from readers and pondered their feedback. By December I finished, with a story 54,000 words long.

This novel is much longer than the serial and departs

from it in several ways. That's partly because the serial was a first draft, and therefore terrible, but also because the formats are so different. The serial was a collection of cliffhangers; the novel I hope is deeper and less tricksy. But this book couldn't have existed without the serial, so I'm indebted to everyone who spent nine months reading it, one freaking page per day. Thank you to those who stuck with it despite the fact that I was sending out a first draft, which is a kind of crime for a writer, or should be. Thank you for the comments, which turned the website into a meta-work (*The Annotated Machine Man*) with ideas, predictions, and explanations. And enhanced, artificially augmented, thanks to those who contributed many, many comments, the most prolific of whom were Pev (still interesting), gStein, CrystalR, Toby O, Electrichead, David, Ben, fredzfrog, Stygian Emperor, Mapuche, coolpillows, Chemical Rascal (puns and haiku on demand), Alex, Ian Manka, Felix, C Leffelman, SilverKnight, Yannick, dabbeljuh, Abgrund, Alan Westbrook, SexCpotatoes, regtiangha, Neville, Adam Speicher (a.k.a. meta-Adam), tim, Katie Ellert ("Where's Lola? *Where's Lola?*"), Ajna, Isaac, Joe M., Justin, towr, Morlok8k, Ballotonia, Sander, Ted, and Robert Bissonnette. Many times I clicked through to the previous day's page with dread, sure everybody must have hated it, but found cheers and jokes and spin-off ideas that buoyed me forward. Before I began, I had considered a warning on the comments page, something like: "Being critical of this thing while I'm still writing it may cause me to lock up creatively." I didn't do that and didn't have to. Readers were far nicer to me than I deserved.

I used many reader ideas. I wasn't sure I should admit that in print, but my legal advice is that you can't copyright ideas, so thanks a lot, suckers. Wait. You didn't type that, did you? Good. Because people would kill for your job, you know.

Thank you to everyone who tossed me an idea. Even the ones I didn't use helped clarify the boundaries of my story's world. My favorite was from Meredith Course, who educated me about brain plasticity and free-roaming neurons. Carl's "Fiber Shield" is from an idea by Kragen Sitaker. Even the first edition cover was chosen with online help, particularly from Reddit: thanks to everyone who contributed their thoughts.

Thank you to Mike Taylor for allowing me to pilfer the heart and soul of his wonderful blog post, "A brief, yet helpful, lesson on elementary resource-locking strategy," which so perfectly depicts why programmers should not be allowed to mix with regular humans that I couldn't do better than to ape it.

Michael Ian Minter is responsible for the original comment quoted above. I don't want to encourage people to go around goading authors. Particularly when the author is me. But Minter essentially convinced me to do this, and I would have blamed him had it gone badly, so I guess I should give him credit now.

Thank you to Jen for her patience on the days I struggled with my daily deadline ("I'm not happy with my page. I have to rewrite my *paaaaage*"), and for telling me it sounded like a good idea to begin with. Ditto to my agent, Luke Janklow, who also made sure this fun experiment in real-time fiction didn't break me financially, by finding enthusiastic fans in Zachary Wagman and Tim O'Connell of Vintage Books, Aviva Tuffield and Henry Rosenbloom of Scribe Publications, and, with Brian Siberell, Cathy Schulman of Mandalay Pictures.

COMPANY

Stephen Jones is a shiny new hire at Zephyr Holdings. From the outside, Zephyr is just another bland corporate monolith, but behind its glass doors business is far from usual: the beautiful receptionist is paid twice as much as anybody else to do nothing, the sales reps use self-help books as manuals, no one has seen the CEO, no one knows exactly what they are selling, and missing donuts are the cause of office intrigue. While Jones wanted to climb the corporate ladder, he now finds himself descending deeper into the irrational rationality of company policy. What he finds is hilarious, shocking, and utterly telling.

Fiction

JENNIFER GOVERNMENT

Taxation has been abolished, the government has been privatized, and employees take the surname of the company they work for. It's a brave new corporate world, but you don't want to be caught without a platinum credit card—as lowly Merchandising Officer Hack Nike is about to find out. Trapped into building street cred for a new line of $2,500 sneakers by shooting customers, Hack attracts the barcode-tattooed eye of the legendary Jennifer Government. A stressed-out single mom, corporate watchdog, and government agent who has to rustle up funding before she's allowed to fight crime, Jennifer Government is holding a closing-down sale—and everything must go. A wickedly satirical and outrageous thriller about globalization and marketing hype, *Jennifer Government* is the best novel in the world ever.

Fiction